Lords of Disgrace

Bachelors for life!

Friends since school,
brothers in arms, bachelors for life!

At least that's what "The Four Disgraces"—
Alex Tempest, Grant Rivers, Cris de Feaux
and Gabriel Stone—believe. But when they meet
four feisty women who are more than a match
for their wild ways, these lords are tempted to
renounce bachelordom for good.

Don't miss this dazzling new quartet by

Louise Allen

His Housekeeper's Christmas Wish
Already available

His Christmas Countess
Already available

The Many Sins of Cris de Feaux
Available now!

And don't miss
The Unexpected Marriage of Gabriel Stone
Coming next month!

Author Note

When I started to tell Cris and Tamsyn's story, I had a very clear image of how it began and also just where it would be set, on the wild and rugged coast where North Devon and North Cornwall meet. I have known and loved this coastline with its towering cliffs, secret coves and tales of smugglers since I was a child. All of the towns mentioned are real, as is Hartland Quay, where Cris's adventure begins, but the villages are imaginary, although based on the places where I spent many happy hours. I also borrowed Hawker's Hut on the cliffs at Morwenstow, possibly the National Trust's smallest and most charming property, for Tamsyn's secret hideaway. If you search online for images, they will give you a vivid picture of the lovely setting.

I do hope you will enjoy the story of how Cris de Feaux, the least likely of the Lords of Disgrace to lose his head and his heart, meets his match in one very independent Devon lady with a scandalous past.

Louise Allen

——

The Many Sins of Cris de Feaux

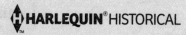
HARLEQUIN® HISTORICAL

Recycling programs
for this product may
not exist in your area.

ISBN-13: 978-0-373-29886-0

The Many Sins of Cris de Feaux

Copyright © 2016 by Melanie Hilton

Printed in U.S.A.

Louise Allen loves immersing herself in history. She finds landscapes and places evoke the past powerfully. Venice, Burgundy and the Greek islands are favorite destinations. Louise lives on the Norfolk coast and spends her spare time gardening, researching family history or traveling in search of inspiration. Visit her at louiseallenregency.co.uk, @louiseregency and janeaustenslondon.com.

Books by Louise Allen

Harlequin Historical

Lords of Disgrace

His Housekeeper's Christmas Wish
His Christmas Countess
The Many Sins of Cris de Feaux

Brides of Waterloo

A Rose for Major Flint

Danger & Desire

Ravished by the Rake
Seduced by the Scoundrel
Married to a Stranger

Linked by Character

Forbidden Jewel of India
Tarnished Amongst the Ton

Stand-Alone Novels

From Ruin to Riches
Unlacing Lady Thea
Scandal's Virgin
Beguiled by Her Betrayer

Harlequin Historical Undone! ebooks

Disrobed and Dishonored
Auctioned Virgin to Seduced Bride

Visit the Author Profile page
at Harlequin.com for more titles.

For the Quayistas,
in memory of a very cheerful week's research.

Chapter One

Cris de Feaux was drowning. And he was angry. The realisation of both came with the slap of a wave of icy salt water in the face and he shook it out of his eyes, cursing, while he came to terms with the fact that he had swum out from the little cove without thinking, without stopping to do anything but shed his clothes on the rocks and plunge into the breakers.

It had felt good to cut through the surf out into deep water, to push his body hard while his mind became mercifully blank of anything except the co-ordination of arms and legs, the stretch of muscles, the power of a kick. It had felt good, for once in his life, not to consider consequences, not to plan with care and forethought. And now that indulgence was going to kill him.

Was that what he had wanted? Eyes wide with shock, Cris went under, into a watery blue-green world, and kicked up to the surface, spitting and furious. He had fallen in love, unsuitably, impossibly, against all sense and honour. He knew it could never be, he had walked away before any more damage could be done and now his aimless wanderings across England had brought him here, to the edge of North Devon and the ocean.

Which was about to kill him, unless he was very lucky indeed. No, he did not want to die, however much he ached for what could never be, but he had swum too far, beyond the limits of his strength and what he could ask of his hard-exercised horseman's body.

Use your head, he snarled at himself. *You got yourself into this mess, now get yourself out of it. You will not give up. I am* not *killing myself for love.*

He studied the shore between sore, salt-crusted lids. High cliffs, toothed at their base with jagged surf-lashed rocks, mocked him, dared him to try to land and be dashed to bloody death. But there were little coves between the headlands, he knew that. The current was carrying him south-west along the line of the shore so he would go with it, conserve his strength until he saw a point to aim at. Even in those few minutes as he hung in the water it had already carried him onwards, but he dared not risk just lying there, a passive piece of flotsam on the flow. It might be the first day of June, but the sea was strength-sapping cold. He could hardly feel his legs, except for the white-hot pain of over-extended muscles and tendons. His shoulders and arms felt no better.

The wind shifted, slapping the water into his face from a different angle. *There.* Above the nearest towering headland, a drift of something against the blue of the perfect sky. Smoke. Which meant a house, a beach or perhaps a jetty. *Swim.* Ignore the pain. Dig down to every last ounce of strength and then find some more. Whatever it was that eventually killed the fifth Marquess of Avenmore, it was not going to be a hopeless love and a lack of guts.

Time passed, became simply a blur of pain and effort. He was conscious, somewhere in the back of what was left of his consciousness, that he could not stay afloat much longer. He lifted his head, a lead weight, and saw land, close. A beach, breakers. It seemed the scent of wood smoke and wild garlic cut through the salt for a second. Not a mirage.

But that is. In the moment of clarity he thought he saw a woman, waist-deep in the water, thick brown hair curling loose on her shoulders, calling to him, 'Hold on!'

Mermaid... And then his body gave up, his legs sank, he went under and staggered as his feet hit sand. Somehow he found the strength to stand and the mermaid was coming towards him, her hands held out. The water dragged at him, forcing his legs to move with the frustrating slowness of dream running. The sand shifted beneath his feet as the undertow from the retreating wave sucked at him, but he struggled on. One step towards her, then another and, staggering, four more.

She reached for him as he took one more lurching step and stumbled into her, his hands grasping her shoulders for balance. Under his numb hands her skin was hot, burning, her eyes were brown, like her hair. There were freckles on her nose and her lips were parted.

This was not a mermaid. This was a real, naked, woman. This was life and he was alive. He bent his head and kissed her, her mouth hot, his hands shaking as he pulled her against him.

She kissed him back, unresisting. There was the taste of woman and life and hope through the cold and the taste of salt and the hammering of the blood where his hands rested against her throat.

The wave broke against his back, pushing them both over. She scrabbled free, got to her feet and reached for him, but he was on his feet now, some last reserve of strength coming with that kiss and with hope. He put his arm around her waist and lifted her against him.

'I do not require holding up—you do,' she protested as they gained the hard sand of the beach, but he held on, stumbling across the sand, over stones he could not feel against his numbed soles. Then, when they reached the grass, his legs finally gave way, and he went down again, hardly conscious that he was falling on to rough grass and into oblivion.

Tamsyn stared down at the man at her feet, Adamnaked, pale, tall, beautifully muscled, his hair slicked tight to his head, his face a mask of exhaustion and sheer determination even in unconsciousness. *A sea god, thrown out of his element.*

You could not live on this coast for long without knowing what to do when someone was near drowned. Tamsyn did not hesitate, for all that her head was spinning and an inner voice was demanding to know what she thought she had been doing just then in his arms. She threw all the towels she had over the still body, then her cloak, dragged her shift over her head and set off at a run up the lane that sloped up past the front lawn of her aunts' house on the left and the steep flank of Stib's Head on the right, shouting for help.

'Mizz Tamsyn?' Johnny, the gardener, came out from the woodshed, dropping the armful of logs when he saw her. 'What's amiss?'

She clung to the gatepost, gasping for breath. 'Get Michael and a hurdle. There's a man down at the shore, half-drowned and freezing cold. Bring him back here and keep the cloak over him. Hurry!'

Her aunts' cook just stared as she burst into the

kitchen. 'Get Mrs Tape, tell her we need blankets and hot bricks for the couch in the bathing room.'

She made herself stop in her headlong dash and open the door into the bathing room more slowly so as not to alarm her aunts. They were there already; Aunt Rosie, tight-lipped with pain, had just reached her armchair after the slow walk from her bedchamber, supported between Aunt Izzy and Harris, her maid. Steam was rising from the big tub, where she took the two long soaks a day that were the only remedy that eased her crippled joints. All three women looked up.

'Tamsyn, dear, your clothes…' Izzy began.

'They are bringing a man up from the beach, he needs to get warm.' Tamsyn plunged her hands into the water, winced. 'Too hot, it will be agony, I'll let some out and run in cold.' She moved as she talked, yanking out the plug, turning on the tap. 'I'm sorry, Aunt Rosie, but I think he will die if we don't do something drastic. I've never felt anyone so frozen.' *Except for his mouth.* 'I've sent Cook for Mrs Tape and blankets, we'll have to use the couch in here for him.'

'Yes, of course. Izzy, Harris, never mind me—help Miss Tamsyn.' Rosie was all practicality as usual. 'Hot bricks, do you think? And lots of towels. Warm them by the range and then they can go on the bed to wrap him in, you must keep replacing them as they cool.' The urgency animated Rosie's face, even as she frowned in anxious thought. 'Poor creature, a fisherman, I suppose.'

'I'm heating that beef broth.' Cook bustled in and held the door open. 'Here they come. There's a lot of him, that's for sure.'

Johnny and Michael had clearly sent for help, for along with them Jason, the groom, had one corner of the hurdle while Molly, the maid of all work, and skinny little Peter, the odd-job boy, struggled with the other.

Over six foot of solid, unconscious man was indeed a lot, Tamsyn realised, as they lowered their burden to the floor. She checked the water—warm, but not hot— and pulled the cloak and towels from him. Aunt Izzy gave a squeak, Cook sucked in her breath and Molly murmured, 'Oh, *my*...'

'For goodness' sake, stop having the vapours, all of you. Haven't you seen a naked man before?' As she spoke she realised that the aunts probably hadn't, even if Cook and Molly had quite *active* social lives and she... *Never mind that now.* 'Lift him up and lower him into the water.'

That brought him round. Cursing, the stranger flailed at the men's hands as he was lowered into the big tub until only his head was above the surface. 'What the hell?' His eyes opened, red-rimmed from the salt. 'Damn, that hurts.' Tamsyn saw him focus on her, then his hands moved convulsively under the water to cover himself.

'Not you, too,' she scolded, dropping a large towel strategically into the tub. 'It doesn't matter in the slightest that you are stark naked. No one is looking and we need to get you warm.'

'I apologise for my language.' The words came out in a mumble through chapped lips that set into a tight line as he closed his eyes.

'That is of no account either. I know this is painful, but we need to warm you.' A sharp nod was his only answer, so Tamsyn reached into the water, took his right hand and began to chafe it. 'Molly, you rub his other hand. And, Harris, could you help Miss Pritchard back to her room? You had best go, too, Aunt Izzy.'

'Nonsense, we will stay right here.' Aunt Rosie was as brisk in her manner as she was slow in her movements. 'Johnny, ride for Dr Tregarth.'

'Don't need a…' Cris began.

'You be quiet, young man. Do as you are told and stop wasting your energy.'

Across the tub Tamsyn met Molly's amused gaze. She doubted whether the man under their hands, who must be about thirty, had been addressed like a stubborn schoolboy for quite some time. He was exceedingly handsome in a severe way and very blond now that his hair was drying patchily. She shuffled along on her knees, dipped her hands into the water and felt for his feet, which recoiled at the touch, bringing his knees above the water and a small tidal wave slopping over the edge.

'I'm sorry if you are ticklish. Can you bear it if we add more hot water?'

'Yes. And not ticklish,' he muttered. 'Taken by surprise.'

And aren't you cross about that, my merman? He was not used to being at a disadvantage, Tamsyn suspected. Certainly he was unused to his body not being under his complete control. She stood up to reach for the hot tap, hoping the supply of hot water would last. As she leaned across him he opened his eyes and looked directly at her.

Tamsyn realised she was wearing nothing but a linen shift that clung to her wet body in a manner that was barely decent and was probably thoroughly unflattering into the bargain. And not only was the stranger looking at her, but the room was full of male staff and a lad who certainly shouldn't be exposed to the sight of the youngest lady of the house in such a state. She topped up the hot water and picked up the cloak from the floor with an assumption of ease. 'I'll just go and put on something…warmer. Keep chafing his hands and feet. Oh, there you are, Mrs Tape—can you make up the couch as a bed and get it warm, please? I'll be back in a minute.' She fled.

It was a perfectly calm and collected exit, on the outside. But it was flight nevertheless. Her hands were shaking as she stripped off the shift, sponged the salt from her skin as rapidly as she could, heedless of drips and splashes. Her hair, curly and wayward at the best of times, was resistant to having the salty tangles combed out, but the pain as the comb snagged and pulled was a welcome distraction.

The stranger surely wouldn't recall that they had kissed in that hot, open-mouthed exchange of life and… well, *desire* on her part, she might as well face it. She couldn't pretend it had been shock and that she had been merely passive. She had kissed him back, she knew she had. Goodness only knew what had made him kiss her. Delirium, maybe?

He probably wouldn't recall being dumped stark naked into a large vat of warm water with an interested audience of most of their household, male and female, either. He would be lucky to survive this without catching an inflammation of the lungs, and that was what she ought to be worrying about, not wondering what had come over her to feel a visceral, dizzying stab of lust for a total stranger.

He had a beautiful body and she had seen it, all of it, and she was not made of stone. She was, after all, the notorious Tamsyn Perowne of Barbary Combe House and she might as well live up to it, once in a while.

But that was quite enough scandal for one day. The

gown she pulled from the clothes press was an ordinary
workaday one with sleeves to the elbow and a neckline
that touched her collarbone. She twisted up her plait,
stabbed a few hairpins into it and topped it with a cap.
There, perfect. She gave her reflection a brisk nod in
the mirror. No one in history ever had inappropriate
thoughts while wearing a cap, surely?

When she re-entered the bathing chamber the couch
was heaped with pillows, towels and blankets. Mrs Tape
was wrapping bricks in flannel and the aunts had retreated behind the screen. Molly was up to her elbows
in the tub, rubbing the stranger's feet with what Tamsyn decided was unnecessary enthusiasm.

'That will do, Molly. I think we had best transfer the
gentleman to the couch.'

'We?' It came out as a croak. He opened his eyes,
narrow slits of winter-sea blue. Perhaps she had over-
estimated the likelihood of him forgetting anything.

'Jason and Michael, help the gentleman out and to the
couch. Come, Molly, behind the screen with you.' She
shooed the maid along in front of her and grimaced at
her aunts. Aunt Izzy was looking interested, although
anything from the mating habits of snails to the making of damson jam interested her. Aunt Rosie wore an
expression of mixed amusement and concern.

'Did he say anything while I was changing?' Tamsyn whispered while splashing, grunting and muffled
curses marked the unseen progress from tub to couch.

'Nothing,' Aunt Izzy whispered back. 'Except, when
we added more hot water, some words in a foreign tongue
we do not know. They sounded…forceful.'

'Perhaps he is a foreigner.'

'I do not think so.' Aunt Rosie pushed her spectacles

further up her nose. 'He looks English to me and definitely a gentleman, not a fisherman, so goodness knows what he was doing in our bay. He reminds me of a very cross archangel. So very blond and severe.'

'Are you acquainted with many archangels, dear?' Aunt Izzy teased. 'And are they all English?'

'He is how I have always imagined them, although I have to confess, he does require a pair of wings, shimmering raiment and a fiery sword to complete the picture and I do not think he is looking quite at his best, just at the moment.'

'Excuse me, ladies, but the gentleman is in bed now.' Michael, their footman, stepped round the screen, his hands full of damp towels. 'I brought one of my own nightshirts down for him. It's not what he's used to, I'll be bound, but it's a clean one.'

'Excellent. Thank you, Michael. Now, if you could just drain the tub and refill it for Miss Pritchard I'll set the screen around the bed and everyone can be private.'

'All the hot water's gone, Miss Tamsyn. Jason's gone to stoke up the boiler.'

'In that case, if you'll help me through to the front parlour, Michael, I'll rest in there.' Aunt Rosie put one twisted hand on the footman's arm. 'I have no doubt our visitor would appreciate some peace and quiet.'

Tamsyn left Aunt Izzy and Molly to accompany Rosie on her painful way to the front of the house, straightened her cap, and, hopefully, her emotions, and went to see how her patient was.

He opened his eyes as she approached the bed. 'Thank you.' They had propped him up against the pillows, the covers pulled right up under his armpits, but his arms were free. His words were polite, but the blue eyes were furious.

'Do not try to speak, it is obviously painful. Have they given you anything to drink yet? Just nod.'

He inclined his head and she saw the beaker on the edge of the tub and fetched it over, sniffed the contents and identified watered brandy. 'Cook will bring you some broth when you feel a little stronger. Sip this. Can you hold it?' He did not look like a man who was taking kindly to being treated like an invalid, whether he was one or not. His long fingers closed around the beaker, brushing hers. The touch was cold still, but not with the deadly chill his skin had held before.

Tamsyn went to fuss with the screen, pulling it around the bed so he wouldn't feel she was staring at him if he fumbled with the drink. She would find some warm water in a moment so he could bathe his sore eyes.

The beaker was empty when she turned back and she took it from his hand, disconcerted to find those reddened eyes watching her with a curious intentness. *Surely he does not remember that kiss?* She willed away both the blush and the urge to press her lips to his again. 'What is your name, sir? I am Tamsyn Perowne and the two other ladies are Miss Pritchard and Miss Isobel Holt.'

'Cri… De…'

She leaned closer to catch the horse whisper. 'Christopher Defoe? Are you a connection of the writer? I love *Robinson Crusoe.*' He shook his head, a sharp, definitive denial. 'No? Never mind. Whoever you are, you are very welcome here at Barbary Combe House. Rest a little and when the doctor has been in I will fetch the broth. In fact, that sounds like him now.' The sound of raised voices in the entrance hall penetrated even the heavy door. 'And someone else. What on earth is going on?' She had barely reached the other side of the screen when the door opened and Dr Tregarth strode in, speaking angrily over his shoulder to the man who pushed through after him.

'Don't be a fool, Penwith. Of course this isn't Jory Perowne. The man went over Barbary Head on to the rocks two years ago, right in front of six dragoons and the Revenue's Riding Officer. He was dead before you could get a noose around his neck and he certainly hasn't walked out of the sea now!'

'That's as may be, but he was a tricky bastard, was Perowne, and I wouldn't put it past him to play some disappearing game. And I'm the magistrate for these parts and I'll not take any chances.'

Squire Penwith. *Will he never give up?* Tamsyn stopped dead in front of the man, hands on hips, chin up so he could not see how much his words distressed her. *Stupid, vindictive, blustering old goat.* She managed not to actually say so. 'Mr Penwith, if you can tell me how a man can go over a two-hundred-foot cliff on to rocks and survive the experience I would be most interested to hear.' That glimpse of the shattered, limp body in the second before the waves took it… She hardened her voice against the shake that threatened it. 'My husband was certainly a tricky bastard, but I have yet to hear he could fly.'

Chapter Two

So, his mermaid in a dowdy cap was a widow, was she? Cris winced as the cracked corner of his mouth kicked up in an involuntary smile at the sharp defiance in her voice, then the amusement faded as the other man, the magistrate, began to bluster at her.

'He wasn't the only tricky one in this household. I wouldn't put it past the pair of you to have rigged up some conjuror's illusion—and don't open those big brown eyes at me, all innocent-like. I know the smuggling's still going on, so who is running it if your husband's dead. Eh? Tell me that.'

'Smuggling's been a way of life on this coast since man could paddle a raft, you foolish man.' Cris liked the combination of logic and acid in the clear voice. 'Long before Jory Perowne was born, and for long after, I'll be bound.' Mrs Perowne spoke as though to a somewhat stupid scholar.

'Don't you call me a fool, you—'

'Penwith, you must not speak to Mrs Perowne in that intemperate manner.' That was the doctor, he assumed.

The magistrate swore and Cris threw back the covers, swung his legs off the couch and realised he was clad only in a nightshirt that came to mid-thigh. With a grimace he draped the top sheet around himself, flung one end over his shoulder like a toga and stalked around the screen, which, mercifully, was sturdy enough not to fall over when he grabbed its frame for support after two strides.

His mermaid—*Tamsyn*—swung round. 'Mr Defoe, kindly get back to your bed.' She sounded completely exasperated, presumably with the entire male sex, him included. He couldn't say he blamed her.

'In a moment, ma'am.' The two men stared at him. One, young, lanky, with a leather bag in his hand, lifted dark eyebrows at the sight of him. That must be the doctor. The other had the face of an irritable middle-aged schoolmaster complete with jowls and topped with an old-fashioned brown wig. 'You, sir, used foul language in the presence of this lady. You will apologise and leave. I imagine even you do not require the doctor to explain the difference between me and a man two years dead?' His voice might be hoarse and cracked, his eyes might be swollen, but he could still look down his nose with the hauteur of a marquess confronted with a muck heap when he wanted to.

Predictably the magistrate went red and made gobbling sounds. 'You cannot speak to me like that, sir. I'll see you—'

'At dawn in some convenient field, your worship?' He raised his left eyebrow in a manner that he knew was infuriatingly superior. His friends told him so often enough. The anger with his own stupidity still burned in his veins and dealing with this bully was as good a way to vent it as any.

'Mr Penwith, my husband was five feet and ten inches tall, he had black hair and brown eyes and his right earlobe was missing. Now, as you can quite clearly see, Mr Defoe is taller, of completely different colouring and is in possession of both his ears in their entirety. Now, perhaps you would like to leave before you make even more of an ass of yourself?' Tamsyn Perowne, pink in the face with the steam from the bath, her brown curls coming down beneath that ludicrous cap, was an unlikely Boudicca, but she was magnificent, none the less.

Cris locked his knees and hung on grimly until the magistrate banged out of the room, then let the doctor take his arm and help him back to the couch. Somehow his muscles had been replaced by wet flannel, his joints were being prodded with red-hot needles and he wanted nothing more than a bottle of brandy and a month's sleep.

'You stay that side of the screen, Mrs Perowne,' the doctor said. 'I'll just check your shipwrecked sailor for broken bones.' He began to manipulate Cris's legs, blandly unconcerned by the muttered curses he provoked.

'Nothing is broken. I swam out too far, got caught by the current and almost drowned. That is all that is wrong with me. Idiocy, not shipwreck.'

'Where did you go in?' Tregarth pushed up one of Cris's eyelids, then the other.

'Hartland Quay.'

'You swam from there and then got yourself out of the current and into this bay? By Neptune, sir, you're a strong swimmer, I'll say that for you.' He produced a conical wooden instrument from his bag, pressed the wide end to Cris's chest and applied his ear to the other. 'Your lungs are clear. You'll feel like a bag of unravelled knitting for a day or so, I've no doubt, and those muscles will give you hell from overwork, but there's no harm done.' He pulled up the bedding. 'You may come round now, Mrs Perowne. Keep him in bed tomorrow, if you can. Feed him up, keep him warm, let him sleep and send for me if he throws a fever. Good day to you, Mr Defoe.'

'I'm not—' *Not Mr Defoe. I'm Anthony Maxim Charles St Crispin de Feaux, Marquess of Avenmore.* With no calling card, no money—and no breeches, come to that, which left him precious little aristocratic dignity. Tamsyn, *Mrs Perowne*, had misheard his mumbled words. The family always used the French pronunciation of their name, but apparently that did not survive gargling with half the Atlantic.

The doctor had gone and Tamsyn was standing at the foot of the bed, hands crossed neatly at her waist, cap perched on her curls, looking for all the world as though butter would not melt in her mouth and not at all like a woman who would call a magistrate an ass or kiss a naked stranger in the surf. He could tell her that kiss might have saved his life, but he suspected that would not be welcome.

'The broth is coming, Mr Defoe.'

Yes, he'd stay a commoner for a while, it was simpler and he had no intention of broadcasting his recklessness to the world. He nodded his thanks.

'Where should we send to inform someone of your safety? I imagine your acquaintance will be very anxious.' She took a tray from the cook and laid it across his thighs. 'Try to swallow the broth slowly, it will soothe your throat as well as strengthen you.'

In his experience women tended to fuss at sickbeds and he had been braced against attempts to spoon-feed him. Mrs Perowne appeared to trust him to manage, despite the evidence of his shaking hand. His arm muscles felt as though he had been racked. 'Traveller,' he managed between mouthfuls. 'My valet is at Hartland Quay with my carriage.'

'And he can bring you some clothes.' She caught his eye and smiled, a sudden, wicked little quirk of the lips that sent messages straight to his groin. *One muscle still in full working order.* 'Magnificent as you look in a toga, sir, it is not a costume best suited to the Devon winds.'

Had he really kissed her in the sea, or was that a hallucination? No, it was real. He could conjure up the heat of her body pressed to his, the feminine softness and curves as their naked flesh met. He could remember, too, the heat of her mouth, open under his, the sweet glide of her tongue. Hell, that made him feel doubly guilty, firstly for forcing himself on a complete stranger and secondly for even thinking about anyone but Katerina. *Who can never be mine.* He focused on the guilt, a novel enough emotion, to prevent him thinking about that body, now covered in layers of sensible cotton.

'You will stay in bed and rest, as the doctor said?'

Cris nodded. He had no desire to make a fool of himself, fetching his length on the floor in front of her when his legs gave out on him. Tomorrow he would be better. Tomorrow he might even be able to think rationally.

'Good.' She lifted the tray and he saw the strength in the slim arms, the curve of sleek feminine muscle where her sleeves were rolled up to the elbow. She swam well enough to take to the sea by herself and he'd wager that she rode, too. 'We know you are stubborn from the way you tried to get up the lane by yourself instead of waiting where I left you. I've just spoken to them and the lads said you were crawling.'

'I was getting there. If I hadn't been weakened by

that…encounter in the sea, I could have walked.' Even as he said it, he could have bitten his tongue. So much for apologising, something that Lord Avenmore rarely had to do. Apparently Mr Defoe was more apt to blunder than the marquess was. He certainly had an unexpectedly bawdy sense of humour.

'An encounter, you call it?' There was a definite spark in the brown eyes and the colour was up over her cheekbones. Indignation seemed to make those brown curls fight free of the cap, too. His one functioning muscle stirred again, complaining that it was in need of exercise. 'That, you poor man, was the resuscitation of the half-drowned. We do it a lot in these parts. I'll fetch you pen and paper.'

And that apparently dealt with the apology. Mrs Perowne was not in the common run of gentry ladies, it seemed. Nor did her late husband seem to have been the kind of man he would have expected to be the owner of this elegant old house, not if the local magistrate was after him with a noose and his widow referred to him as a *tricky bastard.* That clod of a squire had spoken with unfeeling bluntness about her husband's death and yet she had stood up to him, covering her emotions with defiance and pride.

The puzzling Mrs Perowne returned with a writing slope under one arm and a small bowl in the other. 'I'll just bathe your eyes, they look exceedingly sore.'

Cris thought he probably looked an exceeding mess, all over. His hair had dried anyhow, his skin felt as though he'd been sandpapered and doubtless his eyes were both red and squinty. And he needed a shave. What his friends would say if they saw him now, he shuddered to think. Collins, when he arrived, would express himself even more strongly. He regarded the

Marquess of Avenmore as a walking testimonial to his own skills as a valet and did not take kindly to seeing his master looking less than perfect.

'If you would give me the bowl I will bathe them myself.' He had his pride and being tended to while he looked like this did nothing for his filthy mood.

'Very well.' She set the writing slope on the chair beside the couch, handed him the bowl and dragged the screen around the bed. 'My aunt, who suffers from severe arthritic pain, will be taking one of her regular hot soaks shortly. We will try not to disturb you.'

'Mrs Perowne?'

She looked around the edge of the screen. 'Mr Defoe?'

'I am in your aunt's bathing chamber, occupying her couch. I must remove myself to another room.'

'If you do, you will agitate her. She is worried enough about you as it is.' She smiled suddenly, a wide, unguarded smile, so unlike the carefully controlled expressions of the diplomatic ladies he had spent so much time with recently. 'Rest here for the moment, control your misplaced chivalrous impulses and we will find you another chamber at some point.'

Misguided chivalrous impulses. Little cat. She was obviously unused to men who actually acted like gentlemen. Cris twisted the water out of the cloth in the basin and sponged his eyes until the worst of the stinging subsided, then put the bowl aside and reached for the writing slope. Beyond the screen people were moving about, water was pouring into the tub, steam rose. This might be the edge of the country and manners might be earthy, but they certainly possessed plumbing that surpassed that in any of his houses.

He focused on the letter to shut out the sounds of either Miss Prichard or Miss Holt being helped into the bath. Collins was rather more than a valet, more of a confidential assistant, and he could be relied upon to use his discretion.

   …pay the reckoning and bring everything to…

'Mrs Perowne, if I might trouble you for a moment?'

'Sir?' She was decidedly flushed from the steam now. Her pink cheeks and the damp tendrils of hair on her brow suited her.

He recalled her leaning over him to turn on the tap as he lay in the bath and forced his croak of a voice into indifferent politeness. 'Could you tell me how I should direct my man to find this house?'

'Barbary Combe House, Stibworthy. If he asks in the village, anyone will direct him.'

'Thank you.'

   Barbary Combe House, Stibworthy. Do not en-
   quire in the village for Mr Defoe as I am not
   known there, having come by sea. Ensure you
   bring an appropriate vehicle.
   C. Defoe

Collins would not fail to pick up on that. The interior of Cris's travelling coach with its ingenious additions and luxurious upholstery might go unnoticed, but not if the crests on the door panels were left uncovered. It had caused enough of a stir at Hartland Quay to have a marquess descend on a waterside inn, but with any luck the gossip would be fairly localised.

He folded the letter, wrote the address and found a wafer in the box to seal it with, then forced himself to relax. The doctor's advice had been sound, but despite it, when Collins arrived tomorrow he would be out of here and away from the curiously distracting

Mrs Perowne. Back to London, to the normality he had fled from.

Eyes closed, he willed himself to sleep. The room was quiet now, with only the sounds of someone moving about as they tidied up. He was exhausted and yet his eyes would not stay closed. Cris stared at the ceiling. He could *always* sleep when he needed to, it was simply a matter of self-discipline.

He seemed to be somewhat short of any kind of control just at the moment. He hadn't had enough focus to notice when he was in danger of drowning himself and he couldn't even manage to fall flat on his face on a beach without kissing the local widow before he did so. And he was the man the government relied on to settle diplomatic contretemps discreetly, and, if necessary, unconventionally. Just now he wouldn't trust himself to defuse an argument between two drovers in the local public house, let alone one between a brace of ambassadors over a vital treaty clause.

It had all begun when he had first set eyes on Katerina, Countess von Stadenburg, the wife of a Prussian diplomat at the Danish court. Tiny, blonde, blue-eyed, exquisite and intelligent. His perfect match. And she wanted him, too, he could see it in her eyes, in the almost imperceptible, perfectly controlled gestures she made when he was close, the brush of fingertips on his cuff, the touch of a shoe against his under the dinner table, the flutter of a fan. That one kiss.

But she was married and he was the representative of the British Crown. To have indulged in an *affaire*, even if Katerina had been willing, was not only to dishonour her, but to risk a diplomatic incident. And he did not want an *affaire*, he had wanted to marry her. Which was impossible. Honour, duty, respect gave him only one logical course of action. He concluded his business as fast as possible and then he left, taking his leave of her under the jealous eye of her husband as casually as though she was just another, barely noticed, diplomatic wife, a pretty adjunct to her husband's social life.

Her control had been complete, her polite, formulaic responses perfect in their indifference. Only her eyes, dark with hurt and resignation, had told him the truth. He wished, for the thousandth time, he had not looked, had not seen, and that he could carry away with him only the memory of her cool, accented, voice. 'You are leaving the court, Lord Avenmore? Do have a safe journey, my lord. Heinrich, come, we will be late for the start of the concert.'

Finally he felt his lids drift closed, sensed the soft sounds of the house blur and fade. Strangely the eyes that he imagined watching him, just as it all slipped away, were brown, not blue.

'Michael, take this and give it to Jason, please. Tell him to ride to Hartland Quay at once and find Mr Defoe's man.'

'Is he sleeping, dear?' Aunt Izzy looked up from the vase of flowers she was arranging.

'Yes. So soundly I thought for an awful moment that he had stopped breathing.' Tamsyn closed the drawing-room door behind her and went to straighten the book-stand that kept Aunt Rosie's novel propped at just the right angle for her. 'He must be exhausted. I am certain it was only sheer cussedness that kept him going. It would be exhausting enough to swim that distance when the sea is warm, but it is still so cold, and with that current it is a miracle he survived.' She picked up the cut flower stems for Aunt Izzy, then twitched a leaf spray.

'He must be very fit, which is not surprising with that physique. You are fidgeting, Tamsyn.' Aunt Rosie looked up from her book. 'Did wretched Squire Penwith upset you, talking about dear Jory like that?'

'The man is a fool. *Dear Jory* was a tricky—er… devil, but even he could not fly.' She flung herself down on the window seat with more energy than elegance. 'Yes, the squire upset me, with his blustering and his utter lack of imagination. And, yes, I still hate to think about that afternoon.' She stared out over the sloping lawn at the sea, placid and blue in the sunlight, hiding its wicked currents and sharp fangs under a mask of serenity. Jory had lived with its dangers and its beauty and he had chosen it to end his life, which meant she could never look at it the same way again.

She lifted her feet up and hugged her knees. 'And it worries me that Mr Penwith is of no use to us whatsoever with the troubles we've been having. I cannot decide whether he thinks we should suffer as payment for my husband's sins, regardless of what crimes are committed against us, or whether he simply hates me.'

'Or whether he is a lazy fool,' Aunt Rosie said tartly. 'A hayrick on fire—must be small boys up to mischief. Our stock escaping through the hedge—must be the fault of the hedger. Every single lobster pot being empty for a week—must be the incompetence of our fishermen. Really, does he think we are idiots?'

'He thinks we are women, Rosie dear,' Aunt Izzy said, hacking at a blameless fern frond with her shears. 'And not only that, women who choose to live without male protection, which proves we are either reckless or soft in the head.'

'Perhaps he is being bribed to look the other way,' Tamsyn said. She had not mentioned it before because she did not want to upset Aunt Izzy. Even now she did not mention a name.

'Bribed? By my nephew Franklin, I presume.' Izzy might be vague, but there was nothing amiss with her wits.

'He does want us out of here.'

'Out of here and into that poky dower house on his estate where we will be *safe* and where he can *look after us* as though we were a trio of children or lunatics. The boy's a vulture, Isobel,' Rosie snapped, her fierceness alarming in one so frail. 'He wants to get his hands on this house, this estate. He wants Barbary.'

'Well, he can't have it. Papa left it to me for my lifetime and I've a good thirty years left in me, so he will have to learn patience.' Izzy picked up the vase and placed it on the sideboard. 'His foolish little games won't scare me out.'

So long as they stay foolish little games, Tamsyn thought, even as she smiled approval of her aunt's defiance. She rested her chin on her knees and let her gaze rest, unfocused, on the sea. But why would Lord Chelford trouble himself over this one small estate, other than through pique at not being left the entirety of his great-uncle's holdings when he inherited the title? Franklin was spoilt and greedy and he would soon get tired of this game and go back to his life of leisure and pleasure in London.

It was strange, though, that he should have made that offer to rehouse his aunt and her companion now. After all, Aunt Izzy had inherited the life interest in the Barbary Combe estate, the house and the contents when her father, the previous Lord Chelford, died five years ago and she had lived there for ten years before that.

It must be a sudden whim. Or perhaps she was

misjudging Franklin, perhaps his intentions were good and the series of mishaps just after Izzy had refused his offer were nothing but coincidence and bad luck. *Or perhaps the moon's made of green cheese.*

Chapter Three

There was something in the quality of the soft sounds around his bed that was very familiar. Cris kept his eyes closed and inhaled a discreet hint of bay-rum cologne and leather polish. 'Collins?'

'Yes, sir?' Typically there was no hesitation over the correct way to address him.

Cris opened his eyes and turned over on to his back. Collins did not so much as raise an eyebrow at the sudden violence of the swear word.

'Muscle strain, sir?'

'The pain you get when you over-exercise.' Cris levered himself up against the pillow. 'The kind that makes you think your muscles are full of ground glass.'

'Massage,' Collins pronounced, blandly ignoring the reaction that threat of torture provoked. 'I have unpacked your possessions in an upstairs room and the bed is made up, sir. I thought you would wish to transfer there before nightfall. It is five o'clock and the ladies are all in the front room just at the moment.'

Collins was considerably more than a valet. He numbered code breaking, five languages and lethally accurate knife-throwing amongst his less public skills, although he was also more than capable of turning out the Marquess of Avenmore in a state of perfection for any social occasion.

Now he shook out Cris's heavy silk banyan and waited patiently while, swearing under his breath, Cris got out of bed. Collins did, however, wince at the sight of the borrowed nightshirt.

'I've already been carried through the house and dumped in the bath stark naked in front of every female in the place.' Cris eased his arms into the sleeves of the robe and allowed Collins to tie the sash. 'I thought it courteous to cover myself.' The more he thought about it, the more embarrassing it became. He had no reticence about his own body, but being dropped nude and dripping like a half-stunned fish, in front of a gaggle of single ladies was…not good form.

The other man muttered something about stable doors and bolted horses and dropped a pair of backless leather slippers on the floor for him to shuffle his feet into.

'I feel as though I'm a hundred and four,' Cris grumbled as he made his way across to the door.

'If you came ashore here, I would suggest that you had not been swimming like a centenarian.' Collins opened the door and tactfully did not offer his arm. 'Top of the stairs, first on the right, sir.'

'I was swimming like a damn fool, I know that.' Cris walked straight up the stairs without stopping. Swearing in Russian certainly helped. 'You must have assumed I had drowned.'

'I saw no signs of a struggle on the beach when I found your clothes, sir.' Collins followed him into the bedchamber and shut the door. 'I therefore concluded you had entered the sea of your own volition. I confess to a degree of anxiety, especially as you had gone out so early and I had not thought to look for you for some time. I questioned the local fishermen, but they had seen nothing. They did, however, inform me of the direction of the currents and I was about to ride along the clifftops in the hope of sighting you when the message arrived.'

'I was distracted.' Cris ignored the tactful murmur of *Quite, sir.* However discreet he had been, and, in fact, there was nothing to be discreet about, it was close to impossible to keep secrets from Collins. Ominously, the bed was covered with towels and the man was pouring oil into his palm. With grim resignation Cris stripped off and lay face down. 'If you could stop short of actually making me scream I would be obliged. There are ladies around.'

Collins took hold of his right calf and started doing hideous things to the muscles with his thumbs. 'Yes, sir. An interesting household.'

'Mrs Perowne is the widow of a man who leapt off a cliff rather than be arrested and hanged for smuggling and associated crimes.'

'Indeed, sir? Very novel. If you could just bend your knee... Miss Holt, the owner, seems a kindly lady.'

'Is she the owner? I assumed Mrs Perowne was.' *Brown eyes, hot, sweet mouth, the promise of oblivion for a while.* He stirred, uncomfortably aware of how arousing that thought was. 'Ow! Damn it, man—are you attempting to plait those muscles?'

'No, to unplait them, sir.' Collins moved to the other leg. 'Miss Holt welcomed me to her home. That was how she worded it.'

A ruthless massage was certainly an effective antidote to inappropriate erotic thoughts that made him feel unfaithful to Katerina. Which was a pointless emotion.

An indulgence he was not going to wallow in, making himself feel like some tragic victim. They had not been lovers, they had not even spoken of that feeling between them, let alone exchanged protestations of love. There had just been those silent exchanges amidst crowds of others and that one, snatched, burning kiss when they had found themselves alone, passing in a corridor at the Danish royal palace. No words, no hesitation, only her body trembling between his hands, only her mouth sealed to his, her hands on his shoulders, and then her little sob as they tore themselves apart and, without a word, turned and walked away.

It was a relationship that could never be, not without the sacrifice of her reputation, his honour. Cris set his jaw, as much against the pain in his heart as the agony in his overstretched joints. He was a man, he was not going to become a monk because of how he felt for an unattainable woman. Next season he must find himself a bride, get married, assume the responsibilities of his title. He would be faithful to his wife, but not to a phantom—that way lay madness.

Tamsyn Perowne had kissed him back. He smiled into the pillow. It had probably been shock. Doubtless she would box his ears if he took any further liberties. Any fantasies about a willing widow to make him forget his ghosts were just that, fantasies. She was a respectable lady in a small community, not some society sophisticate. He'd be gone tomorrow, out of her life.

There was a tap of knuckles on wood, the creak of hinges and a sudden flap of linen as Collins swirled the sheet over his prone body.

'Oh, I beg your pardon, I had assumed Mr Defoe would be in bed by now, not…' Tamsyn put down the tray on the small table in the window embrasure and tried to forget the brief glimpse of elegant, sharp-boned bare feet as the sheet had settled over the man on the bed. She had seen all of him today, in the sea, in the bath, so what was there to discomfort her so in one pair of bare feet?

'I have brought some more broth.' *Long toes, high arches, the line of the tendon at his heel...* She was prattling now, looking anywhere but at the bed. But it was a small room and a big bed and there wasn't anywhere else to look, except at the ceiling or the fireplace or the soberly dressed man who stood beside the bed in his shirtsleeves, hands glistening with oil. 'It isn't much, and dinner will not be long, but the doctor said to keep his strength up and it will help Mr Defoe's throat.'

'Thank you, ma'am,' the valet said. 'I will see that Mr Defoe drinks the soup while it is hot.'

'Mr Defoe is present, and conscious, and capable of speech, Collins.' The husky voice from the bed brought her head round with a jerk. His eyes were closed, his head resting on his crossed arms, his expression as austere as that of an effigy on a tomb.

'Are you warm enough? Perhaps I should light the fire.' She moved without thinking, touched her fingers to the exposed six inches of shoulder above the sheet, just as she would if it had been one of the aunts in the bed. But this was not one of the aunts and his eyes opened, heavy-lidded, watchful, and she did not seem able to move her fingers from the smooth, chill, skin. When they had kissed, those beautiful, unreadable blue eyes had been open, too. Now she tried not to show any recollection of that moment.

'Yes, I will light the fire.' The words came out in

a coherent sentence, which was a surprise. Her hand was still refusing to obey her. 'You seem a trifle cool.'

'Cool? You think so?' The question had a mocking edge that seemed directed more at himself than at her.

'I will deal with the fire, ma'am.' The manservant's words jerked her back into some sort of reality, mercifully before her hand could trail down below the edge of the sheet.

'Thank you.' Tamsyn twitched the cover up over Mr Defoe's shoulders. 'I'll just…' The blue eyes were still open, still watching her. 'You should drink that soup while it is hot.'

She retreated with what dignity she could muster and did her best to close the door firmly, but quietly, behind her and not bang it shut and run. What was the matter with her? He was an attractive man. A very attractive man, and she had seen the whole of him, so was in an excellent position to judge, and she had been foolish enough to kiss him and she had saved his life. No, probably not. He was determined enough, and strong enough, to have kept going up the lane if he'd had to. He would have walked in through the kitchen door, in all his naked glory—and that would have made for a nasty accident if Cook had her hands full of something hot at the time. The thought made her smile.

'How is Mr Defoe, dear?' asked Aunt Izzy. 'You look very cheerful.'

'Alive, a little warmer and, I suspect, in considerable pain, but his manservant seems highly competent and I am sure he is not going to succumb to a fever.'

'That is good news. I suppose we may rely on his man to contact his wife, let her know he is safe.'

'His *what*?'

'Wife.' Aunt Izzy stopped with her hand on the door into the drawing room.

'Whose wife?'

'Mr Defoe's. He is more likely to be married than not, don't you think? He is very personable, I am sure he is most respectable when he has some clothes on and, if he can afford such a superior manservant, he is obviously in funds.' She cocked her head on one side, thinking. 'And he is probably thirty, wouldn't you say?'

'About that, yes. Not more.' His body was that of a fit young man, but there was something about him that spoke of maturity and responsibility. Doubtless marriage would give him that. It had not made Jory any more dependable, let alone respectable, but the man had been wild from a boy and his sense of duty and accountability was not one that most decent men would recognise.

She had no desire to smile now, which was only right and proper. A woman might look at an attractive man and allow her imagination to wander a little…*a lot.* But a respectable woman did not look at a *married* man and think anything at all, nor see him as anything other than a fellow human being in need of succour.

'Mizz Tamsyn, is it convenient for you to review the list of linen for the order I was going to send off tomorrow?' She looked up to find Mrs Tape at the door, inventory in hand. 'Only you said you wanted to look it over it with me, but if you're busy I can leave it.'

'Certainly. I will come now, Mrs Tape.' She turned and followed the housekeeper. Linen cupboards full of darned sheets were exactly what she should be concentrating on. And then the accounts and a decision about which of the sheep to send to market would keep her busy until dinner time.

All the humdrum duties of everyday life for an almost respectable country widow who should be very grateful for a calm, uneventful life.

'Do you think Mr Defoe will find our dinner time unfashionably early?' Aunt Izzy sipped her evening glass of sherry and fixed her gaze on Tamsyn.

'I am sure I do not know. I suppose seven o'clock is neither an old-fashioned country hour nor a fashionably late town one. But as he is either asleep, or will be having his meal on a tray at his bedside, I do not think we need concern ourselves too much with whether his modish sensibilities are likely to be offended.'

'Mr Defoe strikes me as an adaptable man,' Aunt Rosie remarked. 'Although how I can tell that from the brief glimpses I have had of him—'

'Excuse me, Miss Holt.' It was Jason, hat in hand, at the drawing-room door. 'Only there's a message from Willie Tremayne—a dozen of the sheep have gone over the cliff at Striding's Cove.'

'A dozen?' Tamsyn realised she was on her feet, halfway across the room. 'How can that be? The pastures are all fenced, Willie was with them, wasn't he? Is he all right?'

'Aye, Willie's safe enough, though by all accounts he's proper upset. A rogue dog got in with them and the hurdle was broken down in the far corner, though the lad Willie sent says he's no idea how that happened, because it was all right and tight yesterday.'

'Whose dog?' Tamsyn yanked at the bell pull. 'There aren't any around these parts that aren't chained or are working dogs, good with stock.'

'Don't rightly know, Mizz Tamsyn. The lad says Willie shot it and it doesn't seem to have been mad, by all accounts. Not frothing at the mouth nor anything like that. Just vicious.'

'Oh, Michael, there you are. Find Molly, tell her to put out my riding habit and boots. Jason, saddle my mare.'

'I don't think there's rightly anything you can do, Mizz Tamsyn, not at this time in the evening. Some of the men from the village helped Willie barricade the fence and one of the boats has gone down to the foot of the cliffs to see if there's anything to salvage.' Jason shrugged. 'By the time you get there it'll all be done.' He looked past her to the fireside and lowered his voice. 'I think the ladies are a mite upset, perhaps you'd be best biding here. I'll send the lad back with the message that you'll be along in the morning, shall I?'

She wanted to go, to stand on the clifftop and rage, but it would achieve nothing. She had to think. 'Yes, do that if you please, Jason.'

When she turned back into the room she was glad she had listened to him. Aunt Izzy was pale, a lace handkerchief pressed to her lips. Rosie was white-faced also, but hers was the pallor of anger. 'That was no accident. That was Chelford up to his nasty tricks again. Izzy, that boy is becoming a serious nuisance.'

'He is no boy,' Tamsyn snapped. 'He is thirty years old with an over-developed sense of what is owed to his consequence and no scruples about the methods he uses to get what he wants. If this is down to him, then he is becoming more than a nuisance. I think he is becoming dangerous.'

'Who is becoming dangerous, if I might ask?'

Mr Defoe stood in the doorway, dressed, shaved and very much awake. His eyes were fully open, the flexible voice had lost almost all of the painful huskiness, and the long, lean body was clad in what she could only assume was fashionable evening wear for a dinner on the wilder coasts of Devon—slim-fitting pantaloons, a swallowtail coat, immaculate white linen and a neck-cloth of intricate folds fixed with a simple sapphire pin that matched the subtle embroidery of his waistcoat.

'What are you doing out of bed. Mr Defoe? The doctor said you should rest and not get up until tomorrow.' Tamsyn knew she was staring, which did not help her find any sort of poise. And, faced with this man, she discovered that she wanted poise above everything.

'I am warm, rested and I need to keep my muscles moving,' he said mildly as he moved past her into the room. 'Good evening, Miss Holt, Miss Pritchard. Thank you for the invitation to dine with you.'

Invitation? What invitation? One glance at them had Tamsyn seething inwardly. They had invited him without telling her, for some nefarious reason of their own. They should have left the poor man to sleep. She eyed the *poor man* as he made his way slowly, but steadily, to the fireside and made his elegant bow to the aunts.

Predictably Aunt Izzy beamed at him and Aunt Rosie sent him a shrewd, slanting smile. 'Do sit down, Mr Defoe. I can well appreciate your desire to leave your room. Tamsyn, dear, perhaps Mr Defoe would care for a glass of sherry or Madeira?'

'Thank you, sherry would be very welcome.'

Tamsyn poured the rich brown wine into one of Aunt Izzy's best glasses. At least their tableware would not disgrace them. The house was full of small treasures that Izzy treated with casual enjoyment. She was as likely to put wildflowers into the exquisite glasses as fine wine and, if one of the others protested, she would shrug and say, *Oh, Papa let me take all sorts of things down here. I'm sure none of them are very valuable and I like to use nice objects.*

Mr Defoe stood beside the wing chair, waiting until Tamsyn had completed her task. 'Thank you.' He took the glass, then when she perched on the sofa next to Izzy he sat down with grace, and, to an observant eye, some caution. She suspected his overstretched muscles were giving him hell and he was more exhausted than he would allow himself to show. His features were naturally fine cut, she guessed, but even allowing for that, she detected strain hidden by force of will.

'Again, I have to ask you—who is dangerous? I apologise for my inadvertent eavesdropping, but having heard, I do not know how to ignore the fact that you seem to be in need of protection.'

In the silence that fell the three women eyed each other, then Tamsyn said, 'A rogue dog chased some of our flock of Devon Longwools over the cliff.'

'And moved a hurdle, I gather.' He rotated the glass between his fingertips, his attention apparently on the wine. 'A talented hound.'

He had sharp ears, or he had lingered on the stairs, listening. Probably both. 'That must be coincidence and it is simply a sorry chapter of accidents,' Tamsyn said. 'Tell me, Mr Defoe, do you come from an agricultural area?'

'I own some land,' he conceded. The amusement in his eyes was, she supposed, for her heavy-handed attempt at steering the subject away from the sheep. 'But I do not have sheep. Arable, cattle and horses in the south. This must be challenging country for agriculture, so close to the sea and the wild weather.'

'Everyone mixes farming and fishing,' Aunt Rosie said. 'And we have land that is much more sheltered than the sheep pastures on top of the cliffs, so we keep some dairy cattle and grow our own wheat and hay.' Aunt Izzy opened her mouth as though to bewail the burnt hayricks again, then closed her lips tight at the look from Rosie. 'We own some of the fishing boats that operate out of Stib's Landing, which is the next, much larger cove, just around Barbary Head to the south.'

'A complex business, but no doubt you have a competent farm manager. I am often away, so I rely heavily on mine.'

'Oh, no, dear Tamsyn does it all,' Izzy said cheerfully. Tamsyn wondered why Rosie rolled her eyes at her—it was, after all, only the truth.

'I have to earn my keep,' she said with a smile. 'And I like to keep busy. Are you travelling for pleasure, Mr Defoe? We are beginning to quite rival the south-coast resorts in this part of the world. Ilfracombe, for example, is positively fashionable.'

'Perfect for sea bathing,' Izzy said vaguely, then blushed. 'Oh, I didn't mean…'

'I am sure I would have done much better with a genteel bathing machine—I might have remembered to swim back when my time was up and not go ploughing off into the ocean while I thought of other things.' He smiled, but there was a bitter twist to it.

'Is that what you were doing? I did wonder, for the beach—if you can call it that—at Hartland Quay is hardly the kind of place you find people taking the saltwater cure.' Not, that Mr Defoe needed curing of anything, Tamsyn considered. He looked as though he would be indecently healthy, once rested.

'I was seized with an attack of acute boredom with the Great North Road, down which I was travelling, so, when I got to Newark, I turned south-west and just kept going, looking for somewhere completely wild and unspoilt.'

'And then attempted to swim to America?' What on earth prompted a man to strip off all his clothes, plunge into a cold sea and swim out so far that the current took him?

'I needed the exercise and I wanted to clear my mind. I certainly achieved the first, if not the second.' He stopped turning the glass between his fingers and took a long sip. 'This is very fine wine, I commend you on your supplier.'

'Probably smuggled,' Rosie said, accepting the abrupt change of subject. 'Things turn up on the doorstep. I suppose the correct thing to do is to knock a hole in the cask and drain it away, but that seems a wanton waste and one can hardly turn up at the excise office to pay duty without very awkward questions being asked.'

'There is much smuggling hereabouts?' Mr Defoe took another appreciative sip.

'It is the other main source of income,' Izzy, incorrigibly chatty and enthusiastic, confided. 'And of course dear Jory led the gang around here.'

'Jory?'

'My late husband,' Tamsyn said it reluctantly.

'Such a dear boy. I took him in when he was just a lad, he came from over the border in Cornwall, but his father found him…difficult and he ran away from home.'

'Dear Isobel is a great collector of lost lambs,' Rosie said drily.

'Such as me.' Even as she said it Tamsyn knew it sounded bitter and that had never been how she felt. She managed to lighten her voice as she added, 'My mother was Aunt Isobel's cousin and when she died when I was ten I came to live with her. Jory arrived the next year.'

'How romantic. Childhood sweethearts.' The word romantic emerged like a word barely understood in a foreign language.

'I married my best friend,' Tamsyn said stiffly. She was not going to elaborate on that one jot and have yet another person wonder why on earth she had married that scapegrace Jory Perowne when she could have had the eligible Franklin Holt, Viscount Chelford.

'And speaking of marriage,' Aunt Izzy said with her usual blithe disregard for atmosphere, 'has your man-servant notified your family of your whereabouts? Because, if not, the carrier's wagon will be leaving the village at nine tomorrow morning and will take letters into the Barnstaple receiving office.'

'Thank you, ma'am, but there is no one expecting my return. Now I have set Collins's mind at rest, my conscience can be clear on that front.'

'Excellent,' Tamsyn said briskly. It was nothing of the kind. Either he had a wife he could leave in ignorance with impunity, or he did not have one, and she would very much like to know which it was. Not that she was going to explore why she was so curious. 'Now, tell me, Mr Defoe, are you able to eat rabbit? I do hope you do not despise it, for we have a glut of the little menaces and I feel certain it will feature in tonight's dinner.'

Chapter Four

'What have you gleaned from your flirtation with Cook?' Cris asked as Collins took his discarded coat. The bed was looking devilishly tempting so he sat down on a hard upright chair instead and bent to take off his shoes. The doctor had been quite right, damn him. He should have stayed in bed for the whole of the day and not tried to get up until tomorrow, but everything in him rebelled against succumbing to weakness.

'Flirtation, sir? The lady is amiable enough, but her charms are rather on the mature side for my taste.' Cris lifted his head to glare at him and he relented. 'Cook, and Molly the maid, are both all of a flutter over a personable gentleman landing on Mrs Perowne's doorstep, as it were. That lady is the main force in the household, that's for certain, although Miss Holt owns the property. Very active and well liked in the local community is Mrs Perowne, even though she married the local, how shall I put it—?'

'Bad boy?' Cris enquired drily as he stood up and began to unbutton his waistcoat, resisting the temptation to pitch face down on the bed and go to sleep. It had been a long, long day.

'Precisely, sir. A charismatic young man, by all account, and a complete scoundrel, reading between the lines. But a sort of protégé of the two older ladies, who seem to have regarded him as a lovable rogue.'

'A substitute son, perhaps?'

'I wondered if that was the case.' Collins began to turn down the bed. 'And Molly did say something about it being a good thing he married Miss Tamsyn because otherwise *that little toad* Franklin Holt would have pestered her to distraction. Which I thought interesting, but Cook soon silenced Molly on that topic.'

'Franklin Holt? He is Viscount Chelford, I believe. I think I have seen him around. About my age, black hair, dark eyes, thinks a lot of himself.' Cris put his sapphire stickpin on the dresser and unwound his neckcloth. 'A gamester. I have no knowledge about his amphibious qualities.'

'That is the man, sir.' Collins's knowledge of the peerage was encyclopedic and almost as good as his comprehension of the underworld. 'He has a reputation as someone who plunges deep in all matters of sport and play and he is Miss Holt's nephew. He inherited her father's lands and titles.'

'And he was annoying Miss Tamsyn, was he?' And was more than annoying her now, by the sound of it. But why the ladies should imagine he was responsible for sending their sheep over a cliff, he could not imagine.

Cris pulled off his shirt, shed his trousers and sank gratefully into the enfolding goose-feather bed. 'You know, Collins, I think I may have overdone things this evening. I feel extraordinarily weak suddenly.'

'That is very worrying, sir.' The other man's face was perfectly expressionless. 'I fear you may have to presume on Miss Holt's hospitality for several days in that case. I would diagnose a severely pulled muscle in your back and a possible threat to your weak chest.'

Cris, who could not recall ever having had a wheeze, let alone a bad chest, tried out a pathetic cough. 'I do fear that travelling would be unwise, but I am reluctant to impose further upon the ladies.'

'I understand your scruples, sir. I will find a cane so you may hobble more comfortably. However, it will be agony for you to travel over these roads with such an injury and I confess myself most anxious that you might insist on doing so. I will probably be so concerned that I will let my tongue run away with me and say so in front of the servants.'

Cris closed his eyes. 'Thank you, Collins. You know, you almost convince me of how weak I am. I am certain that if you confide your fears to Cook the intelligence will reach Miss Holt before the morning.'

'Good night, sir.' The door closed softly behind the valet and when Cris opened his eyes the room was dark. He smiled, thinking, not for the first time, that it was a good thing that Collins chose to employ his dubious talents on the side of the government and law and order.

Correct behaviour would be to take himself off the next morning, relieving his kind hostesses of the presence of a strange man in their house. But something was wrong her. Tamsyn Perowne was tense, the vague and cheerful Miss Holt was hiding anxiety and the much sharper Miss Pritchard was on the point of direct accusations. But why would they think that Chelford was behind the agricultural slaughter? The man would have to be deranged and, although Cris had seen nothing in their brief encounters to like about the viscount, neither had he any reason to think him insane.

It was a mystery and Cris liked mysteries. What was

more, there were three ladies in distress, who had, between them, possibly saved his life. He owed them his assistance. If he was searching for something to take his mind off love lost in the past, and a marriage of duty in the future, then surely this was it? There was, after all, nothing else he felt like doing.

Come the morning Cris was not certain that he needed any acting skills to convince his hostesses that he was unable to travel. His exhausted muscles, eased the day before by the hot bath and Collins's manipulation, had stiffened overnight into red-hot agony. After another painful massage session he swore his way out of bed and through the process of dressing. He negotiated the stairs with the assistance of the cane Collins had produced from somewhere and had no trouble sounding irritable when he and the other man took up their carefully calculated positions in the hall in order to have a *sotto voce* argument. He pitched both his voice and his tone to tempt even the best-behaved person to approach the other side of the door to listen to what was going on.

'Of course we are going to leave after breakfast. How many more times do I have to tell you, Collins? I cannot presume upon the hospitality of three single ladies in this way.'

'But, sir, with the risk of your bronchitis returning, I cannot like it,' Collins protested. 'And the pain to your back with the jolting over these roads—why, you might be incapacitated for weeks afterwards.'

'That does not matter. I am sure I can find a halfway acceptable inn soon enough.'

'In this area? And we do not have our own sheets with us, sir!' Collins's dismay was so well-acted that

Cris was hard put to it not to laugh. 'Please, I beg you to reconsider.'

'No, my mind is made up. I am going—'

'Nowhere, Mr Defoe.' The door to the drawing room opened to reveal Mrs Perowne, her ridiculous cap slightly askew as it slid from the pins skewering it to her brown hair. Her hands were on her hips, those lush lips firmly compressed.

The thought intruded that he would like to see them firmly compressed around— *No.*

His thoughts could not have been visible on his face, given that she did not slap it. 'The doctor said you were to stay in bed yesterday and you ignored him, so no wonder you are not feeling quite the thing this morning. If you have a tendency to bronchitis it is completely foolish to risk aggravating it and what is this about a painful back?'

Cris discovered that he did not like to be thought of as weak, or an invalid, or, for that matter, prone to bronchitis, which should be of no importance whatsoever beside the necessity of convincing Mrs Perowne that he should stay put in this house. His pride was, he realised, thoroughly affronted. That was absurd—was he so insecure that he needed to show off his strength in front of some country widow? 'The merest twinge, and Collins exaggerates. It is only that I had a severe cold last winter.'

'Oh, sir.' The reproach in Collins's voice would have not been out of place in a Drury Lane melodrama. 'After what the doctor said last year. Madam, I could tell you tales—'

'But not if you wish to remain in my employ,' Cris snapped and they both turned reproachful, anxious looks on him.

'Mr Defoe, please, I implore you to stay. My aunts would worry so if you left before you were quite recovered, and besides, we are most grateful for your company.' There was something in the warm brown eyes that was certainly not pity for an invalid, a flicker of recognition of him as a man that touched his wounded pride and soothed it, even as he told himself not to be such a coxcomb as to set any store by what a virtual stranger thought of him. Before now he had played whatever role his duties as a not-quite-official diplomat required and it had never given him the slightest qualm to appear over-cautious, or indiscreet, or naïve, in some foreign court. He knew he was none of those things, so that was all that mattered.

But this woman, who should mean nothing to him, had him wanting to parade his courage and his endurance and his fitness like some preening peacock flaunting his tail in front of his mate. He swallowed what was left of his pride. 'If it would not be an imposition, Mrs Perowne, I confess I would be grateful for a few days' respite.'

'Excellent. My aunts will be very relieved to hear it.'

'They are not within earshot, then?' he enquired, perversely wanting to provoke her.

He was rewarded with the tinge of colour that stained her cheekbones. 'You reprove me for eavesdropping, Mr Defoe? I plead guilty to it, but I was concerned for you and suspected you would attempt to leave today, however you felt.'

Now he felt guilty on top of everything else and it was an unfamiliar emotion. He did not do things that offended his own sense of honour, therefore there was never anything to feel guilty about. 'I apologise, Mrs

Perowne. That was ungracious of me when you show such concern for an uninvited guest.'

'You are forgiven, and to show to what extent, let me lead you through to the breakfast room and you may tell me what you think of our own sausages and bacon.'

Cris, ignoring Collins's faint smile, which, in a lesser man, would have been a smirk, followed her into a sunny room with yellow chintz curtains and a view down the sloping lawn to the sea. 'Should we not wait for your aunts?'

'They always breakfast in their room.' Mrs Perowne gestured to a seat and sat opposite. The centre of the table had platters of bread and ham, a bowl of butter and a covered dish. 'Let me serve you, you will not want to be stretching to lift dishes.' As she spoke she raised the dome and a tantalising aroma of bacon and sausage wafted out.

'Thank you.' He meekly accepted a laden plate and tried to work out the enigma that was Mrs Tamsyn Perowne. She was well spoken, confident, competent and a lady, even if she was decidedly out of the ordinary. She was distantly related to a viscount, but she had married a local man who had died one leap ahead of the noose.

'That is a charming portrait on the wall behind you,' he remarked. 'Your aunts do not resemble each other greatly. Are they your mother's relations or your father's, if I might ask?'

'Aunt Isobel is my mother's cousin. Aunt Rosie is not a relation.' Mrs Perowne shot him a very direct glance as though measuring his reaction. 'They left home to set up house together when they were in their late twenties. It was—is—a passionate friendship, as close as a marriage.'

'Like the famous Ladies of Llangollen?'

'Yes, just like that. It was their inspiration, I believe. Are you shocked?'

'No, not at all. Why should they not be happy together?' Lucky women, able to turn their backs on the demands of society and its expectations. But daughters did not bear the same weight of expectation that sons did, especially elder sons, with the requirements of duty to make a good match, bring wealth and connections into the family, provide an heir to title and estates.

'And you?' he asked when she gave him an approving nod and turned her attention to a dish of eggs in cream. 'What led you to make your life here?'

'My father was a naval man and I cannot even recall his face. He was killed at sea when I was scarcely toddling. Mama found things very difficult without him. I think she was not a strong character.'

'So you had to be strong for both of you?' he suggested.

'Yes. How did you know?' The quick look of pleasure at his understanding made Cris smile back. She really was a charming woman with her expressive face and healthy colour. And young still, not much above twenty-five, he would estimate.

'You have natural authority, yet you wear it lightly. I doubt you learned it recently. What happened to your mother?'

'She succumbed to one of the cholera epidemics. We lived in Portsmouth and like all ports many kinds of infection are rife.'

'And then you came here?' He tried to imagine the feelings of the orphaned girl, leaving the place that she knew, mourning for her mother. He had lost his own mother when he was four, bearing the sibling he never knew. His father, a remote, chilly figure, had died when he was barely ten, leaving Cris a very young, very frightened marquess. Rigorously hiding his feelings behind a mask of frigid reserve had got him through that ordeal. It still served him well.

'Do your duty,' was his father's dying command and the only advice he ever gave his son on holding one of the premier titles in the land. But he had found it covered every difficulty he encountered. *Do your duty* usually meant *do what you least want to do* because it was hard, or painful, or meant he must use his head, not his heart, to solve a problem, but he had persevered. *It even stood me in good stead to prevent me sacrificing honour for love*, he thought bitterly.

'Aunt Izzy is a maternal creature,' Tamsyn said. 'She adopted Jory, she took me in.' She slanted a teasing smile at Cris. 'I think she sees you as her next good cause.'

'Do I appear to need mothering?'

'From my point of view?' She studied him, head on one side, a wicked glint in her eyes, apparently not at all chilled by his frigid tone. 'No, I feel absolutely no inclination to mother you, Mr Defoe. But you could have died, you are still recovering, and that is quite enough for Aunt Izzy.' Having silenced him, she added, 'Will you be resting today?'

'I will walk. My muscles will seize up if I rest. I thought I would go along the lane for a while.'

'It is uphill all the way for a mile until the combe joins Stib Valley, but there are several places to rest—fallen trees, rocks.' Mrs Perowne was showing not the slightest desire to fuss over him, which was soothing to his male pride and a setback for his scheme to draw her out.

'Will you not come with me? Show me the way?'

'There is absolutely no opportunity for you to get lost, Mr Defoe. If you manage to reach the lane to Stibworthy, then by turning right you will descend to Stib's Landing. Left will take you to the village and the tracks to either side will lead you to the clifftops.'

'I was hoping for your company, not your guidance.' Cris tried to look wistful, which, he knew, was not an expression that sat well on his austere features.

Tamsyn took the top off a boiled egg with a sharp swipe of her knife. 'Lonely, Mr Defoe?' she enquired sweetly.

Cris did not rise to the mockery. 'It is a while since I had the opportunity to walk in such unspoiled countryside and have a conversation with a young lady at the same time.'

She pursed her mouth, although whether to suppress a smile or a wry expression of resignation he could not tell. 'I have to go and see our shepherd about the... incident yesterday. I am intending to ride, but I will walk with you up the combe until you tire, then ride on from there. There is no particular hurry, the damage has been done.'

Cris wondered whether she was as cool and crisp with everyone or whether she did not like him. Possibly it was a cover for embarrassment. After all, he had come lurching out of the sea, stark naked, seized hold of her and then kissed her, neither of which were the actions of a gentleman. But Tamsyn Perowne did not strike him as a woman who was easily embarrassed. She had an earthy quality about her, which was not at all coarse but rather made him think of pagan goddesses—Primavera, perhaps, bringing growing things and springtime in her wake.

It was refreshing after the artificiality of London society or the Danish court. There, ladies wore expressions of careful neutrality and regarded showing their feelings as a sign of weakness, or ill breeding. Even Katerina had hidden behind a façade of indifferent politeness. *And thank heavens, for that,* Cris thought. Self-control and the ability to disguise their feelings had been all that stood between them and a major scandal. Mrs Perowne could keep secrets, he was sure of that, but she would find it hard to suppress her emotions. He thought of her spirited response to the magistrate, the anger so openly expressed. Would her lovemaking be so passionate, so frank?

It was an inappropriate thought and, from her suddenly arrested expression, this time something of it had shown on his face. 'Mr Defoe?' There was a touch of ice behind the question.

'I was thinking of how magnificently you routed that boor of a magistrate yesterday,' he said.

'I dislike incompetence, laziness and foolishness,' she said. 'Mr Penwith possesses all three in abundance.'

'Doubtless you consider me foolish, almost getting myself drowned yesterday.' If she thought him an idiot she was not going to confide in him, and unless she did, it was going to be more difficult to discover what was threatening the ladies Combe. Not impossible, just more time consuming and, for all he knew, there wasn't the luxury of time.

'Reckless, certainly.' She was cutting into her toast with the same attack that she had applied to beheading the egg. 'I suspect you had something on your mind.'

'Yes,' he agreed. 'That must be my excuse.'

'Mr Defoe.' She laid down her knife and looked directly at him across the breakfast table. 'It is easy to become…distracted when we are hurting. It would be a mistake to allow that distraction to become fatal. There is always hope. Everything passes.'

She thinks I was trying to kill myself. The realisation hit him as he saw there was no smile, no teasing, in those brown eyes. Then he saw the ghost of something besides concern. *Pain. She is speaking of herself. When her husband died did she want to die, too?*

'I know. And there are responsibilities and duties to keep one going, are there not? I was angry with myself for my lack of focus, Tamsyn. I have no desire to find myself in a lethal predicament again because I have lost concentration.'

Cris realised he had called her by her first name as her eyebrows lifted, giving her tanned, pleasant face a sudden look of haughty elegance. She was not a conventional beauty, but he was reminded again what a very feminine creature she was, for all her practicality. 'I apologise for the familiarity, but your concern disarmed me. May we not be friends? I do feel we have been very thoroughly introduced.'

Tamsyn laughed, a sudden rich chuckle that held surprise and wickedness and warmth even though she blushed, just a little. 'Indeed we have… That moment in the sea. I do not normally…'

'Kiss strange men?' Now she was pink from the collarbone upwards. 'If it is any consolation, I do not normally kiss mermaids.' That made her laugh. 'It felt like touching life when I thought I was dying.'

'It was an extraordinary moment, like something from a myth. You thought I was a mermaid, I thought you were a merman, Christopher.'

'Cris,' he corrected. 'St Crispin, if we are to be exact.'

"'And Crispin Crispian shall ne'er go by, from this

day to the ending of the world, but we in it shall be remember'd,'" she quoted, visibly recovering her composure. 'Your parents were Shakespearian enthusiasts? Or is your birthday October the twenty-fifth?'

'Both. My father was much given to quoting Henry V. *"Once more unto the breach, dear friends."* He would mutter it before anything he did not want to do, such as attending social gatherings.'

'How infuriating for your mother.'

'She died many years ago, in childbirth. My father was shot in the shoulder in a hunting accident and developed blood poisoning.' He stopped to calculate. 'It was nineteen years ago, the day before my tenth birthday.' He would not normally speak so openly about their deaths, but he wanted Tamsyn to talk of her husband's fatal plunge from the cliff and his frankness might encourage hers.

'I am so sorry. You poor little boy, you must have been so alone. I was ten when I lost my mother to that epidemic, but at least I had the aunts.'

'There were many people to look after me.' Four trustees, one hundred servants, indoor and outdoor. There had been three tutors, a riding master, a fencing master, an art master, a dancing master—all dedicated to turning out the young Marquess of Avenmore in as perfect a form as possible.

'I am glad of that,' Tamsyn murmured. 'Now, some more coffee before we take our walk?' She passed him the pot, a fine old silver one. 'I cannot delay much longer or Willie Tremayne will think I have forgotten him. I will meet you at the garden gate.'

Cris sat with his coffee cooling in the cup for several minutes after she had gone from the room. This household, and its inhabitants, were unlike any he had encountered before. He supposed it was because, used as he was to palaces, government offices, great houses or bachelor lodgings, he had never before experienced the world of the gentry. Were they all so warm, so unaffected? He gave himself a shake and swallowed the cold coffee as a penance for daydreaming. He had to get his reluctant limbs moving and find a coat or he would be keeping Tamsyn Perowne waiting.

Chapter Five

The garden gate was as good a perch as it had been when she had first come to Barbary, but now it did not seem like a mountain to climb. Tamsyn hooked the toes of her riding boots over a rail and kept her weight at the hinge end, as a proper countrywoman knew to do. The breeze from the sea blew up the lane, stirring the curls that kept escaping from under the old-fashioned tricorn she had jammed over her hair and flipping the ends of her stock until she caught them and stuffed them into the neck of her jacket. She felt almost frivolous, and if that was the result of looking forward to a very slow walk up the lane with an ailing gentleman, then it was obvious that she was not getting out enough.

Mr Defoe—*Cris*—emerged from the door just as Jason led out Foxy, her big chestnut gelding, and she bit her lip rather than smile at her own whimsy. He might think she was laughing at his cane.

'Leg up, Mrs Tamsyn?'

'I'm walking for a little while, thank you, Jason.' She jumped down from the gate and pulled the reins over the gelding's head to lead him and he butted her with his nose, confused about why she was not mounting.

'That's a big beast.' Cris was walking slowly, using the cane, but without limping or leaning on it. She did her best not to stare. He would experience enough of that if he walked as far as Stibworthy and the locals had a good look at his pale tan buckskins and beautiful boots. He might as well have dressed for a ball, as donned that dark brown riding coat and the low-crowned beaver. He clicked his tongue at Foxy and the horse turned his head to look at him. 'Powerful hocks and a good neck on him. Is he a puller?'

'No, he's a pussy cat with lovely manners and a soft mouth, aren't you, my handsome red fox?' She was rewarded with a slobbery nuzzle at her shoulder. 'But I wish you were a tidier kisser.'

That provoked a snort of amusement from the man holding the gate open for her. Possibly references to kissing were not such a good idea. She could still feel the heat of his mouth on hers, in shocking contrast to the cold of his skin. And despite any amount of effort with the tooth powder, she imagined she could still taste him, salty and male.

Two years without kisses had been a long time, and this was a man who seemed to have been created to tempt women. *He probably has several in keeping and has to beat off the rest with his fine leather gloves.* Intimacy with a man to whom she was not married had never occurred to her before now. Was it simply that the passage of time had left her yearning for the lovemaking that she had learned to enjoy? Or was it this man?

She had never seriously considered remarrying, although sometimes she wondered if, given any encouragement, Dr Tregarth might have declared an interest. But it would be unfair to any man when she… *With my past*, she substituted before she let herself follow that train of thought.

Thoughts of illicit intimacy were certainly occurring to her now and the fact that Cris Defoe was walking with a cane and complaining of a bad back and weak chest did absolutely nothing to suppress some very naughty thoughts. They turned up the lane and she wandered along, letting Cris set the pace. The sound of their feet and the horse's hooves were muffled by the sand that filled the ruts in the pebbly turf, and the music of the sea behind them and the song of the skylark high above filled the silence between them.

'Salt from the sea, vanilla from the gorse and wild garlic,' he said after a few minutes. 'The air around here is almost painfully clear after the smoke of towns or the heat of inland countryside, don't you think?'

Cris was not breathing heavily, despite the increasing slope of the lane as it rose up the combe. He was certainly very fit. She remembered the muscles strapping his chest and his flat stomach, the hard strength as she had gripped his bare shoulders in the sea. Unless he developed the chest infection his valet seemed to fear, his recovery should be rapid. 'I do not know about towns— I hardly recall Portsmouth and our local ones, Barnstaple, Bideford and Bude, are small and they are not the kind I think you have in mind. How is your back?'

'My... Oh, yes. Amazingly the exercise has already straightened the knots out of it. You have never been to London, then?'

'No, never.'

And I'll wager you have never had bronchitis in your life and your back hurts you no more than the rest of you does. So what is this nonsense about being unable to endure a coach ride over rough roads?

The track turned as they came out from the trees on to the pastureland. 'There's a fallen tree.' Cris stopped, made a show of flexing his shoulders. 'Shall we sit a while? The view looks good from here.'

And you need a rest? He was a good actor, she would give him that. But she suspected that this man would no more willingly admit weakness than he would ride a donkey, so he must have a good reason other than exhaustion or sore muscles for wanting to stop. 'Certainly,' she agreed, and tossed Foxy's reins over a handy branch. 'Don't mind me, you sit down,' she added over her shoulder. As she turned back to the tree trunk she was treated to a fine display of bravely controlled wincing and the sight of Cris's long legs being folded painfully down to the low seat.

She could go along with it and let him fish for whatever it was he wanted, or she could stop this nonsense now. Jory had been a man who was constitutionally incapable of giving a straight answer, a husband who could keep virtually his entire life, and certainly his thoughts, secret from his wife, and she was weary of mysteries.

'Mr Defoe.' His head came up at her tone and his eyes narrowed for an instant before he was all amiable attention. No, he was doing a good job of it, but she was not at all convinced by this harmless exterior.

'Why so formal all of a sudden, Tamsyn?'

Now he was trying to unsettle her because he knew she was not entirely comfortable with first names. Tamsyn sat down. 'Because I have a bone to pick with you, sir. You are no more in need of a rest than I am. I can believe that you are sore and your muscles are giving you hell, but if you are so sickly that you are about to succumb to a chest infection and you are incapable of riding in a coach over rough ground, then I am the Queen of the May.'

'You are flattening to a man's self-esteem, Mrs Perowne.'

'Why flattening? I imagine you hate being thought less than invincible. Most men do.'

'Ouch. Now *that* hurts. I mean that I dislike being so transparent.'

'You are not. But I saw you stripped to the core yesterday—and I do not mean stripped of clothes,' she added as that infuriating eyebrow rose. She did so wish she could do that… 'You would have kept on going until you dropped dead rather than lie there passively on the beach and be fetched. You hated being weak and in need of help. If your man with your coach had been anywhere in the neighbourhood, you would have crawled a mile to him on your hands and knees rather than admit to needing three women to help you. So why so unwilling to travel now and leave here?'

Cris leaned back against a sapling, folded his hands over the head of his cane and looked at her. It was a long, considering stare with no humour and no flirtation in it. If she was a parlour maid being interviewed, she suspected she would not get the position. If she was a horse for sale, he was obviously doubtful about her bloodlines. When he spoke she almost jumped.

'You may well have saved my life. I am in your debt. There is something very wrong here and if it is in my power, I will remedy it.' From another man there would have been a note of boasting, of masculine superiority over the poor, helpless females. But this sounded like a simple declaration of fact. Something was wrong. Crispin Defoe would fix it.

It had been so long since there had been anyone from

outside the household to confide in, or to lean on, just a little. Even Jory could be relied on only to do what suited his interests. They had been fortunate that he had adored Aunt Izzy and had been fond of Tamsyn. But this man would be leaving, very soon. He did not belong here, he had drifted to Barbary Combe House, borne on the current of a whim that had brought him across England. Soon he would return and to rely on him for anything—other than to disturb her dreams— was dangerous.

'Nonsense. You do not owe us anything, we would have done the same for anyone who needed help. And there is absolutely nothing wrong except for a rogue dog and some valuable sheep lost.'

'You see?' The austere face was disapproving. 'That is precisely why I felt it necessary to have an excuse for lingering here. You are going to be stubborn.'

'I am not stubborn—if anyone is, it is you. You find three women living alone and assume they are incapable of dealing with life and its problems.' She walked away across the grass, spun round and marched back, temper fraying over her moment of weakness. 'We are managing very well by ourselves, Mr Defoe, and I am rather tired of gentlemen telling me that we are not.'

'Who else has the nerve to do that?'

'It takes no particular nerve, merely impertinence.' She took Foxy's reins, led him to the far end of the tree trunk and used it as a mounting block. 'I am sure you can manage the path back.' Cris stood up and took the reins just above the bit. 'Let go at once!'

'Tamsyn, I am not an idiot and neither are you. Something is wrong, your aunts are distressed and who is the other interfering gentleman?'

'Aunt Izzy's nephew considers we would do better

living in a house on his estate. He seems over-protective all of a sudden.'

'Lord Chelford.'

'You have been *eavesdropping*.' Foxy's ears twitched back as her voice rose. 'Hardly the action of a gentleman.'

'Neither is ignoring ladies in distress.' He stood there looking up at her, his hand firm on Foxy's bridle. 'I wish you would get down off your high horse, Tamsyn. Literally. You are giving me a crick in my neck. I happened to overhear something completely accidentally. Collins heard more because he likes to gossip. Now, of course, you may simply be a trio of hysterical females, leaping to conclusions and making a crisis out of a series of accidents—'

'How dare you?' Tamsyn twisted in the saddle to face him, lost her balance and grabbed for the reins. Cris reached up, took her by the waist and lifted her, sliding and protesting, down to the ground. Trapped between Foxy's bulk and Cris's body, she clenched her fist and thumped him square in the centre of the chest. 'You are no gentleman!'

'Yes, I am. The problem is that you do not appear to have any others in your life with whom to compare me. Now, stop jumping up and down on my toes, which is doing nothing for the state of my boots, and come and sit on the tree trunk and tell me all about it.' She opened her mouth to speak. 'And I am the soul of discretion, you need have no fear this will go any further.'

'If you would allow me to get a word in edgeways, Mr Defoe, I would point out to you that I am unable to get off your toes, or move in any direction, because you still have your hands on my person.' In fact they seemed to be encircling her waist, which was impossible, she was not that slim.

'I have?' He did not move, although she could have sworn that the pressure on her waist increased. 'It must be a reflex. I was anxious that you were going to fall off.' He still managed to maintain that austere, almost haughty, expression, except for a wicked glint in those blue eyes that should have looked innocent and instead held a wealth of knowledge and deep wells of experience. *Thank goodness. He is going to kiss me.*

And then he…didn't. Cris stepped back, released her and gestured to the tree trunk. 'Shall we sit down and try this again? I will tie up your horse again, he is becoming confused.'

'He is not the only one,' Tamsyn muttered. Of course he was not going to kiss her. Whoever got kissed wearing a dreadful old hat like hers? Certainly no one being held by an elegant gentleman whose boots would probably have cost more than her entire wardrobe for the past five years.

Cris came back to the tree and she noticed his cane was lying forgotten on the grass. 'What else has happened besides the accident to the sheep yesterday?' he asked as he sat beside her.

'You will doubtless say we are simply imagining things.'

'Try me. I can be remarkably imaginative myself when I want to be.'

'A hayrick caught fire two weeks ago. Our little dairy herd got through a fence last week and strayed all over the parish before we caught them. All our lobster pots keep coming up empty. And now the sheep.'

'All this in the span of two weeks?' When she nodded he scrubbed his hand across his chin and frowned at the now-scuffed toes of his boots. 'Even my imagination is baulking at that as a series of coincidences.' His frown deepened and Tamsyn fought the urge to apologise for the state of his boots. 'May I ask how your aunts are supported financially?'

She saw no harm in telling him, none of it was a secret, after all. 'Aunt Izzy has the use of Barbary Combe House and its estate for her lifetime, along with all the income to spend as she wishes. She also has the use of everything in the house for her lifetime. Anything she buys with the income is hers to dispose of as she wishes, as are the stock and movable assets of the estate. Aunt Rosie has a very respectable competence inherited from her father and other relatives. She has high expenses, of course, because of her health—she paid for the bathing room, which uses a lot of fuel, and she also consults a number of medical men. Both of them live well within their incomes.'

'And you?' Cris said it quite without inflection, as though he were her banker or her lawyer gathering the facts before advising on an investment. And there was no reason why she should not tell him. After all, establishing her non-existent pride was simply another fact for his calculations.

'I have a small inheritance from my parents. Aunt Izzy makes me an allowance and in return I act as her land steward.'

'And your husband?'

The cool, impersonal voice left her no room for manoeuvre. Tamsyn shrugged. 'Jory left me nothing. Or, rather, he had a fishing smack, a small house, nets, gear, firearms... All used in the commission of criminal offences, all seized by the Excise after his death. To have laid claim to anything would have been to admit I was a partner in his activities.'

'And were you?'

'I knew what he was doing, of course I did, even though he kept all the actual details secret. Everyone on this coast knew and I was married to the man, after all. He led a gang of smugglers.'

If she had thought for a moment that she would fob off Cris Defoe with that as an explanation, then she was mistaken, it seemed. 'Smuggling covers everything from bringing in the odd cask of brandy under a load of herring, to a cover for spying, by way of full-scale organised crime accompanied by murder, extortion and blackmail. Where on that spectrum was Jory Perowne?'

'You know a lot about it. Perhaps you are a magistrate yourself and I would be well advised not to compound my indiscretion.' She smiled, lowered her lashes, wondered if she could remember how to flirt. *If I ever knew.*

'No, I am not a magistrate.' That was a surprise. He had said he was a landowner and most landowners of any standing were justices. 'I have been crossing the Channel, back and forth, for ten years and one cannot do that without hearing about smugglers.'

There was a little nugget of information to tuck away and muse upon in that comment. Mr Defoe had been crossing the Channel at a time when England was at war with France, even if it was now five years since Waterloo had brought peace again. Had he been in the army? But the way that he spoke made it sound as though he was still crossing over to the Continent on a regular basis. He could hardly be a merchant, not with his clothes and the indefinable air of *ton*nishness that even a country mouse like her could recognise. And *ton*nish gentlemen did not engage in trade.

Perhaps he is a spy himself and he ended up in the sea after being thrown overboard by an arch enemy in a life-and-death struggle—

'Mrs Perowne? Am I boring you?'

'Not at all, Mr Defoe. I was merely contemplating the perils of the sea for a moment.'

And wondering why your voice sends little shivers up and down my back when you drawl like that when really I ought to give you a sharp set-down for sarcasm.

Just to prove she had been paying attention she added coolly, 'Jory was in about the middle of your spectrum. He ran a highly organised smuggling ring with high-value goods and he was not averse to violence when his business was threatened by rivals or the Excise. But he protected the aunts fiercely, the people hereabouts worshipped him and he looked after them. You probably think me shocking for not condemning him, but he was loyal and courageous and looked after his men, and smuggling is a way of life around these coasts.'

'The Excise must have given you a very difficult time after his death when they were looking for the profits of his activities.'

'They could not have been looking as hard as I was.' The villagers had needed the money when their main local industry collapsed overnight with Jory's death. 'They bullied me and threatened me and finally allowed that I was just a poor feeble woman led astray by a wicked rogue.'

'Could Chelford be searching for hidden treasure on the assumption that Jory Perowne hid his ill-gotten gains somewhere on the estate?' She must have been staring at him with her mouth agape because he enquired, dry as a bone, 'Is that such a ridiculous idea?'

Chapter Six

Despite herself, Tamsyn laughed. 'Ridiculous? No. It is brilliant and I am just amazed that I am such a ninnyhammer that I did not think of it for myself. It is precisely the kind of thing that Franklin would think of—that there must be treasure and therefore a chance to grab it for himself.'

'Then I suggest we search, locate the hoard and thwart Chelford.' The thought of hunting for buried treasure seemed to appeal to Cris.

All men are such boys, even the most impressive specimens. 'Unfortunately, whatever fantasies Franklin might have, I do not believe there is any treasure to be found. The idea that he would think it exists is a good one, but I suspect Jory would have done something truly infuriating with his profits, like putting it in a bank in Exeter under a false name and then forgetting to tell me.'

'Are you certain there is not?' Cris's question had a hopeful note to it.

Yes, he is definitely disappointed. 'There are no secret caves or tunnels. Or, rather, none that I or the villagers don't know about. And Jory had more sense than to bury money in the churchyard in a nice fresh grave or any of the other tricks. He would want it earning interest and to be safe, not where someone might stumble across it.'

'A nice fresh grave?' Cris sounded incredulous. 'You shock me.'

'It is the best way to hide newly turned earth, of course. You wait for someone in the village to be buried, come along that night and do the reverse of grave robbing.' The question was in his eyes and she thought of teasing him some more, but relented. 'And, no, I have never taken part in such a thing. I have more respect for my fellow parishioners, although I suspect none of them would be very surprised or distressed if it happened.' He still looked unconvinced. 'It is difficult for city dwellers to shake off their preconceptions about us rustics who live on the very edge of the country. We are not neatly divided into dyed-in-the-wool rogues and happy pastoral innocents.'

'No, I suspect you are all rather more complex than that.' He watched her from beneath lowered lids, an unsettling appraisal that made her feel anything but complicated.

'I must go.' It was far too comfortable sitting here in the sunshine exchanging ideas, teasing and being teased. Tamsyn stood up and Cris followed her. 'I must see Willie Tremayne and make certain the remainder of the flock are safe.'

'Of course.' He made no move to detain her. But why should he? That moment when he had held her so close as she slid from the saddle and she had thought he was about to kiss her had been nothing more than her imagination. Just because he had kissed her once was no reason to suppose he had any desire to do it again.

'Let me give you a leg up.'

'No need.' She was on the log, and from there to the saddle, as she spoke, chiding herself as she did it.

You have no idea how to flirt, do you? You should have let him help you mount, let his hands linger on your foot or perhaps your ankle. You should have thanked him prettily, as a lady should, not gone scrambling on to Foxy like a tomboy.

'I will see you at luncheon, perhaps.' She waved her free hand as she urged the horse into a canter along the path that led to the clifftop pastures and did not look back.

When she knew she was out of sight she slowed, reined Foxy back to a walk, which was quite fast enough on the rabbit-burrowed turf, and turned her face into the breeze to cool the colour that she guessed was staining her cheeks. Cris Defoe had done nothing at all, other than look at her with warmth in his eyes and hold her a little too close when she dismounted, and yet she was all aflutter and expecting more. A great deal more.

She had no excuse, she told herself as she reached the stone and turf bank and turned along it towards the gate. Nor was there any reason not to be honest with herself. For the first time since Jory had died she had been jolted out of her hard-working, pleasant routine by a man. A handsome—*oh, very well, beautiful*—man. A man of sophistication and education. Someone who could discuss more than the price of herring and the demand for beef cattle in Barnstaple.

He had kissed her in the sea and now she had woken up from her trance, a rather soggy Sleeping Beauty. *Not much of a beauty... But I want him.* To be exact, and to look the thing squarely in the face, she wanted to go to bed with him, get her hands on that lean body, make love with him. She should be shocked with herself, she supposed. But weren't widows allowed more freedom? Couldn't she be a little daring, a trifle dashing? 'I'm my own mistress,' she informed Foxy, who politely swivelled an ear back to listen. 'And I would rather like to be Cris Defoe's mistress, just for a while.'

He was a man who knew about these things, she was sure. Elegant, sophisticated widows probably indicated their availability to him on a daily basis when he was not stuck in the wilds of Devon. And there was the rub. *Sophisticated.* Tamsyn hooked the latch with her riding crop and let Foxy push the gate open, then reined back to hook it closed again. She could attend the local assemblies at Barnstaple or Bideford looking perfectly respectable and well dressed. She would receive a gratifying number of requests for dances, she was never short of a supper partner, but none of those gentlemen had one-tenth of the poise or *finish* that Cris Defoe possessed. And while she entertained with confidence and knew she had nothing to be ashamed of in her education or her manners, her social skills had never been tested in a London drawing room.

Which was not really the problem, Tamsyn told herself as she urged Foxy into a canter across the level ground of the headland. Put her in a drawing room with a duchess and she was sure courtesy and imagination would see her through. But how did one go about indicating one's availability to a man, other than by coming right out and stating one's desires? Or dressing immodestly?

She'd had to do neither with Jory. One day she had bumped into him as she came running across the meadow, late for tea because of a difficult encounter with Franklin. They had clung together, breathless. He had been laughing until he saw the tears she was fighting not to show. They had been old friends, comfortable together. And then their eyes had met and the laughter in his had died, and the comfort was replaced by something that was not at all cosy or familiar, and the next thing his mouth was on hers and...

'Mizz Tamsyn!' It was Willie, hailing her from the far gate, his battered old hat pushed far back so his weathered face was clear to see. He looked grim, but he raised a smile for her as she drew close. Behind him he had the sheep penned under the watchful eye of his black and white Border collie, Thorn.

'A bad business, Willie.' She stayed where she was, not wanting to disturb the remains of the flock any more than she had to.

'Aye, it is that. And deliberate, too. The hurdle was dragged out of the gap and thrown aside. There's no way it could have been pushed out by the sheep, or blown by the wind.'

'I know, you always wire it back into the gap when it isn't being used to move the flock.' She saw him relax a little. 'Does anyone recognise the dog?'

'No, it's not from round here. Scrawny, mean-looking beast, but not mad, I reckon.'

'Someone brought it in, especially?'

'Aye, that'll be it. Someone got a grudge, Mizz Tamsyn? Folks is starting to talk, what with the ricks and all that. Isn't anyone local—you know that. We all owe too much to you and the ladies, and no one forgets Jory Perowne, not round here.'

'No, it isn't a grudge, Willie. I think someone is out to scare us, though. Tell people to look out for strangers, will you?'

'We will that.' He grinned suddenly, exposing his

tobacco-stained teeth. 'Not likely to be yon merman you fished out, that's for sure.'

'He's no merman, Willie. Just a gentleman who got caught in the current when he was swimming.'

'Ha! Fool thing to be doing, that swimming lark. They do say that folks are visiting Ilfracombe specially to get in the sea in wooden huts on wheels and they pay to be ducked by hefty great females. Pay good money! What they be wanting to do that for, Mizz Tamsyn? 'Tis foolishness.'

'Some doctors say seawater is good for you, Willie.'

'Huh! Good for drowning in, more like.'

'Well, they must find something good about it, given how hard it is to get to Ilfracombe with the roads like they are.'

'That what yon gentleman was doing, then? Sea bathing for his health?' He nodded, obviously pleased that he had solved the mystery. 'He'll be some weedy invalid then, all spindleshanks and a cough.'

'Not *quite*.' Tamsyn managed not to smile. There was absolutely nothing spindly about Cris Defoe. 'But he will be staying with us for a while longer. For his health.'

'Will he now?'

Tamsyn knew the tone. It could be roughly interpreted as, *Some of us will take a look at him and we'll sort him out proper if he's up to anything with Jory Perowne's widow.* She appreciated their loyalty, but there were times when the fact that the whole closeknit community knew everyone's business made her want to scream with frustration.

'Yes, he will. Now, do you think we ought to pay some of the lads to watch the animals at night for a while?'

'Good idea.' Willie, distracted from the thought of a strange man under the Barbary Combe House roof, leaned his elbows on the gate and settled down to a discussion of who was reliable and whether one lad alone was more reliable than two or three, all egging each other on for mischief.

Cris stood up and, now that he was alone, permitted himself the indulgence of a long, slow stretch. His muscles were still sore across his shoulders and deep in his thighs, but the walk uphill had done them good. By tomorrow he would be himself again, and now he needed to walk, stride out and work up a sweat and distract himself from the memory of a pair of amused brown eyes and the novelty of a woman who seemed to say exactly what she thought.

Why that was arousing he was uncertain, and he was not sure he wanted to explore why that should be. It was bad enough, every time he got close to her, to find himself imagining her naked under him as the surf pounded on the beach and the sun beat down hot on his back. The fantasy had kept him awake in the small hours of the night, too. It felt disloyal to Katerina, it disturbed his conscience and it was discourteous to his hostess.

Cris surveyed the rough track that led onwards towards the head of the valley. It looked challenging enough to drive any thoughts of sex out of his head for a while. How the blazes Collins had got the carriage over this road without breaking an axle was a minor miracle, he decided as he jumped a particularly evil pothole. He had thought the roads to Hartland Quay were bad enough, but this area appeared to have had nothing done in the way of road-making since before the Romans.

By the time he walked into the village he had taken off his coat, his body felt warm and limber and he had worked up a healthy thirst. There had to be an alehouse hereabouts. He surveyed the main street, which forked where he stood, the other arm presumably running to his right down to the quayside. The road was lined on both sides with single-storey cottages, some thatched, some with slate roofs. The whitewashed walls bulged and looked as though they were made with clay, but the quality improved slightly as the street rose from the fork, with a few two-storey dwellings, a public house with a faded sign showing a galleon in full sail swinging outside it, a shopfront and, rising behind the rooftops, the stumpy grey tower of the church.

Cris shrugged on his coat again and turned to walk up to the Ship Inn. The street was roughly cobbled, with narrow slate pavements raised on either side and, although he could see no signs of prosperity, neither did it look poor or neglected. A woman came out and emptied a pot of water into a trough of flowers that stood beside her door, stared openly at him, then went inside again, shooing a small child in front of her.

Two more women came down the street, baskets on hips, skirts kirtled up to show their buckled shoes and a glimpse of ankle. They smiled at him as they passed and broke into shy laughter when he doffed his hat. He kept it in his hand as he ducked under the low lintel of the inn door. 'Good day, gentlemen.'

The half-dozen men in the taproom fell silent, stared at him with the calm curiosity he was beginning to expect, then there was a murmur of greeting before they went back to their ale. He heard the click of dominoes from the table next to the window. The big man behind the bar counter waited, silent, as Cris made his way between stools and settles, then nodded. 'Good morning, sir. What can I do for you?'

'A pint of your best, if you please.' Cris leaned one elbow on the bar and half turned, letting the others take a good look at him. 'Is this cider country?'

'No, sir. Nor hops, neither, so we've no beer. We brew our own ale. Or there's brandy,' the landlord added.

'Your ale sounds just the thing at this hour.'

The brandy, no doubt, was French and smuggled. Cris picked up the tankard that was put in front of him and took a long swallow, then a more appreciative mouthful. 'A good brew.'

'Aye, it is that.' The man nodded, unsmiling, well aware of his own worth. He went back to polishing thick-bottomed glasses and Cris drank his ale and waited.

Finally one of the dominoes players slapped down the winning tile and shifted in his seat to look across to the bar. 'You be the gennelman down at Barbary?'

'I am.'

'Mizz Tamsyn fished you out the sea, is what we hear.'

'She found me staggering out and the ladies were kind enough to let me recover at their house.'

'Huh. Swimming. Don't hold with it, just makes drowning last longer.'

'It certainly seemed to go on a long time,' Cris agreed, straight-faced, provoking laughter from the other tables. 'I was most grateful to the ladies. Popular landowners hereabouts, I imagine.'

'Miss Isobel is that and all. A proper lady, for all that she's a bit scatty sometimes. Miss Rosie does a power of good for the school, too, poor lady, despite her afflictions. But Mizz Tamsyn makes certain it all runs right and tight.' There was a murmur of agreement round the room.

'They're having a difficult time just now, I understand. Rick fires, the sheep over the cliff.' Around him the dim room fell silent. Cris took another swallow of ale and waited.

'Nothing that won't get sorted. Mizz Tamsyn's one of ours now.' There was a warning in the voice from the shadows.

'What manner of man was her husband?' Now the silence was tangible, thick.

'Another one of ours,' the dominoes player said, putting down a tile and placing both formidable fists on the table. 'We look after our own. No need for strangers to get involved.'

It was said pleasantly enough, but the threat was quite plain. He was an outsider, this was not his business and if he continued to probe they would assume the worst and take action. He couldn't blame them for it, for all that it made life damnably difficult. Time to change the subject. 'Fishing good at the moment?'

As he spoke the latch on the door beside the bar snicked up and Dr Tregarth walked through, rolling down the cuffs of his shirt, bag under one arm. 'Your daughter will be fine now, Jim. It was a clean break. Just make sure she puts no weight on that leg until I say so or it will grow out of line. Now, where did I put my coat?'

'Here, Doctor.' The innkeeper produced it from behind the bar. 'I'm rightly glad to hear it ain't worse, given that she went down the stairs top to bottom. The little maid was crying fit to break her heart. What do I owe you?'

'A jug of ale and my noon meal will suit me just fine.'

He shrugged into the coat. 'I've got to go down to the Landing, but I'll be back directly.'

'Old Henry's rheumatics, that'll be,' the other dominoes player remarked.

'There's no privacy to be had around here,' the doctor said, turning with a grin, then saw Cris. 'Mr Defoe. How the blazes did you get up here?'

'Good day to you, Dr Tregarth. I walked.'

'Sore?'

'Some,' Cris returned, equally laconic. 'Exercise eases it, I find, once I get going.'

'First mile's the worst, eh?' Tregarth made for the door. 'I'll be back for that slice of pie, Jim. Make sure these rogues don't eat it all.'

'I'll walk with you, if you've no objection.' Cris laid a coin on the bar. 'Thank you, landlord. Good day, all.'

Outside, they walked in silence for a few yards. 'That will have provided more excitement than the last pedlar in the village a month ago,' the doctor remarked as he turned downhill. 'You'll be a major source of gossip and speculation for many a day.'

'More interesting than wondering how a strange dog got into Mrs Perowne's flock on top of a chapter of other incidents?'

'You've heard about that, then?' The other man's voice was carefully neutral.

'I have. Do you have any theories?' Cris ducked under a washing line slung across the street.

'As you say, a chapter of accidents.'

'I said incidents, not accidents.'

'At the risk of sounding rude, Mr Defoe, what concern is it of yours?' The doctor reached out the hand not encumbered with his medical bag, seized a runaway toddler by the collar and passed him back to his pursuing, breathless, mother. 'He's in fine form, Mrs Pentyre.'

Cris tipped his hat to the mother, sidestepped the struggling child. 'The ladies at Barbary Combe House may well have saved my life. It is clear something is wrong and, as a gentleman, I owe them my help.'

'And you know about agricultural matters?' Tregarth enquired. There was more than a hint of warning in his tone.

'Some. I know more about plots and sabotage, scheming and secrets.'

'And no doubt I wouldn't get a straight answer if I asked how you came by that knowledge. Mrs Perowne is an attractive lady.'

They had cleared the last cottage and the street bent into a rough track. Cris sidestepped sharply, forcing the doctor into the angle of the wall and a gate. 'Are you suggesting that I have dishonourable intentions towards the lady, Tregarth? Because if so, I am quite willing to take offence.'

Chapter Seven

Cris watched the other man's eyes darken, narrow, and wondered if he was about to be asked to name his seconds. He knew he was being hypocritical because his thoughts, if not his intentions, were downright disgraceful as far as Tamsyn Perowne was concerned, but if he did not react he risked damaging her reputation with one of the pillars of the local community.

'Naturally, if you give me your word, sir.'

'That I do not wish Mrs Perowne harm? You certainly have my word on that, although as you do not know me from Adam, I am not sure how you judge the worth of the assurance.' What the devil was wrong with him? If he was observing this encounter, he would assume he was trying to force a fight on Tregarth, as though they were rivals for Tamsyn.

Oddly, the doctor relaxed. 'I trust you. Judging character is one of the tricks we medics must acquire, just as a horseman learns how to judge an unreliable animal. You, sir, have an odd kick to your gait, but I judge you are not vicious.'

'Thank you, for that,' Cris said drily, stepping back. He thought he had found an ally. Tregarth straightened his coat and they fell into step, as far as the surface of the track would allow. 'Miss Holt has a nephew.'

'The charming Lord Chelford. An acquaintance of yours?'

'I have encountered him in London. I would trust him as far as I could throw him. Possibly rather less if he had a deck of cards in his hand.'

Tregarth laughed. 'I suspect Tamsyn would say the same.' There was an awkward silence as the doctor realised he had used her first name. Cris did not comment, but noted it. 'He pressed her to marry him, quite persistently, and did not like getting *no* for an answer.'

'Before she married Perowne?'

'Then—and again after she was widowed. The first time she took refuge in marrying Jory, the second she had the iron in her soul and she sent him packing with no help from anyone.'

'Where did the iron come from?'

They rounded another bend and the land to the south fell away, giving a view of the sea and another towering headland. Tregarth nodded towards it. 'Black Edge Head. For a woman to see her husband hunted to his death it's either going to break her, or temper her steel.'

'He jumped from that?' Cris stared at the sheer face, the sea crashing at its foot, the snarling rocks. 'That is a long way down to regret an impulse.'

'Jory Perowne did not work on impulse. He was a realist and no coward. A man can dangle for half an hour on the gallows if the authorities are determined to make him suffer and Perowne had his pride. He would never have let them take him alive and jumping from there certainly made an impression.'

'And that old fool of a magistrate really thought he had to check that a strange man under Mrs Perowne's roof was not her husband? After he went over there in front of witnesses?'

'They never found the body and Jory was a legend. He had charisma, magic. No one would be surprised if he walked dripping out of the sea one dark night. Cornwall has King Arthur and, of late years, we had Jory Perowne. But if he does come back it will be as a ghost. Enough men saw him hit those rocks to know he died that day.'

Tamsyn had chosen marriage to a brigand who sounded like a swashbuckling rogue from the last century rather than submit to a man who would have given her status and title, if not happiness. She had survived seeing her husband's horrific death and lived with the consequences, and now she supported and protected two charming, and apparently unworldly, ladies. She ran an estate, kept a tart tongue in her head and she kissed like an angel. Cris was beginning to wonder who needed protection from whom.

'But where is he?' Aunt Izzy enquired plaintively for the fourth time. 'I cannot believe you simply abandoned the poor man like that and rode off, Tamsyn. Why, he might be collapsed in a ditch from exhaustion.'

'I did not abandon him, he is not a *poor man* and there are no ditches anywhere around there.' Exasperated, Tamsyn eyed the walking cane she had picked up when she rode home past the fallen tree. 'He was walking perfectly well and he can hardly get lost around here. He will turn up when he wants his luncheon, I have no doubt. He is a man, after all.' There was no doubt about that either. She braced her shoulders against the sensual little shiver that ran through her at the thought. She should tell them that Cris Defoe had exaggerated his weakness in order to have an excuse to stay there and protect them, but she suspected Aunt Rosie would be indignant and that Aunt Izzy would make a hero out of him.

'Here he comes now, from the beach,' Rosie said from her seat by the window.

'The beach?' And so he was, striding up over the lawn as though he had never experienced so much as a mild muscle twinge in his life. But how did he get there without being seen?

Cris raised his hat when he saw Rosie, then turned to take the path round to the kitchen door. Like all of them he had developed the habit of ignoring the front entrance. He obviously felt at home at Barbary Combe House and, strangely, the aunts, who were so protective of their privacy, seemed quite comfortable that he had become part of the household in only two days.

'Mr Defoe is back so I'll serve luncheon, shall I, Miss Holt?' Mrs Tape enquired. Through the open door his booted feet taking the stairs two at a time sounded quite clearly.

'By all means,' Tamsyn muttered as Aunt Izzy agreed with the housekeeper and they both went to help Aunt Rosie to her feet. 'Let us females wait upon the convenience of The Man.' She was thoroughly out of sorts and it was not helped by the fact that she felt guilty for being so scratchy. The aunts enjoyed having a man in the house again—Izzy to fuss over, Rosie to sharpen her wits on—and she was being a curmudgeon about it.

Booted feet clattered down the stairs again and she realised why she was feeling like this. The house had a man inhabiting it again for the first time since Jory's death. There were the male staff, but they were different; they did not fill the space in the same way. Nor did she desire them.

The sight of Cris as he came into the room affected her as though he had touched her, instead of immediately going to Aunt Rosie's side to offer his arm. Tamsyn tried to ignore the hollow feeling low down in her belly and the sensation that she was altogether too warm.

Whatever Cris Defoe had been doing had left him with colour on his cheeks and a sparkle in those blue eyes and he looked exactly what she had thought all along—a splendid male animal in his prime. *And a more cunning one than I have been giving him credit for.* But was he using his intelligence to help them or had he some other motives? Surely he could not be in league with Franklin? No one would risk drowning like that. Yes, he had been interested in Jory's legendary hoard…but the same objection held. All he'd have needed to do if he had wanted to be 'rescued' and taken in was to sink a boat in their bay or stage a fall from a horse outside the house.

'You came from the direction of the beach, Mr Defoe,' she observed when they were all seated. 'A remarkable feat, considering where we parted.' He looked at her with a faint smile. 'Do have a nice pilchard.'

'Thank you, but I feel sufficiently fishy for one day.' He sliced some ham and offered it to Aunt Rosie. 'I begged a ride back from one of the fishermen at Stib's Landing and his craft is liberally encrusted with fish scales. Dan Cardross, I think? He was going to lift his crab pots and said this was on his way.'

Dan had been Jory's right-hand man. Tamsyn tried not to read any significance into that. 'You had a long walk.'

'I went up to Stibworthy, had a pint of ale in the inn, encountered Dr Tregarth and walked with him down to the harbour. I will admit to being glad of the boat ride back,' he added to Aunt Izzy, who was making anxious noises about *overdoing it* and *recklessness*.

Tamsyn believed none of it. If he had needed to walk back, then Cris Defoe was quite capable of doing so. 'You must rest this afternoon,' she said, sweetly solicitous. 'Perhaps your manservant can give you one of his massages.'

'You are all consideration, Mrs Perowne, and I must admit, the thought of bed is a temptation.' His lids lowered over the sinful blue eyes, the only acknowledgement that he was teasing her with a *double entendre* that went right past the two older ladies. 'But I have correspondence to attend to, which will be restful enough. How does one get a letter to the post from here?'

'Jason will take it up to the Ship Inn, which is our receiving office. The post boy comes in every day except Sunday at about eleven, delivers the mail, picks up our letters and takes them to Barnstaple. Post going out of the county is taken to Bristol by one of the daily steam ships and from there by mail coach. A letter you send up tomorrow morning will be in London in three days.' Tamsyn delivered the information in a matter-of-fact tone, refusing to allow him to see the image that the conjunction of *Cris Defoe* and *bed* and *temptation* conjured up reflected in her expression.

'Steam ships?'

'They have been a boon for this coast because our roads are so bad. That is how the visitors to Ilfracombe and Instow arrive. We have quite a little sea-bathing industry in North Devon these days.'

'That is what gave us the idea for the bathing room,'

Aunt Izzy explained. 'I read how beneficial for rheumatic complaints the new hot-seawater baths are, but of course, Rosie could not tolerate the rough roads to reach Ilfracombe from here. So we decided to build our own.'

'Ingenious. Would you object if I made sketches of the plumbing? I am tempted by the thought of hot baths in my own houses.'

'Houses?' He had more than one? Aunt Izzy shook her head at Tamsyn's abrupt question but Cris showed no offence at her curiosity.

'The house in the country and a *pied-à-terre* in London,' he said vaguely. 'Would you pass the butter?'

Tamsyn handed him the dish. 'How lovely, to be able to go to London whenever you please.'

'Shops?' Cris enquired. He was teasing her, she could tell. The infuriating man did not so much as smile, but she was learning to watch for the slight dimple that appeared at the corner of his mouth when he was hiding amusement and the crinkle of laughter lines at his eyes.

'Of course.' She would not be drawn into a defence of shopping. 'And bookshops and theatres and the sights—St James's Palace and Carlton House and the parks.'

'You enjoyed your season, then?'

'I never had one. But as for the social round and the Marriage Mart, I am not sorry to have missed those.'

'Your absence was society's loss, Mrs Perowne. Think of all the bachelors deprived of the opportunity to court you, all the balls and assemblies ungraced by your presence.'

'I am sure those bachelors survived heart-whole. After all, they had no idea what they were missing.'

Aunt Izzy laughed and turned to Rosie. 'Do you remember at that assembly in Exeter, the evening before my eighteenth birthday?' In moments they were lost in reminiscence over some private joke.

'Yes, the poor souls have been languishing in ignorance,' Cris said slowly, answering Tamsyn, ignoring the laughter beside him. He raised his glass of ale to his lips and sipped, his eyes on hers as he did so. 'It is incredible that one can continue for years unaware of a gaping hole in one's life.'

Surely he did not mean that he recognised her as something missing from his life? No, he must mean that she was existing here, cut off from the world, not realising what *she* was missing. That was more likely. How very…*humiliating* to be pitied. 'And it is incredible how difficult it can be for some people to recognise when others are happy, just because they value different things,' she retorted.

There was a sudden flare of emotion in Cris's eyes. 'I think we may be at cross-purposes, Tamsyn.'

'Probably because we come from two very different worlds.' So, he had not meant to insult her, but the exchange had served to remind her how distant from polite society she was, here at the edge of England, cut off by sea on one side and rough tracks on the other. She was country gentry, teetering on the verge of slipping into something else since her marriage. The small resources that she felt gave her everything she needed were pitiful against the wealth that Cris Defoe was obviously used to with his beautiful boots and elegant coats, his valet and his London home. She must seem pathetically provincial and unsophisticated.

And in danger of slipping into self-pity and unjustified feelings of inferiority. I'd like to see him striking a bargain in a cattle auction or setting up a village school or teaching himself French from books ordered from an Exeter bookshop. I would like to see one of the elegant ladies of his acquaintance running a farm and a fishery.

They finished the meal in polite, prickly silence with each other, letting the two older women take the burden of conversation. *How complicated men are*, Tamsyn thought as she dropped her napkin on the table and nodded her thanks as Cris pulled back her chair for her when, finally, Aunt Izzy stopped chattering and noticed that they had all long since finished eating.

He went to offer his arm to Rosie and Tamsyn followed them out. 'That is a good walk with wonderful views that you took this morning,' Rosie was saying as he led her to the drawing room. 'It must be five or six years since I could manage it. I should not repine, this is a lovely house and I have an ever-changing view of the sea from the garden, but I confess that I miss being able to stride along the clifftops, see the expanse of the ocean and Lundy Island in the distance with the ships sailing by.'

If they could spare the money she would have the track up to the village made into a proper lane, with a surface levelled and graded by Mr McAdam's new method, but it would cost more than they could spare and Aunt Rosie would no doubt protest at the idea of spending so much on something intended for her pleasure alone.

'A penny for your thoughts?' Cris had stopped beside her at the foot of the stairs and was regarding her with a quizzical smile. Tamsyn realised she must have been standing there, staring blankly at the front door.

'I was speculating on road building,' she admitted. 'An expensive investment.'

'You, Mrs Perowne, are a constant source of surprise to me,' he murmured. 'You will allow me to stay for a few more days, despite my pretence of feebleness being exposed?'

'I suppose so.' Her dark mood lifted as rapidly as it had descended. 'I can hardly cut short your seaside holiday, now can I?'

'Holiday?' Cris's mouth twisted into a wry smile. 'It was hardly that.' He turned to climb the stairs.

'What was it, then?' She reached out and touched his hand as it gripped the carved ball on top of the newel post.

For a moment she thought he would not answer. Then he twisted his hand to catch hers within it and lifted them, joined, to his lips. 'A journey from reality, from the loss of a dream, from the acceptance of what is inevitable,' he murmured against her fingers. 'Perhaps that is the definition of a holiday.' His breath was warm, the touch of his lips no more than the brush of a feather. His fingertips were against the pulse of her wrist and he must have felt the thunder of the blood, the surging response, the desire.

It was madness, a dangerous madness if it could be so powerful when ignited by such a light touch, such a gentle caress. *I want him and he would not say* no *if I came to his bed.* But how did one carry on an *affaire*, however brief, under the same small roof as two doting and observant aunts? And how could she risk it—her reputation…*my heart*…for a few moments of pleasure with a man who would be gone within days?

Behind her, from the window embrasure out of sight of where they stood in the hallway, she could hear her aunts discussing their latest order to be sent to the circulating library in Barnstaple. Innocent, safe pleasures. This was not innocent and not safe and suddenly she had no desire for either. Tamsyn reached up and slid her fingers into Cris's hair, just above his nape, pulled down his head and lifted her face to his. One kiss, surely she could risk that?

Chapter Eight

Hᴉis kiss was not tentative, nor respectful. Certainly it took no account of where they were. Cris turned from the stair, took her in his arms and swept her back against the front door, the length of his body pressed against hers, the thrust of his arousal blatant, thrilling. Tamsyn twisted and got her hands free so she could lock them around his head, the shape of his skull imprinted on her palms, the heavy silk of his hair caressing across her fingers.

Her mouth was open to him, his tongue forceful, demanding that she open more, let him taste her, explore her. She pulled back so she could nip at his lower lip, making him growl, low and thrilling, the sound reverberating from his chest to her breast, before she drove her own tongue into his mouth, refusing to allow him mastery. If this was to be nothing else, there would be equal desire, equal responsibility.

They broke apart, panting. Tamsyn wondered if she looked as stunned and wild as he did, with his hair tousled, his eyes dark. She reached behind her, turned the doorknob and staggered back on to the porch, pulling him with her. 'Summer house.'

Without waiting to see if he was following her she

ran across the lawn, round the corner of the dense shrubbery that sheltered one side of the garden, and into the little summer house that looked out over the beach. Cris followed her, the door banging closed behind him. Tamsyn collapsed on the bench, her knees failing her.

Cris stood with his back against the door as though glad of its support. 'What in Hades was that?' he demanded. 'I've been on the edge of an avalanche in the Alps and it was rather less violent. It was certainly less frightening.' She realised that he was smiling. It transformed the austerity of his face, changed him from beautiful to real.

'I thought a kiss would be…' *Nice? Do not be ridiculous.* 'I wanted to kiss you again.'

'You will get no argument from me on that score.' He still had not moved from the door.

'I noticed.' She could feel her lips twitching into an answering smile. It had not occurred to her that there might be anything amusing in giving in to this attack of desire. 'That is all it can be, you realise that? Just a kiss. This is quite inappropriate.'

Cris's smile deepened at the prudish word. 'With so many other people around, perhaps. But lovers have always found ways and means to be together.'

'We are not lovers.' Tamsyn found she had lost the desire to smile.

'Not yet.' Cris pushed away from the door and went to sit at the other end of the bench, out of touching distance unless they both stretched out a hand. 'There was something, there had to be, right from the start, in that moment of madness on the beach. I am not married, Tamsyn, and you are not an innocent. What is to stop us?'

Reputation, risk, prudence? 'And you are not committed to anyone?' she asked, wondering suddenly why such an attractive, eligible man should be unattached.

He did not answer her immediately and when she looked at his profile she found he had closed his eyes as though to veil his thoughts.

'Cris?' she prompted.

His eyes opened and when he turned his head to look at her the smile was on his lips alone. 'No, I am not committed to anyone.' He got up, a sudden release of energy like an uncoiling spring. She jumped. 'You are correct. This is quite inappropriate. You might have been married, but that does not give me the right to treat you like one of the sophisticated London society widows. They know the game and how to play it and they move in circles where these things are understood.' Cris opened the door and stepped out on to the daisy-spangled lawn. 'Forgive me.'

By the time she had realised what he was doing and had reached the door, he was striding away towards the house. The front door closed firmly behind him. A succession of Jory's riper curses ran through her mind.

Damn him! That was not about me, or at least, not entirely about me. There is someone and I made him think of her. Now you have got exactly what you told yourself you wanted, Tamsyn Perowne. You got your kiss and that was all. You are safe, respectable. And frustrated.

The tables had turned so fast she had been taken completely unaware. One moment she had been hesitant and he eager, the next she had pushed aside her qualms and he was backing away. She tried to make some sense of those past few hectic minutes. Cris had been a gentleman—once he had stopped kissing her like a ravening Viking pillager. She had said it would be inappropriate and he had agreed. And, just as she was telling herself that she should seize this opportunity and argue against herself, her question about other women had stopped him in his tracks. He had said there was no one else now, but she must have made him face a memory that hurt.

Tamsyn went down the slope of the lawn and took the steps to the foreshore. The sea had always helped her think, but now, as she watched the Atlantic waves come rolling in to end a thousand miles' journey in a frill of harmless lace on the sand, she knew there was nothing to think about. She wanted Cris Defoe, beyond prudence and reason and despite knowing quite well that he would leave this place very soon, whatever she felt or wanted. That meant that she had a decision to make. Was she capable of seducing a man—and would it be right to do so?

'Muscles paining you, sir? Would you like a massage?' Collins got up from the window seat looking out to the track up towards Stibworthy and put down what looked like a book of German grammar.

'No. Thank you.' Cris bit back the oath. His fault, his temper, and no need to take it out on Collins. He would think about what had just happened later when he had his breathing under control and some blood had returned to his brain from where it was currently making itself felt. 'I need paper and ink. Wax. And a seal.'

'Not your own, of course, sir.' Collins removed a key from his watch chain and opened the large writing box that sat on the dresser. 'The plain seal?' He laid a seal on the table in front of the window and set out paper and an ink stand with steel-nibbed pens, then struck a flint to light a candle. 'Which colour wax, sir?'

'Blue.' Cris picked up the seal and rolled it between his fingers. His own seal ring, securely locked away, showed the de Feaux crest, a phoenix rising from flames, a sword in one clawed foot. *From Ash I Rise, In Fire I Conquer.* The crest was an ancient pun on the similarity in pronunciation between *feu*—fire—and *Feaux.* This version showed only the flames, but it was known to his friends.

'Cipher, sir?'

He thought about it, then shook his head. 'No. Can you see anyone in this household opening a guest's correspondence?'

Gabriel Stone was in London, up to no good as usual, and perfectly placed to send Cris information about Franklin Holt, Viscount Chelford. Gabe might be Earl of Edenbridge, but he was also a gambler, a highly successful, ice-cold, card player, and he would know just what Chelford was about, whether he was in debt and any other scandal there was to be had.

Send whatever intelligence you can find—and especially anything about Chelford's relationship with his aunt, Miss Holt, of this address, and his inheritance of her estate after her death.

He put down the pen and stared out of the window as he ran through the things he wanted Gabe to find out.

He wished he could ask him to send down a couple of burly Bow Street Runners, or better still, a couple of doormen from one of the tougher gambling hells, but they would stick out like daffodils in a coal cellar down here. Then his eyes focused on the stony track and he smiled. Of course, that would kill two birds with one stone. He dipped the pen again.

You recall that little incident in Bath and our two Irish friends? If you can locate them and send them here with their equipment, I have use of both their old trade and their willingness to use their fists.

All correspondence should be directed to Mr C. Defoe.

He folded and sealed the letter, addressed it to *The Earl of Edenbridge*, then folded it within a second sheet and addressed that to his solicitor in the City, sealing it for the second time. However scrupulous his hostesses might be about other people's correspondence, there was no need to raise questions over letters to the aristocracy.

'Thank you, Collins. If you take that down I am told someone will take it to the receiving office in the village. That will be all for the moment.'

Alone, he got up and prowled around the room as he finally allowed himself to think about Tamsyn and that kiss. It was like unravelling tangled string, sorting out what he felt, what he ought to feel, what she wanted— what was right. She was not an innocent, but neither was she experienced with men other than her husband, he could tell that. Whatever she had been doing since Jory Perowne's death, Tamsyn had not been sharing the beds of any local gentlemen. This was a tiny, unsophisticated community where everyone knew everyone else's business and where a reputation lost would be common currency within hours. If this…attraction…flirtation… madness…whatever it was, went any further, then he would have to be very careful indeed.

And what was he thinking of anyway? Part of his anatomy was sending him very clear signals indeed, but it had been months since he had lain with a woman, not since he had set eyes on Katerina. He could simply be suffering from an attack of lust, which was something very different from what he had felt for Katerina. To have even thought of another woman while he was seeing her every day had been impossible. But she was far away and unobtainable and always would be, and he, as he kept reminding himself, was not cut out for celibacy.

Cris sat on the window seat and stared at a clump of gorse. It was sentimental tosh to feel that kissing another woman was disloyal to Katerina. She had never been his, he had never been hers, they had never spoken the words he read in her gaze, that he felt in his heart.

But the desire he felt for Tamsyn was shaking his certainty about his feelings for Katerina. Was it love? He felt uncomfortable with the doubt. It had certainly been more than pure lust. But was desiring Tamsyn just a selfish need to lose himself in a passionate encounter that he would walk away from in a few days?

Perhaps he should tell her who he was. Cris examined the idea and realised he was enjoying the freedom too much. For the first time as an adult he had none of the burdens of his title on his shoulders, none of the demands or the expectations. He was just Cris, a man who was attracted to a woman and who saw the need to protect her from the danger that threatened them. It would do them no good to know who he was, only make them feel awkward.

The whole thing was academic, anyway. He had kissed Tamsyn as though he was about to rip off her clothing, there and then in the hallway. He had almost had her standing up against the door, like some drab in a back alley, and he had topped off a thoroughly unpolished performance by informing her that she was not from the sophisticated world he inhabited. If Tamsyn would give him the time of day next time they met, then it was more than he deserved.

Something moved on the road. Cris focused and saw it was Jason, a satchel slung on his shoulder, riding up the track. The mail was on its way. Now he just had to remind himself who he was, what he was, and somehow recapture the man he had been before that wild impulse had sent him off the road at Newark, driving across country into oblivion.

There was absolutely nothing like a pile of account books for setting a woman's feet firmly on the ground. Or, in the case of the farm's accounts, in the mire. Nothing was adding up this afternoon, not the price of oats, not the farrier's bill, not even the egg money. Tamsyn gritted her teeth, turned over a sheet of paper covered in crossings-out and started again. All that was wrong with her, as she was very well aware, was that her brain was off with the fairies, her body was pulsing with desire and more than half her attention was focused on listening for footsteps on the stairs.

'Letters, Mizz Tamsyn.'

She jumped, sending her pen in one direction, the account book in another and a large ink blot on to her page of calculations. 'Jason, you startled me.'

'Sorry, Mizz Tamsyn.' He came into the room and emptied the contents of the satchel on to the table. 'You were daydreaming, it looked like.'

'Er…yes.'

Dreams of night, not of day. Of beds and rumpled sheets and mindless pleasure. And impossible dreams. There had been a moment as she daydreamed that she had heard wedding bells. And that would never be. Her stomach cramped with remembered pain and she bit her lip before she could turn back to the waiting groom.

'Thank you, Jason.' She dabbed at the spreading blot, made it worse, screwed up the whole sheet in sudden exasperation and began to sift through the pile of post. Several newspapers, two days out of date, a notification from the circulating library that three novels she had asked for were now available. Several bills, including another from the farrier, an invitation to dine at the vicarage in a week's time when the moon was full and the roads consequently less hazardous, and a letter with their solicitor's seal.

Something about leases, or perhaps an answer to her query about buying that small warehouse in Barnstaple she'd had her eye on. The heavy paper, expensive, like Mr Pentire's excellent services, crackled as she broke the seal and started to read.

'What?' The shriek hurt her throat, but that did not stop the next words being wrenched out. 'The *swine*. The utter, unmitigated *swine*.'

There was a thunder of boot heels down the stairs, Aunt Izzy's cry of, 'Tamsyn? What is wrong?', then the door flew open to reveal Cris with, of all things, a pistol in his hand.

'What is it?' He cast one searching look around the room, then strode in, jerked her out of the chair and into the curve of his arm. 'Who was it? Where did they go?'

Aunt Izzy hurtled into the room, gave a cry at the sight of her niece in the clutches of a man holding a gun, and collapsed into the nearest chair. 'What happened? Why do you have a gun?'

'What gun?' The question came from the doorway where Aunt Rosie, grim-faced and clutching the poker in one arthritic hand, clung to the doorpost.

'There is nobody, Aunt Izzy, please be calm. Cris, put that thing down and let me go. Aunt Rosie, let me help you.'

He beat her to the doorway, taking her aunt gently by the arm and thrusting the gun into the waistband of his breeches. 'It isn't loaded, which is more than I can say for this poker. Do let me take it, Miss Pritchard. Mrs Perowne, what provoked that scream?'

'Pure temper.' She picked up the letter and flapped it at them. 'This is from Mr Pentire, our man of business. Our bankers wrote to him because they had received information that we were about to withdraw all our funds to meet sudden and unexpected debts. In effect, that our credit was no longer good. And half today's post is bills—word must be spreading. Pentire has reassured the bank, but now we may expect a flood of demands for payment of all our accounts and it may take months for confidence in our credit to be restored.'

All energy gone, Tamsyn sank down in the chair and dropped the letter.

'Can you afford to meet all your creditors in full?' Cris asked.

'Yes, I never let accounts run on and we always settle up completely. Luckily we are almost at quarter-day when the rents will come in. But it is the principle of the thing and it will put doubts into the minds of people who do not know us well. This must be the work of Franklin, I cannot believe anyone else has a grudge against us and would do a thing like this.'

'But Franklin can have no grudge,' Aunt Izzy protested. 'I know you do not like him, dear, and I have to admit he is a sore disappointment as a nephew, but—'

'But nothing,' said Aunt Rosie. 'Tamsyn's right.

The man wants us out of here. I just wish I could work out why.'

'We are not moving and that is that,' Aunt Izzy said, with remarkable firmness.

'Forgive me, but does your right of possession here rely upon your residence?' Cris hitched one hip on the table edge and looked round at the three of them. 'If you move away, what becomes of Barbary Combe House and the estate?'

'I retain ownership and the revenues,' Izzy said promptly.

'And your nephew knows this?'

'Certainly.'

'So he would not gain control of it until, forgive me again for being so blunt, your death?'

Izzy gasped, Rosie went pale. Tamsyn got a firm hold on her panicking imagination. 'But Franklin offered you a house on his estate, Aunt Izzy. I agree he wants us out of here, but I do not think he is too worried about the estate as such. The farms brings in enough for our needs, but hardly the sort of income that will rescue him from some financial crisis, and land prices are very poor, so selling it would hardly help either.'

She looked at Cris and found his gaze fixed on her face. Of course, there was Jory's mythical treasure. If Franklin got them out of the house he could helpfully supervise getting it prepared for tenants—all to help his dear aunt Isobel—and search to his heart's content. 'There is no need for alarm about your personal safety, Aunt Izzy.' She directed a narrow-eyed look at Cris, daring him to say any more. 'I have organised some watchers for the livestock and we are quite secure down here. Any stranger would be spotted a mile away, we are so remote.'

'Of course. I am being over-cautious, and over-imaginative, too.' Cris stood up. 'I am sorry, Miss Holt, ladies, for alarming you.'

'No need for that.' Aunt Rosie was brisk. 'You talk a lot of sense, we should take more care. Help me back to the drawing room, Isobel. No, you stay here.' She waved a twisted hand at Cris as he came forward to help her. 'Soothe Tamsyn's ruffled feathers before she calls Franklin out for his idiocy.' She gave a wicked little cackle of laughter. 'I would lay several guineas on her being the better shot.'

Cris closed the door behind her and turned back. 'My apologies.'

'For what?'

'For alarming your aunts…and for what happened in the summer house.'

'They are made of sterner stuff than it might seem,' she said. 'And nothing happened in the summer house.'

'That, perhaps, is what I should be apologising for.'

Chapter Nine

Now, perhaps, was the moment to be bold, to reach out and admit, frankly, that she would welcome him as her lover, that she wanted him, that he had nothing to fear from her, that she would not cling or make demands. But that shadow—the one that had killed the heat of desire in his eyes—that haunted her. She would not be a substitute for another woman, nor would she demand he forget.

'There is nothing to apologise for in behaving like a gentleman.' She shrugged and smiled, making it light, slightly flirtatious. Unimportant. 'I was uncertain and you, very thoughtfully, did not press me. Now, if you will excuse me, I must finish these accounts or we really will be in a pickle if any more demands for payment come in.'

She thought he was going to offer his help with the books, but a smile, as meaningless and pleasant as her own, curved his mouth and he nodded. 'Of course. I will leave you in peace.'

Tamsyn stared at the account books for a long while after he had gone. The path of virtue was the right one to take, and the least embarrassing, as well as the decision that would carry no risks at all, for either of them. Safe.

'Safe is dull, safe kills you with rust and boredom,' Jory's voice seemed to whisper in her ear.

'Take care,' she had pleaded with him so often. *'Do not take risks.'*

'Risk makes your blood beat, fear tells you that you are alive,' he would respond with that charming flash of teeth, the smile that was as enchanting as Hamelin's Piper must have been. The smile he had given her before he had turned and sprinted for the cliff edge and oblivion.

And risk made you dead, Jory, Tamsyn argued back now, in her thoughts.

Yes, his voice seemed to echo back. *But I lived to the end.*

A week later Cris was still installed in the back bed-chamber, Collins had his feet firmly under the table in the kitchen and both of the older ladies protested strongly whenever Cris suggested that he really should be moving on. Not that he wanted to, not until he heard from Gabe and had a clearer idea of what Chelford might be up to, and not until his surprise for Aunt Rosie arrived.

The ladies insisted he call them Aunt Izzy and Aunt Rosie, exclaimed with pleasure over each small service he did for them, made a great fuss over him—even when he tangled Izzy's knitting wool into a rat's nest or beat Rosie at chess. He needed a holiday, they insisted, and his presence was as good as one for them, too. Again, as it did almost every day, the truth was on the tip of his tongue, and once again he closed his lips on it. Hiding his identity was becoming dangerously addictive, like losing himself in drink, and he justified it to himself again, as he did every time. He needed the rest, he was doing no harm to anyone.

The only blight on this amiable arrangement was Tamsyn. She protested that they should not detain him, that he must be bored or uncomfortable or, when he choked over one of her more blatant attempts to dislodge him one dinner time, in need of a London doctor.

None of this made him want her any less. He found himself in a state of arousal which long punishing walks along the cliffs, or up through the woods, did nothing to subdue. If he couldn't stop reacting like a sixteen-year-old youth soon he was going to have to resort to several cold swims a day. That particular form of exercise he had been avoiding, wary of encountering Tamsyn, who apparently saw no reason to curtail her own daily swims just because there was a man in the house.

He wanted her, he admired her spirit and her directness, her love of her aunts, her work ethic, her courage and her humour. Taking her as his lover would be healing, he sensed, provided he could manage a short-lived *affaire* without harming her in any way. On the other hand, finding a bride, plighting his lifelong fidelity and affection, that was another matter altogether. That would be a betrayal of Katerina. As soon as he thought it he felt uncomfortable, as though he was dramatising himself and his feelings. But if he was in love with Katerina…

He came in through the front door that morning after an unsatisfactory, brooding, walk on the beach, trying to conjure up the memory of Katerina and finding it damnably difficult, and found Tamsyn in the hallway arranging flowers in the big urn at the foot of the stairs. 'Can I be of any help? That looks heavy.'

'It will be staying here, thank you for offering.' A polite smile, a polite exchange, a not-very-polite urge to sweep the basket of foliage on to the floor and take her here and now, on the half-moon table amidst the flowers and the moss.

Cris pushed the fantasy back into the darker recesses of his imagination, from whence it should never have escaped in the first place, and took the stairs to his bed-chamber two at a time. Increasingly he found it difficult to be in Tamsyn's company and pretend there was nothing else he wanted beyond a polite social friendship.

Collins was sorting out laundry and managing to take up most of the space in the room in the process. 'I'll be out of your way in a moment, sir. I've just got to put these shirts away, the rest can wait.'

'No, carry on.' Cris took off his coat, tugged loose his neckcloth as he went to stand in the window embrasure and stare out over the roofs of the stable yard to the steep lane. Someone was coming, a rider, low-crowned beaver hat jammed on over windswept curling black hair, and behind him the roof of a carriage was just visible with, strapped on top, something that looked like a giant coffin with windows.

It was Gabriel. He had come himself without warning, riding into a situation he knew hardly anything about and quite apt to let all of Cris's secrets out of the bag if he wasn't stopped. Cris threw up the casement, climbed over the sill and dropped the ten feet to the rough grass path behind the house.

'Sir!' He looked up to see Collins leaning out. 'May I assist, sir?' He kept his voice to a discreet whisper. It was not the first time both he and Cris had left a building by way of the window and Cris suspected that the valet enjoyed missions where there was a strong element of cloak and dagger work as much as he did.

'Lord Edenbridge is riding down the lane, I need to head him off.' He was off, running, before Collins could reply, shouldered his way through the narrow gap in the shrubbery behind the house and sprinted up the lane past the entrance to the service yard.

Gabriel reined in, his hand on the hilt of his sword, the moment Cris emerged. The horse, battle-trained, went down on its haunches, ready to kick out, then Gabriel relaxed, clicked his tongue and the horse was still.

'My good fellow,' he drawled as Cris arrived at his stirrup. 'I am looking for my friend Cris de Feaux. Elegant, well-dressed gentleman, a certain dignity and refinement in his manner. Anyone answering to that description around here?'

Cris shoved the hair back out of his eyes. 'Buffoon.'

'*I* am a buffoon? By the sainted Brummell, what have you done to yourself? Your hair hasn't been cut, you're as brown as a farm labourer—and your clothes!' He surveyed Cris from head to foot. 'What the devil has happened to you?'

'I just climbed out of the window. What are you doing here? I wanted information, not the dubious pleasure of your company. And it is *Defoe,* not *de Feaux.*'

'It all sounded intriguing and I needed to remove myself from temptation in London.' He shrugged when Cris raised an interrogative brow. 'A sudden impulse of decency in regards to a woman.' His habitually cynical expression deepened. 'A lady. I thought it better to remove myself before I discovered that I was on the verge of becoming reformed. So here I am, complete with the cargo from Bath, armed to the teeth and looking for adventure. And, judging by the state of the roads hereabouts, this is probably the end of the known world, so adventure should be forthcoming.'

'You will fit right in. There are smugglers hereabouts and I would guess we're about two generations from pirates.' With his unruly black hair, his gypsy-dark eyes, his rakehell attitude and the sword at his side, Gabriel Stone, earl or not, looked as though he was up for any criminal activity. 'Listen, we must make this fast. I am plain Mr Defoe and you had better be simply Mr Stone. This is not a part of the world used to the aristocracy and I do not want to cause complications.'

'Or raise expectations. I assume there's a woman in the case?'

'A lady.' Gabriel grinned at the echo of his own phrase. *Lord, Tamsyn married one rogue, I just hope for her sake she doesn't take a fancy to this one...* 'There's some kind of trouble and I haven't got to the bottom of it yet, but until I do, there are two ladies of a certain age who would be better for some protection whether they want it or not.'

'Hence our Irish friends?' Gabe looked over his shoulder at the carriage with its incongruous load.

'Exactly. I'll just have a word with them, then we'll go on down to the house. The ladies will offer you a bed, I have no doubt. You'd best accept unless you want to make your way back to Barnstaple today—there isn't more than an alehouse for ten miles in any direction.'

He went up to the carriage, nodded to the coachman, and opened the door. The inside was filled with Gabe's luggage and two very large Irishmen. 'Good day to you, me lord!' the black-haired one exclaimed. 'And a pleasure it is to be seeing you again.'

'Seamus.' Cris nodded to his red-headed companion. 'Patrick. Now listen. I am Mr Defoe—forget I ever had a title. I've a couple of very nice ladies who need an eye keeping on them, but they aren't to know that. As far as they are concerned I've sent for a sedan chair for the one who can't walk far and the two of you are here to train up a couple of likely local lads. And you'll have trouble finding the right ones, if you catch my drift?'

Seamus cracked his knuckles and grinned, revealing a gap in his front teeth. 'Someone causing them grief, eh? Don't like bullies who upset nice old ladies, do we, Patrick? You can rely on us, Lord…Mr Defoe, sir. We're doing very nicely with the bodyguarding business you helped us with, it's a pleasure to take a job in the country for you, that it is.'

Patrick, a man of few words, grunted.

'Unload the chair now,' Cris decided. 'Get it set up, then follow us down in ten minutes. You'll be a surprise for the ladies.'

What they would make of two massive chairmen, Irish as most of the Bath chairmen were by long tradition, goodness knew. These two had waded into the action when Cris and Gabriel had found themselves cornered in a dark alleyway by a gang who did not take well to Gabe's legendary game-winning skills with cards. When the dust had settled and the four of them had been binding up their injuries and drowning the bruises in brandy at the nearest inn, Cris had suggested they might find acting as bodyguards a profitable sideline. After he had put some business their way the two were building quite a reputation and they made no bones about expressing their gratitude.

'Tamsyn, there is a carriage at the gate,' Aunt Rosie called. 'And a gentleman on a horse. Who on earth can it be?'

She jammed the rest of the flowers into the vase with more haste than care, whipped off her apron and threw open the front door. And there was Cris, who only ten minutes before had been upstairs while she had been filling vases at the foot of those stairs the entire time. She shot him a questioning glance as she approached, blinked at the sight of shirtsleeves and loose neckcloth, and blinked again when she saw the man dismounting from a raking bay horse. Presumably she was not dreaming and transported into some Minerva Press novel, so this was not a dashing gentleman highwayman. She took a deep, appreciative breath. Goodness, but he certainly looked like every fantasy of such a romantic character.

'Mrs Perowne, may I introduce my friend, Mr Gabriel Stone.' Cris gave her a very old-fashioned look as though he knew exactly what she thought of the newcomer. 'I wrote to him on a business matter and did not make myself clear that posting the information would be sufficient.'

Mr Stone doffed his hat. 'Mrs Perowne, my apologies for the intrusion. Just as soon as my coachman can work out how to turn the carriage on this track, we will be on our way.'

'Mr Stone.' She inclined her head in response to his half-bow. 'Are you in haste, sir?'

'No, ma'am, not at all.'

'Then you must stay. If your man takes the carriage further down he can turn where the lane opens out to the beach. Then the stable yard is just up behind the house. Oh, I see Mr Defoe is already organising him.'

And Mr Defoe wants you to stay, now you are here. I wonder just what that matter of business is.

She turned towards the house, inviting the intriguing Mr Stone to follow her as Cris strode across the lawn to rejoin them.

'If Miss Holt and Miss Pritchard are able to come to the door, I have a small gift for Miss Pritchard. I will go and fetch her a chair out to the porch.' He was gone before she could ask what possible present could necessitate Aunt Rosie coming outside.

It took a few minutes for Michael to carry out a chair and for Aunt Rosie to be settled on it and introduced to Mr Stone. There was the sound of feet on the stones of the lane and then, completely incongruous in the wilds of the Devon coast, two burly men appeared carrying a sedan chair between them. Cris opened the gate and they marched across the lawn, deposited the chair in front of Aunt Rosie, opened the door between the shafts and whipped off their hats.

They were certainly an imposing pair in their dark-blue coats, black tricorns and sturdy boots. The sedan chair gleamed and the seat was deeply padded. 'Would you care to try it, ma'am?' the black-haired man enquired in a broad Irish accent.

'Why…' For a moment Aunt Rosie seemed lost for words. 'Why, yes, I would. But we have no city pavements here, you will find it hard going.'

'We're from Bath, ma'am, and that has hills as steep as you'll find anywhere and cobbles like walking on ice. We're strong lads, that we are. We won't drop you, ma'am.'

'You brought them here?' Tamsyn asked Mr Stone as they watched Michael and Cris help Aunt Rosie into the chair. He nodded as the men picked up the poles and set off smoothly around the lawn, then through the gate and off up the hill.

'I'll be able to go with her on my mare.' Aunt Izzy ran across the grass and took Cris's arm as he stood watching the chair's progress up the lane. 'We can go for picnics and Rosie can visit our friends again and go up on the clifftops. Oh, thank you, Mr Defoe.'

'Mr Stone brought them,' he said with a smile.

'But you sent for them.' Tamsyn joined them at the gate. 'How long can they stay?'

'The chair is yours to keep. Seamus and Patrick will stay until they've found you a pair of local men to train in their stead.' He looked down at her, his face austere again. 'They are very reliable men, I can vouch for them. Very strong, honest. No harm will come to your aunts with them around.'

The chair was returning and Aunt Izzy ran out to join it. Tamsyn hardly noticed her going. 'You sent for bodyguards,' she said as the realisation struck.

'That is a side benefit. I thought of the sedan chair when your aunt was saying how difficult it was to get around, then I remembered these two. Will it be a problem feeding them? They probably eat like bullocks.'

'No, not at all, and there is space in the living quarters over the stables. But, Cris, you don't truly believe we are in danger, do you?'

Mr Stone, who had strolled over to the wall to watch the progress of the chair, remarked, 'Rider coming. Looks military.'

Cris joined him, leaving her question unanswered. The horseman reined in, his way blocked by the sedan chair, and even at that distance Tamsyn could see the colour in his face and the angry set of his mouth. He did not like being held up and neither did he seem to enjoy being stared at.

The chairmen came back into the garden, took the chair right up to the seat and began to help Aunt Rosie out. She and Izzy immediately broke into animated conversation, then fell silent as the stranger dismounted at the gate and strode in.

Around her Tamsyn was conscious of the men closing up. The two chairmen were standing in front of her aunts like a solid wall of muscle. Cris and Mr Stone flanked her. This was ridiculous. It was only one man, apparently on official business judging from his dark-blue tailcoat with insignia on the high collar and the naval sword at his side.

'Sir?'

He halted in front of her and made a sketchy bow, lifting his tall hat as he did so. 'Ma'am. I am looking for the householder.'

She was aware of his gaze shifting between the two large men beside her, Cris dishevelled in shirtsleeves, Mr Stone managing to look piratical despite his sober, conventional clothing. 'My aunt, Miss Holt, is the householder. And you are?'

'Lieutenant Ritchie, newly appointed Riding Officer for this beat of the coast. And I was told it is Mrs Perowne that I need to speak to.'

Was it her imagination or had Cris growled, low in his throat.

'I am Tamsyn Perowne.' She tried to sound calm and welcoming, but the man's hard, unfriendly gaze was setting her hackles up. 'And Mr Defoe and Mr Stone are our house guests.' She should invite him in, she knew. The Riding Officer had about the same status as the doctor or the curate and would expect to be received in gentry houses, but she did not want this man, who seemed to radiate hostility, over their threshold. 'What can I do for you, Lieutenant Ritchie?'

'The Revenue service has been informed of a new smuggling gang in these parts. What can you tell me of it, Mrs Perowne?'

'Nothing whatsoever. There is no gang here, not since—'

'Not since your late husband's death?' he enquired.

'Precisely.' She took a hold on her temper, sensing that her supporters would react violently at any sign of distress from her. A fight on the front lawn was the last thing they needed. 'I imagine smuggling still goes on, here and there, in a minor way, but I defy you to find any stretch of coastline in England where it does not.'

'And so it will remain while the local gentry take such a casual attitude to law-breaking. Ma'am.' The last word sounded like an afterthought. 'I came to give fair warning that we will be on the alert hereabouts now.'

'There is no *gang*, Lieutenant Ritchie. And I can only assume you mean you wish to advise us to take care and lock our doors. Any other *warning* would be nothing short of insulting.'

'Take it as you will, ma'am,' he snapped.

'Mrs Perowne is too much of a lady to respond to an insult in kind.' Cris took one step forward. He sounded perfectly calm and yet his tone held a threat that sent a shiver down her spine.

'And you are, sir?' The Riding Officer's square chin set even harder.

'As Mrs Perowne said just now, Crispin Defoe, a visitor.' Now he sounded as haughty as a duke.

'Gabriel Stone. *Another* visitor,' the mocking voice on her other side echoed, equally arrogant in its own way.

Ritchie's gaze rested on the faces in front of him, then shifted as though to study the chairmen. Tamsyn could almost feel them glowering behind her. 'Good day to you, gentlemen. Ma'am. You appear to have quite a private army here, Mrs Perowne.' He touched his whip to his hat, turned the horse and clattered back up the lane.

Chapter Ten

Tamsyn turned to find that the two Irishmen had taken Aunt Rosie inside by the simple method of picking up the armchair she was sitting in and carrying it into the house.

Aunt Izzy remained, her face creased with puzzlement. 'What an unpleasant man. I couldn't hear all of what he was saying, but he seemed almost aggressive.'

'Merely a jack-in-office,' Cris said. 'Newly appointed and officious. Nothing for you to worry about.' He turned and looked at Tamsyn. 'If he tries to cause any trouble, I will deal with him.'

It was necessary to take in a breath right down to her diaphragm. Somehow *she* was going to have to deal with this crisis and the aunts' willingness to live without men suddenly became very understandable. Her life was far too full of them—Riding Officers trying to scare her, the mysterious Mr Stone arriving without warning and securing an invitation to stay without the slightest effort, large Irish chairmen who were carrying Aunt Rosie about as though they had been in her service for years and now Cris calmly announcing that he would *deal with* a government official.

'And just how will you do that?' she demanded. 'Forgive me, Mr Defoe, but you are hardly the Duke of Devonshire, are you?' He stood there, competent hands on admirably slim hips, the breeze from the sea stirring the thin white linen of his shirtsleeves, a glimpse of skin at his throat, a long green stain that looked remarkably like lichen up the length of one buckskin-clad thigh. 'But of course, dukes do not go scrambling out of windows, do they?'

Behind him Mr Stone gave a snort of laughter. 'Cris, a duke? He certainly acts like one on occasion, I will give you that.' He appeared to find the idea inordinately amusing.

'Mr Stone, perhaps you would excuse us for a moment? No doubt you would like to freshen up after your journey. If you cannot see either of my aunts when you go inside, then our housekeeper, Mrs Tape, will take care of you.'

'Very crisp,' Cris remarked as his friend, still chuckling, strolled off towards the front door.

'I feel very crisp. In fact, I feel positively brittle. Just what, exactly, is going on, Mr Defoe? Why are you climbing out of windows and threatening Revenue officers and why does the idea that you are a duke convulse your exceedingly relaxed friend with amusement?'

'You are allowing yourself to become agitated, Tamsyn.' He touched her cheek with the back of his hand. 'You are quite flushed. Come and sit in the summer house and compose yourself.'

Grinding one's teeth was not ladylike, but then she did not feel so very ladylike, just at the moment. 'By all means, let us go to the summer house.' She waited until he had stepped into the shadowy interior behind her, then swung round and jabbed an angry finger into the middle of his chest. He caught her hand and held it, pressing the palm against the warm linen. Somehow she managed not to let her fingers curl, gathering the fabric up, pulling him closer.

'Being married to Jory Perowne was not all joy, but at least he never patronised me, never treated me as though I was incapable of looking after myself and never, ever, told me I was becoming *agitated* when I was rightfully annoyed!'

'But you aren't married to me, Tamsyn.' If she had not been flushed already, the suggestive growl in his voice would have turned her cheeks crimson. 'Was I being patronising? I apologise if I was.' He did not let her go and his fingers curled around hers as he took a step forward, trapping their joined hands between their bodies.

'No, you were not. Not until you told me I was becoming agitated,' she conceded. Stepping back would be admitting that his closeness, his touch, affected her. Confessing that she had found his presence at her side had given her strength was too much like accepting weakness. She lifted her chin instead and made herself meet the cool blue eyes. 'Up to then you were merely... lordly.'

Cris shrugged. 'London style, that is all. Take no notice of Gabriel, he finds the idea of his old friend being a duke amusing, the sarcastic devil. Do I seem like a duke to you? After all, I am the kind of man who almost drowns himself in foolish swimming incidents, climbs out of windows and is acquainted with Bath chairmen.' His face was austere, but she recognised the slight crease at the corner of his eyes, the start of a smile he was not allowing out.

She was not going to let him get away with charming her into smiling back at him. 'Explain the window.'

'The chair and the men were a surprise for your aunts. I wanted to stop Gabriel and make sure they arrived with it all set up for her.'

And you could not have run downstairs and out through the door? No, not without alerting me, she answered herself. Cris had wanted to talk to Gabriel Stone first. The pair of them made her uneasy. They had an aura of power and confidence about them, something that went beyond mere competence. They were used to being obeyed and to making things happen. Their way.

Tamsyn moved forward, closer, until she could feel the beat of his heart against her fingers, could see his pupils dilate with surprise, or perhaps, pleasure. 'Tell me,' she murmured sweetly, and he bent his head, to listen, or to kiss. 'Do I seem a helpless little female to you? Do I appear unable to take care of myself and my aunts? Do you think that I need a big, strong man to protect me?' She did smile then, showing her teeth in a clear warning that she could, and would, bite if provoked.

She expected Cris to respond with an attempt at mastery, a hard kiss to show her what she was missing. Or perhaps a display of affronted male pride and a declaration that she did not know what she was talking about and had quite misunderstood him. Instead he did the last thing she expected. He laughed.

It was infectious, open, genuine, and she laughed, too, not knowing why, only that this was completely disarming.

And *then* he kissed her. There were perhaps three seconds to make up her mind on how to react and she was aware of each of them in the thud of her pulse. Three seconds to decide whether to be charmed, or to be resentful, to be mastered or to fight. Or, perhaps, to meet him on equal terms.

One, two, three… Cris lifted his head, eyes watchful. He would not force her, she knew that. Whatever else this man was hiding from her, it was not a willingness to ill treat a woman. Tamsyn wrapped her arms around his neck, pulled his head to hers again and nipped at his lower lip, deliberately provoking. He laughed again against her lips, then probed with his tongue, risking her teeth, provoking in his turn.

This was the man from the sea, the man she had kissed in the surf without knowing why, only that it was right and she wanted him. Then they had been naked and that had been right, too, and they were wearing far too much now. Her hands ran down over the thin linen of his shirt, over the long, beautiful muscles of his back, down to the waistband of his breeches and she tugged, impatient, careless of rips.

He stepped back, breaking the kiss, to let her pull the shirt free and over his head, then his own hands were busy with buttons and pins and her gown was sliding from her shoulders, down to her feet and she was back in his arms, his skin hot and smooth under her palms, his mouth hot and urgent on the swell of her breasts above the neck of her chemise.

'Yes,' she said, closing her teeth on the tendon where his neck met his shoulder, biting gently, tasting his skin, tasting him. *'Yes.'*

'Cris!' The shout from outside froze them in place.

'Hell's teeth.' Cris stepped back, looked round wildly for his shirt. 'I must be out of my mind—the middle of the day in a confounded *shed* in the garden within a stone's throw of the house and a dozen people. Are you all right?' He dived into his shirt, dragged it on, stuffed it into his breeches while Tamsyn just stood and looked at him. 'Get dressed! What are you doing?'

'Looking at you.' She wanted to smile at the sight of him, uncharacteristically harassed and urgent, dishevelled and flatteringly aroused. This was not the cool, calm and mysterious Mr Defoe, this was another man altogether and she was charmed as well as attracted. The sound of Mr Stone's voice calling Cris came closer.

'Dress, Tamsyn!' He found the ends of his neckcloth, whipped it into some sort of knot, then moved to get between her and the door with its old glass panels fogged with salt spray. Through them, as she turned, she could see the blurred figure of the other man standing with his back to them. He seemed to be scanning the beach.

Suddenly seized with Cris's urgency, she pulled up her gown, fumbled the fastenings closed, twitched the skirts, patted at her hair. 'Am I decent?'

'More or less. You'll be the death of me, woman.' He pushed in a few of her hairpins and smiled at her, suddenly tender, his hand cupping her cheek. 'Do you want to be ruined?'

'Yes, please,' Tamsyn said demurely.

'But not here—'

The door swung open behind him. 'There you are. Cris, what the blazes are you doing?' Gabriel Stone took a step inside, took one look at her, turned on his heel and went out again. 'Or, rather, why the blazes are you doing it here and now?' he enquired without looking back.

'Insanity,' Cris said without turning, his smile still promising things that made her feel reckless and eager. He stroked his fingers down her cheek and murmured, 'We'll talk.' Over his shoulder he asked, 'Is the coast clear?'

'Completely.' Gabriel Stone stepped aside to let them

out on to the gravel in front of the summer house. 'Everyone is in the yard admiring the sedan chair and arguing about which of the locals might be employed to carry it.' He was still looking out to sea, presumably tactfully sparing Tamsyn's blushes. She was amazed to discover she did not have any. 'It will be a while before you can find two men suitable, I would suggest, Mrs Perowne. They need to be matched in size and strength, have good balance and endurance. Carrying a sedan chair is harder than it looks.'

'You suggest I do not search too hard?' She grappled to focus her mind on the issue and not on her pounding pulse, the excited flutter low in her belly, the ache in her breasts, the need to reach out and touch the man by her side. 'But how long can these two men stay?'

'As long as I am here, I will pay them,' Cris said. 'Call it a return for my board and lodging,' he said when she began to protest. 'When I leave they will stay for as long as you choose to employ them because this is their work these days.'

'Bodyguards? You cannot pay for them as well as give us the chair.'

'It is for my own peace of mind,' Cris said. He offered his arm to her and she slid her hand into the crook of his elbow. Mr Stone fell in on the other side and offered his arm as well.

'I feel very well protected between two gentlemen,' she remarked lightly as they strolled across the grass. The switch from reckless passion to a sensible discussion was disorientating, and the presence of Gabriel Stone with his rakish understanding at finding them in a compromising position in the summer house only added to the feeling.

Gabriel Stone chuckled.

'What is so amusing?' she asked.

He turned thick-lashed dark brown eyes to study her. 'In London you will find many who would say we are a disgraceful pair and that you are not safe with us at all. Certainly we would not add to your respectability.'

'You would not? Mr Defoe seems entirely respectable to me.' *Except when he kisses me. You, on the other hand...*

'We are two of four close friends, referred to bitterly by the dean of our university as the Four Disgraces. We worked hard at proving him right and did not lose the habit when we went out into the world. Two of us have married this year, so are probably removed from any further temptation to be disgraceful, but Cris and I have a reputation to uphold.'

'Speak for yourself,' Cris said. 'I am, as Mrs Perowne says, *entirely* respectable.'

'You cultivate the appearance of it, but underneath you are as much of a rakehell as the rest of us.' Mr Stone tucked Tamsyn's hand more firmly into his elbow. 'If you saw Cris at court, doing the pretty amongst the ambassadors and the courtiers and the politicians, to say nothing of their wives, you would not recognise this man in his shirtsleeves facing off with Riding Officers.'

Beside her Cris seemed to go still, although he continued to walk, his steady pace unchecked.

'You are often at Court? I thought you said you were a landowner.'

'I am. I just happen to be well connected enough to attend St James's, which is nothing very unusual. It is hardly as exclusive as its habitués would like to make out.' He shrugged. 'I find politics and diplomacy interesting. Unlike Gabriel who is as close-lipped as a clam most of the time and as indiscreet as a village gossip when he does open his mouth.' There was an undertone of threat in the teasing words.

There was something he was not telling her, although she could guess what it was. Crispin Defoe was not the country landowner he pretended to be, he was someone who mingled in society, someone used to London. Someone used to authority and privilege. So what was he hiding? And, more to the point, why was he hiding it?

Try as she might, she could not think of any reason that Cris might be a danger to her, or to those at Barbary Combe House. He had come into their world by accident and the fact that he was being less than open about his own life was probably simply reticence and not in any way sinister. *And I want him.* Was her desire for him blinding her to concerns she should be feeling? No, she decided. Franklin made her uneasy, unsettled, suspicious. Cris made her feel safe, even when she knew her feelings were definitely *un*safe.

Aunt Izzy came to the front door, saw them and waved. 'Dinner in thirty minutes,' she called. 'We have quite lost track of time with all this excitement and Cook is threatening a disaster with the fish if we are late.'

'I must go and tidy myself up,' Cris said. 'Return to my entirely respectable self.'

'And I will show you to your room, Mr Stone. Hot water will have been taken up for you.'

'I'm confused.' Gabe lounged into the dining room, where Cris, decently washed, dressed and combed, was waiting for the rest of the household.

'*You're* confused? I can't imagine what you are doing here—and don't give me that line about curiosity. You are never so curious as to put yourself out with a journey of over two hundred miles to one of the most inaccessible parts of England.'

'I told you, I'm removing myself from temptation and telling myself I am not quite such a rogue as to ruin a respectable young lady.' He shrugged when Cris lifted an eyebrow. 'And Kate is worried about you. She thinks you are in love and moping. But the timing is awry, unless you met Mrs Perowne earlier this year.'

'Kate said…' *Hell's teeth.* Had he been that obvious when he and Gabriel had visited their old friend Grant Rivers, Lord Allundale, and his new wife, Kate? He had thought he had concealed his heartache over Katerina very effectively behind his usual cynical exterior. Apparently not.

Thinking about Katerina did not bring the jab of pain he had become used to. The shock of that realisation almost took his breath away. Was he so shallow, so hard-hearted, that he could shrug off the heartbreak of true love, simply because he was distracted by a lovely woman and a mystery?

Unless, of course, he had not been in love in the first place. Cris moved down the length of the room, away from the door and into the deep window embrasure to absorb that thought.

'Kate was mistaken,' he said quietly. 'There was a woman I could not have. It preoccupied me for a while, that is all.' It occurred to him that there had never before been something that the Marquess of Avenmore wanted badly, yet could not have. Was that all that had been wrong with him? An attack of pique, added to sexual frustration and a heady dose of forbidden romance and he had thought himself in love? If that was the case, he was not at all sure how that made him feel.

The doubt made him almost dizzy. Ridiculous. He was never doubtful, certainly not to the extent of rocking on his heels as though he had drunk too much. Cris steadied himself with one hand on the window frame. He was always in command of his emotions, clear about his motivation. But now… Had he almost drowned himself out of sheer inattention because of the *delusion* he was in love?

Gabe, card-player *extraordinaire*, was watching his face, his own expressionless. He did not have to say anything. It was obvious he thought that Cris had ricocheted from one unsatisfactory *amour* to another.

'I was not in love.' *I think. Perhaps. Damn it, I should know, surely?* 'I am not in love,' he repeated more firmly. 'And I do not intend to find myself in love. I intend to leave here when I am confident that the ladies are no longer in any danger and I am then going to find myself a suitable, sensible wife. Kate hardly knows me. What she calls moping was merely the gloom brought on by contemplating matrimony.'

Gabriel's mouth twisted into a wry smile, but he did not respond to the attempt at levity. 'So what, pray, was going on in the summer house just now? And what is this I hear about you almost drowning yourself?'

'If I have to explain to you that Tamsyn and I are verging on the edge of an affair, then it is you we need to worry about, not me. As for the near drowning, I underestimated the power of the currents off this coast. I was not paying attention, that is all.'

'You always pay attention, Cris,' Gabriel murmured. 'And you are never transparent. Now I can read you like a book and you lose focus almost fatally. I think—'

Whatever he thought was, mercifully, interrupted by Aunt Rosie being helped into the dining room by the footman, Isobel and Tamsyn behind her. Cris let out the breath he had not been aware of holding and set his face into the blandest and most neutral of all his diplomatic expressions.

Chapter Eleven

Cris ate and smiled and kept up his share of the conversation, which was not difficult when the two older ladies could talk of little else but the wonder of the sedan chair and all the expeditions they could take with Isobel riding her hack and Rosie being carried, safe and comfortable at her side. He had taught himself to carry on a dinner-party conversation in three languages while puzzling over a coded letter, planning a meeting and thinking about a new pair of boots. This cheerful domestic meal, even with Gabriel's sardonic eye on him, was child's play.

It gave him the opportunity to think about the self-revelation Gabe had forced on him. He had, somehow, deluded himself that he had fallen in love with Katerina and that was inexplicable. Yes, she was an attractive, intelligent woman—what he knew of her, which was very little. Yes, she had been attracted to him. But that was all. He had never been in love before, he was not in love now. There was no point in trying to convince himself that he had not lost temporary control of his reason over a woman.

It could have been a disaster. If he had not been so

strong with himself about duty, honour and the need to protect both their reputations, the whole affair could have blown up into a diplomatic scandal, meant ruin for Katerina and probably someone dead on the duelling ground. And he would be a disgrace, tied to a woman who was quite intelligent enough to see through whatever protestations of devotion he made to her once their ruin had been accomplished.

What had come over him? He was not some green youth talking himself into love with an unobtainable beauty. He was, on the other hand, a mature man facing the prospect of making a suitable marriage and resenting it. He had always prided himself on his detachment and his independence and the only relationship that he had ever allowed to become personal, to matter, was his friendship with Gabe, Grant and Alex Tempest, Viscount Weybourn.

Was that what this was about? Had he armoured himself against the faceless, unknown, woman he was going to marry by telling himself that his heart was already taken, that marriage was a matter of form, of convention and of convenience, something that would not get close to him, could not hurt?

'Mr Defoe?'

It took him a moment to remember that was who he was, that someone was speaking to him. It seemed that he had been over-confident and his dinner-party skills had disintegrated along with everything else. 'I am sorry, I was distracted for a moment.'

'I was just remarking what a spectacular sunset there is this evening,' Aunt Rosie remarked.

The wall behind her was suffused with pink and those with their backs to the windows turned to admire the sight as the hot red disk of the sun dropped into the sea.

'You almost expect to hear it sizzle,' Tamsyn said as the colour faded. She rang the little hand bell by her side plate and when Michael came in, she gestured to him to light the candles. 'There will be a full moon tonight.'

'A smugglers' moon?' Gabriel asked.

'Certainly, if there is a big run, then moonlight helps, especially if they are going to load it straight on the ponies and head inland,' Tamsyn explained, surprising Cris with her lack of reticence in talking about the subject. 'But the men know the coast so well that they can land with only the aid of a few dark lanterns on shore.' She sent him a quizzical look. 'You don't want to take any notice of what that Riding Officer said. That's just some foolish rumour. There's no serious smuggling going on around here these days. I would know.'

She kept them entertained with tales of the last century when the gangs ruled the coast, then teased the two men with local ghost stories.

'I'll be safe riding back tomorrow, will I?' Gabriel demanded with mock alarm. 'No fear of finding Old Shuck loping at my heels, or headless horsemen or drowned sailors or any of those other horrors in broad daylight?'

'Surely you are not leaving us so soon, Mr Stone?' Isobel asked. 'Do stay a little longer. I am sure you cannot have had time to discuss your business with Mr Defoe yet.'

'This evening after dinner, ma'am…' Gabriel began.

'Not after the long day you have had,' Rosie said firmly. 'You relax this evening and see to your business tomorrow morning, then we can all take a picnic up on to the clifftops to celebrate my wonderful new sedan chair.' When he hesitated she reached out her twisted fingers and touched the back of his hand. 'Won't you indulge me with your company? We are so quiet here that a charming and intelligent guest is too precious to lose.'

'Ma'am, you overwhelm me with your hospitality. I would be delighted.' It brought Cris out of his uncomfortable thoughts to see Gabriel succumbing to the charms of a woman old enough to be his mother, if not his grandmother. He normally avoided respectable older women like the plague and confined his conversation, and his attention, to high-flyers and dashing society matrons.

Tamsyn rang the little bell again and got to her feet as Michael came in. 'We will leave you gentlemen to your port and nuts.'

Amidst the minor flurry of helping Rosie from the room Cris drew Tamsyn aside. 'Where can we talk?'

'Talk?' She looked up at him and blushed. 'The summer house at midnight.'

'That is too close to the house—and uncomfortable for…conversation,' he said, making her blush harder.

'Uncomfortable for talking? I think not. But I will take you on a walk, if you are not frightened of meeting Black Shuck. Wear good boots for rough ground. Coming, Aunt Izzy!'

When he turned back Gabriel had returned to his seat and was pouring ruby port into the pair of fine Waterford crystal glasses Michael had set out for them. He raised his glass and sniffed. 'Excellent port, duty paid or not.'

Edgy, Cris picked up the other glass and walked round the room to study a pair of sketches in the alcove by the fireplace. 'They've some nice pieces here.

I like the ladies' style—Miss Isobel in particular will take some earthenware jar from the local potter, fill it with wild flowers and stand it on an exquisite Sheraton side table and it will look perfect.'

'Stop fidgeting, it isn't like you.' Gabriel watched him, lids half-lowered over his gypsy-dark eyes. 'I like your fierce little widow.'

'She isn't mine.' Cris dropped into the nearest chair and reached for the wine. 'We may have a…thing. For a short while, that is all.' That was all it could be, of course. He knew exactly the sort of wife he needed, his father had explained that to him, young as he was. Marquesses married for dynastic reasons—connections, land, bloodlines. Tamsyn stirred his blood, but she was an obscure widow of a scandalous marriage without any of the attributes that would make a permanent connection acceptable in his world. But, as a widow, then a discreet *affaire* was perfectly acceptable.

'A *thing.*' Gabriel rolled his eyes. 'Are you quite certain that my friend Cris de Feaux has not been kidnapped by smugglers who put you in his place? I am missing the articulate, smooth, cynical man I know.' Cris lobbed a walnut at him. He caught it one-handed and cracked it between his long card-player's fingers. 'Joking aside, if there is something wrong, tell me, I'll help.'

'I know. And there's nothing wrong with me.'

Liar. My brain is scrambled eggs, all the blood in my body is heading straight for my groin and I have no idea what I've been thinking for the last few months.

'But there is plenty amiss here. I'll be interested to hear what you found out about Chelford tomorrow. Meanwhile, pour me some more of that excellent port and tell me the latest London news.'

* * *

'You are here already?' Cris followed the thread of lamplight across the grass to the dark lantern that was set on the step of the summer house.

'I am always prompt.' A hint of laughter, a suspicion of a nervous tremor, a suggestion of excitement. He could not see Tamsyn's face in the shadows, but he knew, quite certainly, that they would be making love that night.

'Where are we going?'

'Follow me.' She picked up the lantern and handed him another, its shutter closed so that only the heat of it and the smell of burning tallow told him it was alight. She crossed the lawn, heading away from the lane, opened the shutter of her lantern a little to show him the stones sticking out of the wall to make a stile and climbed nimbly over. 'We can open the lanterns more now,' she said as the ground began to rise. 'This sheep track winds around the side of the headland, we'll be out of sight of the house in a moment.'

She walked steadily up the steep path, moving with the confidence of someone who was both fit and familiar with where she was going. As they climbed the moon came out, full and brilliant, painting the short turf with abrupt black shadows. They gained the top and Tamsyn strode out, not waiting to see if Cris followed her, then turned abruptly, right on the edge.

'Take care!' He reached for her as she dropped out of sight, then relaxed as he saw she was on a lower path, cutting down below the lip of the cliff by about the height of a tall man. Once they were down it became flat and smooth, just wide enough for one person. Tamsyn ducked, moved sideways and, with an unexpected creak of hinges, vanished into the cliff face.

Cris opened the shutter of his lantern to show a squat hut, built back into the face of the cliff. From what he could see in the flickering lamplight it had been constructed from sea-weathered wood, perhaps hauled up from the beach below. The roof was turf and in the moonlight he could make out the needle-point leaves and round heads of sea thrift, sharp against the midnight sky.

He bent to get under the low lintel and found a square space, long enough for a tall man to lie down in. Across the back was a platform of crude planks. Tamsyn dragged a metal trunk out from under it and Cris crouched to help her, inhaling the scent of old lavender as she opened the lid and hauled out a thickly padded quilt.

They spread it on the planks, then added the pillows she took from the trunk along with a pile of blankets. Tamsyn patted the bed they had created. 'Close the half-door and come and sit here.'

It was divided like a stable door and he did as she asked. All that was visible as they sat there was the sea, filling half the view with the sky above and the reflection of the moon trailing silver across the waves. Tamsyn sighed and leaned into his side, so Cris put an arm around her shoulders and pulled her in snugly.

'An old haunt of yours?'

'It must have been a looker's hut once.' He made a questioning sound and she explained. 'A watcher for the Revenue service. But it was long abandoned when Jory and I found it as children. Later, when things were… difficult, I would sleep here sometimes because it is so peaceful.'

'Difficult? You mean when your husband died?'

She was silent for a moment as though thinking his

simple question through. 'Yes. It was my special place when I wanted to be alone and being alone helped sometimes.'

'Tamsyn.'

'Hmm?'

It had to be said. 'You know I am not staying, that I will be gone in a week or so.'

'Of course.' She wriggled upright and the air struck cool where she had been pressed, warm and soft, against his side. 'We are about to have the conversation about not getting attached and do I really want to do this and you respect me, but...'

There was a trace of amusement in her voice, so he let himself be frank. 'Yes, that was exactly it. You may rely on me to be very careful, but if there are consequences, I also rely on you to let me know.'

'Of course,' she said abruptly. 'I am not worried about that.' The shimmer of amusement had gone now, she sounded almost sad. This businesslike discussion was neither erotic nor romantic, he supposed.

'Tamsyn, if this does not feel right to you, we will go back now. And don't think I am going to sulk, or leave immediately or be less anxious to help you and your aunts.' He turned on the hard bed, reaching to caress her cheek. 'This matters to me, my mermaid. I'll not hurt you.'

'Mermaid?' She laughed, low and husky, the sound like an intimate caress. 'I thought you were a merman, coming out of the sea like that. If you wish to make a woman cautious, you should not appear looking quite so desirable.'

'I was ice-cold, half-drowned and probably covered in goosebumps.' He began to nuzzle her neck and she tilted her head to give him better access.

'I did not notice the goosebumps. I noticed the muscles and how blue your eyes were and your...proportions.' Her hand slid to the fall of his breeches in graphic demonstration. Her breath was coming in little gasps now as his flesh rose to meet her hand.

Cris lifted his head to look at her in the dim lantern light. 'My proportions? It was freezing, I doubt I had any proportions to speak of.'

'Oh, yes, you did. I was most...ah...impressed.'

'Hussy.' Ridiculously flattered, he stood and closed the half-door, then fully unshuttered both lanterns. 'If we are going to take any clothes off, I want to keep warm, regardless of how well I stand up to the cold.'

'You first.' She was sitting with her legs drawn up, her arms wrapped around them, her chin resting on her knees, those great dark eyes watching him. Cris stripped as fast as he could, given that he had to stoop under the low ceiling. It was not cold, but it was cool enough not to want to prolong undressing. And besides, he was beginning to desire nothing more than to be skin to skin with Tamsyn now, to discover whether her body was as tempting warm and dry as it had been wet and shivering.

He sat on the edge of the bed to pull off his boots and she reached out to run her hand down his spine, lingering over each bump of vertebrae. 'I love your back.'

It was difficult to pull off a pair of Hoby's boots when a desirable woman was beginning to twine herself around you. Cris persevered, resisting the temptation to tear off her clothes, rip open his breeches and take her with his boots on. It was an arousing prospect, but he did not know her well enough to judge whether she would find that exciting or insulting.

Barefoot, he stood up to pull off his breeches and she

came up on her knees, her hands sliding over his torso, her mouth trailing down his ribs. Cris stilled, breathing hard, his hands arrested on the fastenings of his falls as he tried for some self-control. Much more of this and she would have him spending like a green youth. He could not remember when a woman had made him quite this aroused so fast.

He kicked off his breeches and to his relief she sat back on her heels and just looked. 'If you touch me, I won't answer for the consequences,' he warned as she gave a low hum of approval.

'Very well.' She began to undress with a straightforwardness that matched his own, shrugging off a simple gown to reveal nothing beneath it but bare woman.

Cris almost swore, swallowed the oath and kept his eyes fixed on her fingers as she pulled the long braid of her hair over her shoulder and began to loosen it. 'Your hair is beautiful.'

'Thank you.' She bent her head and shook it so the mass of dark brown shifted and fell, wavy from the plait. When she looked up it covered her breasts, shadowed the junction of her thighs as she knelt on the bed. 'Cris…' Her voice trailed away, then she seemed to gather her courage. 'I have only slept with one man before. I will not have the skills of the lovers you are used to.'

'You have the skill to bring me to my knees,' he said, and went down on them beside her, pulling her beside him on to the mattress and dragging the blankets up over them. 'I desire you intensely. Can you doubt that?'

'No.' She buried her face in the angle of his neck and shoulder, suddenly shy, it seemed. But her hands were not shy, or clumsy.

'You are sure?' He had never doubted his self-control

before, now he knew that a few more moments of this and he was lost.

'Sure.' Tamsyn slid under him, like the sea creature he had imagined her as, and her damp, hot, softness met his desperate body and he drove into it and stopped, almost shuddering with the pleasure of it, his weight on his elbows, his forehead resting on hers. *'Ah...'* she murmured, and her hands fastened on his shoulders and her legs curled around him until her heels were in the small of his back.

'You are perfect,' he said on a breath that was almost a gasp. 'Perfect.' Then he ceased to know where her body ended and his began as they moved together. It was as though they had done this a thousand times together and yet never before. There was a rightness, a harmony, balanced by a freshness and the wonder of discovery. Somehow he hung on until her eyes opened wide and then closed in ecstasy and she convulsed around him. Somehow he found the strength to withdraw and find his release, straining against the strong, soft, wonderful body in his arms.

For a while he lay dazed, conscious only of their heartbeats, their breathing, the sound of the sea crashing far below. Then he rolled to one side and Tamsyn came with the movement, curling around him, her head on his chest, her body relaxed and trusting. Her lips moved against his skin with silent words, or, perhaps a kiss, then she was still. He sensed her slipping into sleep and closed his own eyes.

But oblivion would not come. He was utterly relaxed, utterly satisfied, warm, content and completely awake, and his mind was apparently determined that he would enjoy none of it. A few months ago, before Katerina, he would simply have been grateful to have experienced such mutually satisfying lovemaking. The fact that he hardly knew Tamsyn, that she was from another world completely, would not have mattered. They were mutually attracted, he could make love with her without compromising her and it would have been a perfect idyll, one that would be ended naturally with a departure that she expected and accepted.

But now he could not help examining his motives, his desires. He was not in love with Tamsyn, but he no longer knew what that meant, not after the shock of self-realisation over Katerina. Was he just using her? But she was not an innocent and she had her own needs, too. The urge to toss and turn, pummel the pillow, had to be suppressed because of the woman draped, limp and trustful, over him.

He should return to London, find a suitable bride, court her, wed her, he told himself. And then stay faithful to her. Gabe the ultimate cynic, was prepared to believe that their friends, Alex and Grant, had fallen in love, but to hear him talk about this was as rare an event as finding a unicorn in the back garden. According to him the remaining two disgraceful lords had no excuse for tying themselves to some woman's apron strings. If he explained his thinking to his friend, Gabriel would laugh at him, tell him that this attack of conscience, of sobriety, was the onset of old age.

Cris opened his eyes and stared up at the weathered old wood of the roof while Tamsyn's curls tickled the underside of his chin. If twenty-nine was old, then he might as well open that door, go back down the cliff and walk back into the sea to finish the swim that had brought him here.

Chapter Twelve

'What is wrong?' Tamsyn swam up out of the sleepy, satisfied haze and found Cris beside her, his arm heavy across her waist. She could feel the tension in him, despite the sprawl of his long body. 'I can hear you thinking.'

He laughed, an almost convincing sound, but she had come to know him very quickly over the past week and he was not amused.

'Are you regretting what we have done?' she demanded, wriggling round so she could sit up and look at him properly.

'No.' This time the smile was quite genuine, a small, sensual twist of his lips. 'I was brooding, that's all. Gabriel would say I am getting old.'

'Truly?' Feeling wicked, she slid one hand under the blanket and explored. 'I don't think so.'

Cris caught her hand, but did not move it from where it lay, her fingers lightly curled around the hardening length of him. 'Mentally old.'

'A sudden attack of responsibility? That is very ageing.' She tried to make a joke of it, but he only frowned.

'No. I've always been responsible, I think.' He

shrugged. 'I was brought up to be, to accept who I was, what I needed to do to fulfil that role.' There was an edge of bitterness there that puzzled her. What kind of burdens had his upbringing laid on him? 'Whatever hell I might have been raising, I always did what needed to be done, looked after the people who relied on me.'

'As you are doing here,' Tamsyn pointed out.

'I don't like men who try to get what they want by intimidating those who can't fight back.' He winced as she closed her fingers rather too tightly. 'I know you can stand up for yourself, but you shouldn't have to. I told you I wouldn't stay long. I must go home, settle down, stop doing things like this.'

She found her fingers had curled into claws. Cris closed his eyes as she let them rake gently over his hot flesh instead of digging them in. 'What exactly is *this*?'

'Making love without commitment.' His hand tightened over hers, moved.

'There is someone you should be settling down with? Someone to whom you should be committed?' She kept her voice light, surprised by the sharp lance of envy.

'No, there is no one.' His face was slightly averted, she wished she could read it. 'There should be. Duty. Responsibility again, I suppose.' His hips rose as she stroked down and up. '*Ah*. That is so good.'

'If there is no one, then you are not being unfaithful.' She thought his face tightened, but that might simply have been the effect of what she was doing to him. 'I believe you are simply experiencing the melancholy and introspection that sometimes comes after lovemaking.'

'*La tristesse*, the French call it. Well, I'm not suffering from melancholy now.' He kicked away the blanket, reached for her and held her so he could torment her right nipple with teeth and lips. Then he suddenly let go and she collapsed on to the bed with him in a tangle of limbs and kisses, and forgot jealousy, and worry, in bliss.

'Tamsyn, dear, have you been sleeping properly?' Aunt Izzy peered anxiously at her over the fruit bowl in the middle of the breakfast table. 'You look a trifle heavy-eyed.'

'I am sure Tamsyn is perfectly relaxed, dearest,' Rosie said before Tamsyn had a chance to collect herself from her improper recollections. Her aunt's smile was bland. *She knows.*

As for the expression on Mr Stone's face, the man was looking so innocent that it was bound to be false. Presumably he was quite well aware what had passed last night between his friend and herself.

'Too much time spent with the account books, that is all I am suffering from,' she said. 'I am looking forward to our picnic lunch. That will wake me up.'

They went their separate ways after breakfast. The two men strolled down to the waterside, deep in conversation, presumably to do with whatever business had brought Gabriel Stone there in the first place. Aunt Rosie went for her hot soak to get herself, as she said, 'In prime condition for my jaunt.' Aunt Izzy shut herself in the kitchen with Cook to create the perfect picnic luncheon and that left Tamsyn staring at the farm's feed bills and trying to focus.

She had to get the accounts straight in case they were sent any more invoices following the mischief with the bank and the damage to their reputation for creditworthiness. It was important and urgent and every time she smoothed her hand over a page in the book all she could feel was Cris's skin under her palm. When she nibbled the end of her pen, all she could think of was his mouth on hers, and once she let her mind wander along those paths, then the heaviness settled low in her belly and the little pulse started its wicked beat between her thighs, and her breasts ached.

I want him again. Now.

It frightened her, a little, the intensity of the need. She had been celibate for all the long months since Jory had died, that must be it. She was a young woman, used to lovemaking. Of course she missed it, even though she had submerged the need as deep as her grief for Jory. That was why last night had been so *magical*. She took the word, turned it in her mind, shivered. There was something charmed about the way Cris had come to her out of the sea, almost out of the jaws of death, something other-worldly about his blond beauty, those haunting blue eyes. If she was not an adult, modern woman she might start imagining things, supposing he had come from some mysterious world of Celtic legend to help her. She had read Scottish tales of Selkies, seal people who came out of the sea to seduce human beings. They would always return to the water, leaving their earthbound lovers desolate.

That was a depressing turn of thought, but of course Cris would leave, she accepted that. Whoever he was, whatever his life at home and in London, he was a man who moved in circles far removed from her rustic, unsophisticated world. Even if he had wanted her in any other way than for this brief, amorous, encounter, then he would not when he knew the truth about her. All men wanted heirs. She realised her hand was resting over her stomach and snatched it away, angry with herself for still yearning, still grieving for what she had lost and could never have.

She had never had illusions about men. Jory had loved her in the only way he knew, as a familiar part of himself. They had married out of desire and because she had loved him in so many ways, although none of them was the romantic love she had always dreamed of. He had wanted to keep her safe because he was fond of her and she was one of his possession. And she had wanted to *feel* safe, a ridiculous illusion with Jory, who did not know the meaning of the word when it applied to himself.

She propped her chin on her cupped palm and stared out of the window overlooking the garden, trying to shake the mood, and saw the men were pacing back and forth along the long seawall at the end of the lawn. Then they broke apart, faced each other. Gabriel Stone drew the sword from the scabbard that seemed to be permanently at his side and she was half out of her seat before she realised that he was demonstrating something. He parried, Cris moved fluidly to one side, then in a blur of movement was behind him, reaching for his sword arm. Stone disengaged, moved out of trouble. They faced each other again, armed against unarmed. Then Cris shifted again, she saw Gabriel's head turn, he recovered, just too late and the sword went spinning out of his grasp and speared point-down, quivering in the grass.

He flourished an elaborate bow, retrieved the weapon, wiped the point carefully and sheathed it. Cris draped one arm around his shoulder and they began to walk up and down again.

Tamsyn sat down with a thump, closed her mouth, which was inelegantly open, and frowned at the two men. That had been disgracefully arousing and it had also been a demonstration of speed and skill and of complete trust. There would have been no fencing button on the point of that sword. One slip and Cris could have been badly hurt. Or if he had been less accurate, his friend might have been wounded in the disarm. They obviously knew each other very, very well.

She wondered why Gabriel Stone was armed with a sword. Gentlemen carried pistols with them in saddle holsters, or in their carriages when they travelled, but usually these days only military officers wore a sword at their hip. It suited him, she decided, went with the slightly sinister presence, the dark, mocking eyes. If Cris trusted him, then she must, but he unnerved her.

Whereas Cris confused and delighted and confounded her. She indulged herself by watching the tall figure sauntering along, silhouetted against the sea, then made herself look down and wrestle with the columns of figures once more.

The picnic expedition set off at eleven o'clock. Aunt Rosie was helped carefully into the chair, the men stepped between the carrying handles, ducked their heads under the leather straps, took a firm grip and lifted. Tamsyn mounted Foxy, Aunt Izzy was helped on to her placid hack, Bumble, and Jason loaded the pack pony with the rugs and hampers.

As Gabriel Stone mounted his own horse, Tamsyn looked down at Cris. 'You are going to have a long walk, I'm afraid.'

'Collins is saddling my horse. Didn't you realise he's been in your stables eating his head off ever since Collins brought the carriage over?'

'No one mentioned it and I've been too busy to visit the stable yard.' Which just went to show how distracted she had been by Cris's presence. Normally nothing stopped her from doing the complete rounds of the house and outbuildings daily.

A raking hunter emerged from the gate further up the lane. There was no one at its head, but when Cris whistled and walked out on to the track it trotted down and butted him in the chest with its big head. 'This is Jackdaw.'

'Because he is black?'

'And wicked and thieving,' Cris said, as he swung up into the saddle. 'Stop that.' The black tossed its head as though in denial that it had even thought about taking a chunk out of Gabriel Stone's bay. 'You are old enough to know better.'

'But not very old.' Tamsyn edged Foxy closer and Jackdaw snorted and rolled his eye.

'He's just four.'

'And not English, I think.' There was something about the powerful rump and the set of the animal's head that seemed different.

'Danish,' Cris said shortly and moved off after the sedan chair.

'Denmark?' Tamsyn said out loud. She had never encountered anything Danish before.

'He shipped him back.' Gabriel Stone brought his bay alongside Foxy. 'It's a nice beast and worth the effort and the cost.'

'You mean Cris…Mr Defoe, has been to Denmark?'

'Oh, yes, last mission he was on.' Gabriel said it vaguely, as though he was not creating even more mysteries. She had a very strong suspicion he knew exactly what he was doing. *Stirring the pot, Mr Stone?* Cris reined in and joined them again, presumably wary of what his friend was saying about him.

'Mission?' she asked, obediently playing Gabriel's game.

'Diplomatic.' Cris's expression did not change, but

Jackdaw sidled across the lane uneasily. 'I occasionally help out.' He managed to make it sound as though he handed the drinks round at embassy parties.

'Help who out? The government, you mean?' She dropped her hands without meaning to and Foxy broke into a trot, jolting her inelegantly for half-a-dozen strides until she got control.

'The Foreign Office. When they want someone who isn't, shall we say, a fixture in the diplomatic circles I drop in on…situations. Help out.'

Do you indeed? She was beginning to wonder just who this man was. The government used him as a part-time diplomat, and, she suspected, in tricky circumstances. He was tough, fit and capable of disarming the dangerous-looking Mr Stone, he could afford to import horses from the Continent and he had time to spend on a little local difficulty in a remote Devon hamlet.

Tamsyn tried to think of a question that did not sound like the bare-faced curiosity that it was. The trouble was, she found the mystery only added to the attraction, which was a dangerous state to be in.

Infatuated, she told herself severely. *That's what you are. You should settle for a nice, ordinary man, like Dr Tregarth. He is pleasant-looking, intelligent, hard-working, respectable, stands up for himself…*

He might even be willing to accept her the way she was. At least he would understand it was not her fault.

She lectured herself all the way up to Stibworthy and had just reached the conclusion that she did not fall for men like the doctor because they obviously did not find her attractive enough to show any interest, when the little procession met him striding down the street.

'Why are you blushing like a rose?' Cris enquired,

his voice carrying to Gabriel Stone, who twisted in the saddle, grinned at her and only made things worse.

'*Shh!* Good day, Dr Tregarth.' She waved, but he was by the sedan chair, smiling and nodding approval to Aunt Rosie while the chairmen set down their burden and stretched.

'Good chap, but too staid for you.' Cris moderated his voice, just a little, but he was still speaking loudly enough for Mr Stone to hear, judging by his expression. 'If he doesn't notice that you blush when you catch sight of him, well, one despairs of the fellow.'

'I am not blushing over Doc…over anyone. I am just a little windblown, that is all. I should have worn a veil.'

'Do you own one?' Cris enquired, all innocence.

Tamsyn brought Foxy tight up against Jackdaw and muttered, 'Do stop teasing me, you provoking man.'

'But I like it when you blush. It makes me wonder what I must do to provoke that pretty colour when we are alone.' His voice had dropped to an intimate murmur. 'Ah, so that's the trick of it,' he said, his eyes laughing at her as the heat flooded her cheeks.

She was saved from having to reply by the chairmen lifting their burden again and the party setting off once more.

'Where are we going?' Gabriel Stone reined back to ask.

'Up through the village and then we turn north on to the headland above Barbary Combe House. There's a wonderful view from up there.'

It was not her aunt's favourite, that had always been the prospect from Black Edge Head to the south, but Tamsyn knew she was far too tactful to take them to the scene of Jory's final confrontation with the militia.

'Mrs Perowne.' Dr Tregarth stepped out into the

street as they passed him. 'A word in your ear, if I
may. I did not want to worry your aunts.' He cast a rapid
glance at the retreating sedan chair party.

'We will ride on,' Cris said with a nod to Gabriel.

'No.' Tregarth held up a restraining hand. 'I think it
would be a good thing if you heard this, too, Mr Defoe.
There is word going around that Jory Perowne's gang
is active again. They say the sign of the silver hand
has been chalked up on walls, even on the door of the
Revenue's building in Barnstaple.'

'That's impossible.' Tamsyn bit back the rest of the
words that sprang to her lips and made herself think
calmly. 'I suppose someone could be using the old
name, the sign. This is what that objectionable Mr
Ritchie was hinting at the other day, I suppose.'

'There is more.' Tregarth looked up at her, his face
serious under the brim of his low-crowned hat. 'There
are not only rumours, there is speculation as well. People are asking if the Silver Hand is operating again, and
who is leading it?'

'I have no idea. Jory had no lieutenant. A second in
command, yes, but no one who could take control of a
gang like that.' Then Cris's intake of breath, the earnest
expression on the doctor's face, made her realise what
Tregarth was worried about. 'They think it is something
to do with *me*? That is preposterous. Smugglers would
not take orders from a woman.'

'They might from Jory Perowne's woman.'

'No.' She jerked Foxy's head round, used her heel
and sent him cantering up the street towards the vanishing picnic party. The Silver Hand gang working again?
It was impossible. Surely she would know if someone
with Jory's skills and deviousness and leadership had
set up the network again anywhere near here. But all

she could be certain of was that it was not her leading even one rowing boat, let alone a gang. Yet if someone who knew her as well as Dr Tregarth could look at her with that question in his eyes, then others might think it, too. People who were far more dangerous than a friendly village doctor.

Pounding hooves caught up with Foxy before she reached the others. Cris and Gabriel fell in, one on either side of her, and she reined in to a walk. She did not want to talk about this within earshot of the aunts.

'Silver Hand gang?' Cris asked.

'Jory had inherited a silver charm. A hand, about two inches long, broken off a religious statue by the look of it. The story was that it was a relic from the Armada shipwrecks, found by an ancestor who had a ring fixed to it and who wore it round his neck on a chain. When Jory inherited it he wore it, too.' She remembered it hanging against his chest, the silver chain glinting through the curling dark hair. When he had been feeling defiant—which was often—he would wear it outside his shirt, answering questions about it with the bland assurance that it was simply an heirloom and it wasn't his fault if people used it as a symbol.

'It became part of the mythology around him,' she continued. Trust Jory to have to be dramatic. 'The men would chalk a hand on casks when they left them on doorsteps, so people knew who to thank for the gifts the gang left in return for silence. Not that anyone would have betrayed Jory and the others. When the Revenue put up posters advertising a reward, someone would always scrawl the hand over it.'

'And where is it now?' Gabriel's question jerked her out of her memories.

'He was wearing it when… It was round his neck

that day.' She had seen it in that moment when he had turned to face her, the moment she realised now was when he had made up his mind to jump and save them both the horror of a trial and an execution. If only she'd had his courage, could have stayed strong and defiant, not collapsed with shock and lost the only thing she had left of him.

'You wouldn't need the actual object,' Cris said thoughtfully, jerking her out of her memories. 'Not with something so well known. I suppose there isn't another, it would be unique.'

It was a question. 'There is another,' she admitted. 'Jory had a replica made for me as a wedding gift.' *Other women get earrings, a pretty gown, flowers from their lover. I get a smuggler's talisman.* 'But it isn't the same as his. He had our names engraved on mine, with a heart and an anchor.'

'Where is it?'

'Locked up in the strongbox with the legal papers and our bits of jewellery. I am not wearing it next to my heart, if that is what you want to know.'

'I know you are not.' Cris's whisper made the blush come back like the flooding tide. 'But it might be a good idea to get it hidden away somewhere a search party couldn't find it. The Riding Officer might see it as a sign of guilt, not as a love token.'

'Yes, I suppose you are right, but I cannot believe they would take it as far as searching the house.' But they had when Jory was alive. It had become almost a routine, tidying up after a party of Revenue men, or the militia, had rummaged in the cellars, the attics, under the beds, through the haystacks.

The ground beneath the horses' hooves began to level out. They were through the trees and at the edge of the clifftop pasture now and off to the left was the head of the path that she and Cris had climbed the night before.

'We are right above the house, surely?' Gabriel stood in his stirrups to look down.

'It is the only way up unless you are on foot. There are few rabbit holes up here—too many buzzards keeping them down—so we can gallop.' She turned Foxy off the track and gave him his head. Behind her she heard the sound of the other two horses in pursuit. Foxy, excited by the competition, stretched out his head and she laughed aloud with the thrill of it as they thundered across the clifftop.

They were neck and neck, the three of them, as she reined in. 'Take care now, it dips down to the next stream, we'd best turn back.'

They trotted behind Gabriel, who spurred his bay into a gallop again. 'Are we climbing our cliff path tonight?' Cris asked.

'Or…' She blushed saying it, it seemed so forward. 'I could come to you. I was thinking about it this morning.' More blushes when he sent her a swift, smiling look. 'Your room is so isolated, no one would know.'

'And the bed is softer,' Cris agreed, his face perfectly composed. Ahead across the clifftop they could see the picnic party flapping out rugs, setting up the folding chair that had been strapped on the pack pony. Cris leaned across, caught her round the waist one-handed, and dropped a rapid, searing kiss on her lips. 'And I am not. Softer, that is.'

'Cris!' She was still laughing, and still flushed, when they reached the others.

'Oh, it is so good to hear you laughing out loud again, my dear.' Aunt Rosie smiled up from her chair set amongst the scattered picnic things. 'And I could laugh like a girl, too. Thank you so much, Mr Defoe, Mr Stone, for this wonderful gift. And to my two stalwart bearers.' She beamed at the chairmen who were lifting tankards to their mouths. 'Just look at this view—you can see Lundy in the distance, see, gentlemen? And—' She broke off. 'Who is this coming?'

A procession was wending its way along the track they had just used. Three men on horseback, three militiamen on foot, the white cross-belts stark against their scarlet coats, muskets at the slope on their shoulders.

Cris nudged Jackdaw closer to Foxy's side. Gabriel moved his big bay until it stood between the advancing party and Aunt Rosie's chair.

'Squire Penwith,' Tamsyn said as the party approached closer. She found her voice was not quite steady. She sat up straighter in the saddle and got it under control. 'And the coroner, Sir James Trelawney. And someone from the Revenue by the look of his uniform.'

The group halted at the edge of the spread rugs.

'Sir James, Squire Penwith. Good day to you.'

'Mrs Perowne. Ladies.' Sir James lifted his hat. 'I apologise for interrupting your picnic.'

'I have no doubt it is a matter of urgency, Sir James.' She managed to sound just a trifle haughty, she was glad to hear.

'It is, Mrs Perowne. I very much regret to say that the Riding Officer, Lieutenant Ritchie, has been murdered.'

Chapter Thirteen

'Murdered?' Foxy backed as Tamsyn's hands clenched on the reins. 'How? When?'

'Last night, in Cat's Nose Bay. He was shot in the back,' the rider in uniform said harshly. 'I am Captain Sutherland of His Majesty's Revenue Service.'

'That is appalling news indeed,' Cris said before she could do more than gasp. 'But might I ask why you accost these ladies here with such a tale, told so brutally?'

'I will be holding the inquest on the body of Lieutenant Ritchie. I require the attendance of Mrs Perowne to give evidence and to answer questions.' Sir James narrowed his eyes at the two men so protectively close to the women. 'I do not believe I have had the pleasure of your acquaintance, gentlemen. Sir James Trelawney, Coroner for this district, at your service.'

'Crispin Defoe, of London and Kent. My friend, Gabriel Stone, of London. Your servants, sir.' Cris, his voice perfectly civil, managed to make the polite introduction sound like a declaration of war, without one word out of place.

From horseback Gabriel bowed. As he straightened his hand lay lightly on the pommel of his sword. The two chairmen lumbered to their feet, pewter tankards tight in their massive fists.

'The inquest will be held in two days' time. I require Mrs Perowne to reside at my house, chaperoned, naturally, by my wife, until then.'

'You are *arresting* me?'

'You have a warrant?' Cris no longer sounded civil.

'I have not. Nor am I arresting Mrs Perowne. This is for her own protection.' The coroner was icy. Beside him the Revenue Officer was glaring at Cris, and Squire Penwith was flushed with anger, or excitement, Tamsyn thought, wondering why she did not feel more frightened. Sick, yes, but not as terrified as she ought to be. But Cris was there, of course. It was time she stood up for herself.

'Against what am I being *protected*?' she enquired.

'Against the members of the gang responsible for this outrage,' Trelawney snapped. 'They will not want you giving evidence, I'll warrant.'

'The implications of that statement are insulting, Sir James.' Cris cut across her furious reply. 'To say nothing of prejudicial to a fair hearing. I see you are escorted by the militia. If you are fearful for Mrs Perowne's safety, then I suggest that stationing them outside her house on guard will be more than adequate. It might also persuade the lady not to take a civil action for wrongful arrest, unlawful detention, kidnapping and defamation of character.'

'Defamation?' Penwith spluttered. 'A smuggler's moll has no character to be defamed, sir!'

Cris jerked his head at Gabriel, who circled his horse and brought it in on Foxy's other side. As soon as he was in position Cris walked Jackdaw forward until the big black was nose to nose with Penwith's horse.

'On the last occasion we met, sir, I suggested a meeting in a field. At dawn. That still seems to me to be an admirable idea.'

'Duelling is illegal,' Penwith said. His horse began to back up; Jackdaw pressed in closer.

'So it is,' Cris said silkily. 'A minor disadvantage. A greater one in this case is that it requires two *gentlemen* who both possess a little courage.'

'Enough of this.' The coroner directed a scornful glance at Penwith. 'Your suggestion is sound, Mr Defoe. Sergeant Willis, you will deploy your men at Barbary Combe House and deliver…*escort* Mrs Perowne to my court the day after tomorrow for a ten o'clock hearing. Good day to you all. Enjoy your picnic, ladies.'

'Insolent wretch,' Aunt Rosie said, her voice cutting through the clear air. 'I knew him when he was a boy, and he was a pompous little no-account then.' Sir James's ears turned scarlet, but he did not turn. 'And as for that jackass Penwith, you are wasting your time attempting to arrange an affair of honour, Mr Defoe. He has none.'

'Cris—'

He rode back, dismounted and held up his hands to her. 'Courage, Tamsyn. They are blustering. It can only be a bluff. Now come down, eat this wonderful picnic, admire the view.'

'Of course.' She managed a smile. 'I cannot let those idiots spoil Aunt Rosie's special day.'

'That's my girl,' he murmured as she slid into his hands, down the length of the hard steady body. 'I'm here, they won't hurt you.'

She stood for a moment, just leaning into him, feeling the strength and the reassurance flowing from him to her, wishing she could put her head on his shoulder.

Instead she pushed away and walked towards the militiamen. *Do not weaken. He won't be here forever.* 'Sergeant Willis, isn't it? Do make yourselves comfortable. None of us are going anywhere for a while and I am certain our picnic will stretch to give you your luncheon also.'

'Ma'am.' The sergeant looked hideously uncomfortable. He cleared his throat and looked round as though for inspiration.

'Might I suggest your men stand guard, one at a time on rotation, while the rest of you sit over there with our staff and refresh yourselves?' Cris scanned the surrounding area. 'I feel certain that the country hereabouts is open enough to give good warning of the approach of dangerous gangs of smugglers intent on subverting Mrs Perowne's evidence.'

'Er…yes, sir. Just as you say, thank you, sir. Perkins! You heard the gentleman. On patrol for half an hour, then you, Downton.' They marched off stiffly.

Tamsyn fought a rather hysterical giggle. 'This would be funny. If it—'

'Wasn't,' Cris finished. 'Quite. A very bad farce. Come and sit down.'

She managed a rueful smile for the aunts, both of whom, she was relieved to see, were fuming rather than fearful. 'I simply cannot believe that there really is a large-scale smuggling operation going on,' she said, once they were settled with slices of raised pie and cheese and apples. 'Things were becoming more difficult even before Jory died. With the end of the war and the changes in taxes, there just isn't the range of things to smuggle to make it worthwhile. Not on this coast, at any rate.'

'I suppose they cannot overlook a murder,' Aunt

Rosie said, obviously struggling to be fair. 'But they must be demented to think Tamsyn has anything to do with it.'

'After the inquest it will be quite apparent there is no evidence.' Gabriel sprawled with careless elegance across one corner of the rug, a chicken leg in one hand. 'I assume you have been nowhere near this Cat's Nose Bay, Mrs Perowne?'

'Not for several weeks,' she said. 'But I know it. It was one of Jory's favourite landing beaches and it is probably still used for some small runs. But violence has never been the way down here, not since Jory was running things. He always found a way to slip past the militia and the Revenue. Someone must have been desperate, or cornered.'

'You don't shoot a man in the back if he's cornered you,' Cris pointed out drily.

Aunt Izzy was beginning to look anxious. Tamsyn took a deep breath and found a smile from somewhere. 'The inquest will be held in Kilkhampton, so I will be able to get some shopping done at that excellent milliners Mrs Holworthy recommended. We must make a list of what we need.'

Always assuming I am not being hauled off to the lock-up right after the inquest.

Her tone and smile must have been suitably optimistic, for Aunt Izzy brightened up and reminded her that there was also a very good stationers and they needed sealing wax and black ink.

Somehow they managed to ignore the militiamen marching up and down, a discordant flash of scarlet in the corner of the eye, however hard everyone looked the other way and pretended they were not there.

Eventually Rosie announced that she was becoming

a little tired and perhaps they should return. The picnic was loaded on the pack pony, the sedan chair set off down the hill and the two men flanked Tamsyn with the militiamen bringing up the rear.

'Right, now we are out of earshot of your aunts, let's have a serious discussion about this,' Cris said briskly. Tamsyn felt an irrational wave of relief that he was not going to pretend everything would be all right. It was not and she needed help, not soothing. 'First thing, we get that silver hand of yours out of the house.'

'How? They will stop any of us leaving, I am certain. And if they search, they will search everyone's possessions.'

'I've a secret compartment in my carriage. It has defeated virtually every border guard on the Continent. If you go and get the hand out of the strong box immediately when we get back, then I'll find an excuse to be in the stables, getting Jackdaw settled.'

That was a relief. She pushed to the back of her mind the question of why Cris needed a secret compartment in his carriage.

'I am assuming this is another of Chelford's little games,' he continued.

'Franklin? But this is murder…' She thought about it while Cris rode on in silence, waiting for her to catch up with his reasoning. 'He spreads rumours about a new smuggling gang, he shoots that poor man and somehow implicates me? That would explain Sir James's confidence. But there cannot be any evidence.'

'That is what is worrying me,' Gabriel said. 'It means that something has been fabricated and it is likely to be something so obvious that even that blockheaded coroner will swallow it.'

Perhaps, after all, it would be nice to be treated like

a damsel in distress and not be subjected to this bracing dose of reality. As if he sensed her wavering courage Cris reached out and closed his hand over hers on the reins. 'Don't worry, we're here. If you can just get it clear in your mind that you are not going to be hauled off to gaol and hanged, you can relax and enjoy this.'

'Relax!' It came out as a shriek before she could help herself. 'How do you expect me to enjoy this?'

'We are going to tie Chelford in knots,' Gabriel said with relish. 'Hang him up by the ba—that is, by the toes and leave him swinging in the wind.'

'There is no need to mince your words for me, Mr Stone,' Tamsyn said crisply. 'I like the idea of suspending Franklin by the balls. It appeals very much indeed.'

'To which end, I'd be glad if you'd go back to London, Gabe, and carry on with the investigations we discussed this morning.' Cris released her hand with a small squeeze.

'After the inquest. I might pick up some more information there.'

'Mr Stone is here for more than the delivery of the sedan chair, is he not?' she demanded.

Cris shrugged. 'He has been investigating Chelford in London for me.' He leaned forward so he could look at his friend across her. 'There was no reason, other than incorrigible curiosity, for him to have come down here himself instead of writing.'

'I told you,' Gabriel said laconically. 'I am running away from a woman.'

It was not until they reached Barbary Combe House that Tamsyn realised that the two of them had managed to keep her distracted and laughing with their inconsequential teasing, all the way back. She let Cris help her down from Foxy, allowing herself the indulgence, this time, of sliding down his body, and then stayed close, enjoying the heat and the feeling of strength and the evidence that her body next to his aroused him.

She was conscious of the sergeant watching them and deliberately raised her voice as she broke free from Cris's supporting hands. 'If you wait just a moment, I will bring you what is left of the herbs that the farrier gave me for Foxy's sore hoof. If Jackdaw is favouring his off hind, it might help.'

The militiamen made no move to stop her as she ran into the house, through to her study, and took the key to the strongbox from its hiding place behind the desk. The old lock creaked and protested as she turned the big key, but it opened easily enough and she rummaged quickly, burrowing beneath the documents for the box with the silver hand. It was not there.

She searched again, then once more, tossing the papers out on to the floor, heedless of deeds and indentures mixing with a roll of banknotes. There was no box except the aunts' jewellery and those boxes were all too small, or too flat, to hold the pendant. There was no silver hand, not even the chain. She scooped it all back, just as it was, slammed the lid on the chaos and locked the strongbox, then ran to hide the key and on to the stillroom to find a mixture of harmless herbs.

'There was no need to hurry so,' Cris said when she reached his side again. He was talking to one of the militiamen and gave him the sort of look that always made her want to slap a man. *Silly female, still, we have to tolerate them, don't we?* it said. The sergeant smirked.

He is getting him on his side, Tamsyn realised. 'What I was looking for was not there any more,' she said brightly. 'But I thought this might help with any swelling.'

Cris took the bowl from her hands, sniffed it. 'To be applied as a poultice? Can you show Collins?' He glanced at the militiaman. 'We are just going up to the stables. Are you coming?'

'Don't see how I needs to, sir.' The man shifted his feet uncomfortably. 'Load of foolishness, if you asks me. The sergeant said I was to watch the lane, not follow anyone about. Dan's round the back, Sarge is looking at the beach. You're not going nowhere, are you, ma'am?'

'No, I am not. You're Willie Downton's brother, aren't you?'

'Yes, ma'am. Jed. I liked Mr Jory, I did. I'd known him since I was a boy. They've no cause to be hounding his widow, not no how.'

'Well, thank you, Jed. But you must obey your orders, I don't want to get you into any trouble. If you stand there, then you are keeping an eye on the stable yard and the lane.'

In the yard Collins was unsaddling Jackdaw. 'Is he favouring the off hind?' Cris asked. The man grunted, his gaze sweeping the yard and surroundings while Cris ran his hand down Jackdaw's leg and lifted the hoof.

Tamsyn came and studied it, close by his side. 'The hand has gone,' she whispered. 'And the chain. Nothing else is missing, not even a roll of banknotes or the jewellery.'

'When did you last see it?' Cris made no attempt to moderate his voice and Tamsyn copied him. Being seen whispering would only look suspicious.

'Months ago. It was in a black bag. I wouldn't notice it unless I was looking especially for it.' She bit her lip in thought. 'I haven't seen it since before Franklin was last here. He could have taken it easily.'

Cris made a remark to Collins about Jackdaw's hoof,

handed him the herbs and took Tamsyn's arm to walk back down to the house.

'He must have been planning this ever since Aunt Izzy refused to move to the dower house,' she said, as they went in through the kitchen door.

'He has taken an object that not only ties you in closely to your late husband, but is a potent symbol of his smuggling activities.' Cris sounded grim.

She swung round to face him. 'You are worrying me now.'

'And you are not already concerned?' His wry smile sent a jolt of panic through her. 'There is no point in me treating you like some feather-headed chit and pretending everything will be all right without us putting some effort into it. What would Chelford think would happen to your aunts if you were hauled off to prison to await trial?'

'He would never believe they could manage on their own.'

'He would expect them to retreat, trembling, to your aunt Isobel's nearest male relative for shelter.'

'But they would not. They would hire a steward, take on more men.'

'He underestimates them, in effect. But he is only going to discover that too late.' Cris kept going, through the bathing room and into the drawing room, which was deserted.

'I confess I would rather he did not have to find out that way.' Somehow she kept her voice from trembling. Murder was a capital offence.

Cris turned, frowned. 'You think I would let it get that far? You do not have much faith in me, do you?'

'What can you do? They must have some evidence, even if it is false.' She wanted to wring her hands, pace about. Instead she made herself stand still, look the thing firmly in the eye and face facts, deal with it.

'The day after tomorrow is the inquest, not a trial. It is to establish the cause of death and to record the circumstances. Come here.' He pulled her to him a little roughly, held her, and for a second she thought his hands shook. Then he was stroking one firmly down her back as though soothing a spooked horse and his voice, which had roughened, was steady and reassuring. 'Tamsyn, I swear to you that I will keep you safe.'

'Why?' She jerked away before the safety of his body, the reassurance of his arms, left her so weak she would not be able to stand on her own two feet. 'You don't belong here, you hardly know me. Why should you get involved in this mess?'

Cris answered without stopping to analyse it. 'Because I probably owe you my life. Because I like you, and your aunts. Because you are my lover. And, when you come right down to it, I'll be damned if that little weasel Chelford gets away with this. Whatever it is.'

And because dealing with this keeps my mind from thinking about all those things I don't want to deal with. The mess I got my head into over Katerina. Thinking about the wife I must acquire. My respectable future and how to fill it. Leaving you.

'Oh. That is certainly a comprehensive list.' There was a hint of a smile now and her colour was coming back. He had not liked her calm, her control. It had looked too much like shock to him. Either that or an inability to see just how serious this might be if it was not dealt with hard and ruthlessly. He wanted her aware of the dangers, but confident and ready to fight. It shook him, how much he worried about her. For a moment there he had almost let his feelings overwhelm him. He had wanted to kiss her senseless, overwhelm her with assurances, treat her like some fragile little miss who had to be tucked away in cotton wool.

And that was foolish because he would be gone soon, back to London, back to his own, real life, and Tamsyn would be here, carrying on with hers, needing to stand on her own two feet. Just as soon as she was out of danger.

'Tell me your plans,' he said, pushing her to think, watchful that he did not push too far.

'Cheer up the aunts, get the accounts straight, choose the best outfit for appearing at an inquest—and carry on racking my brains for some hint as to what Franklin is up to.' Her chin was up, her voice was steady. Yes, she was all right to leave now. Fussing over her would only make her more unsettled.

'That sounds comprehensive to me. I'll go and find out what Gabriel's plans are. He should be heading back to London as soon as possible.'

'Cris.' Tamsyn was half turned from him, the colour up charmingly on the curve of cheek that was visible to him. 'Tonight…'

'Will you come to my bedchamber? It is quite isolated, as you said.' Now that sweet curve was rosy with embarrassment. 'I do not keep Collins hanging around after dinner. If you were to drop by for, shall we say, a nightcap at about eleven I think you might find me unable to sleep.' It was unexpected, the way he felt his heartrate kick up, how his body was already hardening at the thought.

This is a pleasant diversion. A temporary thing. A reaction. I will forget her and this world of fishermen and smugglers and sheep soon enough when this is all over and I am back in London.

Even so, for all that cold water dash of realism, he found he was looking forward to the night with the eagerness of a young man with his first lover.

Chapter Fourteen

'Cris!'

'What?' he demanded with more aggression than good manners.

'I have addressed two full sentences to you and you sit there gazing out of the window like some lovelorn youth. What is the matter with you?' Gabe sauntered into the drawing room and hitched one hip on to the table edge.

'Thinking. You have to concede, there is plenty to mull over.'

'And none of it the sort of thing that might put a foolish smile on your lips,' Gabriel jibed. 'I shall have to send a letter to Alex and Grant with the news that Cris de Feaux has been seen to smile.'

In a moment he would be blushing and that *would* be worthy of a newspaper headline. What the devil was wrong with him? Denmark had apparently confused him far more than he was letting himself believe. 'I've been known to, usually when you aren't around to aggravate me.' Cris waved a hand vaguely at the window. 'It is a pleasant view.'

Gabe made a complicated sound of derision. 'Views, my left buttock. This is developing into something decidedly murky.'

'The view?'

'The persecution of Mrs Perowne.' He grinned. 'Which sounds like the title of some Minerva Press novel.'

'Knowing Chelford that is probably where he got the idea.' The feeling of relief that Gabe would be there, at his back, for one more day, was worrying. He had always operated alone, been confident and self-sufficient. Now there were niggling thoughts about the danger to Tamsyn, about his own ability to keep her safe when he had no idea where the next threat was coming from. 'I was telling myself that Chelford did not have the brains to set up something like this merely as a distraction for another attack, and Patrick and Seamus are a regiment in themselves, but even so, I'm glad of someone here in case things do awry at the inquest.'

'I've got your back,' Gabe said. He gave Cris's shoulder a buffet, then left his hand there for a moment. It was as close a demonstration of emotion as Cris had ever experienced from him. Gabe stood up, pulled out a chair and sat square to the table, producing the inevitable pack of cards from somewhere about his person. He dealt two hands, flipped them both over and began to play against himself.

'Something else strange happened today,' Cris told him about the missing silver hand.

'And what does that mean?' Gabriel threw down the cards he was holding and frowned. 'I don't like the way that it was taken without any apparent damage to the lock.'

It had been at the back of Cris's mind, too. 'Chelford used to run tame here when he was younger. He would have been the kind of sneaky brat who would steal copies of keys so he could pry.'

'That and the fact that I don't think any of the servants here are disloyal makes it almost certain it is him, or some agent of his. Provided you don't need me here after the inquest, I'll go back to London, see what I can do to trace his recent movements.'

'Thank you.' There was no need to say anything more effusive than that.

Gabriel gathered the scattered pack with one sweep of his long-fingered hand and stood up. 'I like her, Cris.' He paused at the door and looked back. 'But don't get in too deep. You are who you are and she is…'

'Intelligent, interesting, strangely beautiful?' Cris enquired coldly, wondering why he did not get up and land Gabe a facer. Wondering at his own depth of anger, the way the need to hit the other man had just surged up from nowhere.

'A smuggler's widow and exceedingly ineligible for—'

He did get to his feet then. 'I know. Don't say it.'

'—someone in your position,' Gabe said and left with the ease of a man who had a great deal of practice in extricating himself from dangerous gaming hells.

To hell with him. Gabriel liked to tease and he particularly enjoyed poking at Cris, simply because he knew his friend valued self-possession and self-control. 'I like to see ice cracking,' he had admitted once with his wicked smile. 'It is more exciting to skate on.'

Cris glanced up at the mirror over the fireplace, kept his face completely emotionless as the cold blue eyes stared back at him. Could Gabe see something he could not? Was the ice cracking?

The wind was getting up, fretting at the old house, worrying at a loose slate here, a shutter there, send-

ing the rags of cloud scudding across the full moon
so that the clear white light that reflected on the polished boards of the passageway kept vanishing, plunging Tamsyn into darkness for seconds at a time.

But she knew every inch of the house and the creaks
and groans were not frightening, merely a useful cover
for any noise she might make. It seemed strange to be
creeping around Barbary like this, as though she had
left behind the impulsive, passionate girl years ago and
had grown sensible and staid. Not that she and Jory had
ever misbehaved here. Before he had shaken her by offering marriage they had been friends and she would
have no more flirted with him than she would a brother.

After they were married there had been many places
for lovemaking, places that Jory found stimulating in
direct proportion to how outrageous and dangerous they
were. She wondered now, as she had begun to increasingly in the months before his death, whether it was
that edge of danger that aroused him and not her at all.

On that thought she arrived at Cris's bedchamber
door. What did *he* see in her? She halted before the
threshold and stood, fingers closed around the handle,
and felt her confidence draining away to her chilly,
bare feet. Convenience, perhaps. Or novelty. She was
presumably unlike the ladies with whom he normally
mixed. Or he felt pity for the poor widow, who must be
pining for the attentions of a man.

The door opened and, as she was clutching the handle in a death grip, she was towed into the room and
fetched up sharply against the solid wall of silk-covered
muscle that, she realised after a moment's ineffectual
flailing, was Cris in a heavy brocade robe.

'Wait a moment.' He reached around her, closed
the door quietly and then put something down on

the dresser by the door. The light of the one chamber stick that stood there sparked fire off the chased silver mounts of a small, sinister pistol.

Tamsyn suppressed an exclamation and managed a coherent question. 'What are you doing with that?'

'When someone stands outside my bedchamber door at almost midnight, shifting uneasily from one foot to the other so that the boards creak, in my experience they are either there to cut my throat or to join me in bed.'

His arms were around her now, holding her against him so her senses were full of the feel of silk and skin and the scent of man and the thrill of his hands stroking lazily down her spine to cup her behind and pull her up against his erection.

'Does it happen very often?' she asked, the words muffled as she explored the tantalising vee of bare skin exposed by the neck of his robe.

'Which? The assassins or the offers?'

'Either.' The crispness of hair tickled her lips. She used the point of her tongue to probe into the dip at the base of his throat and his breath caught. 'Both.' The offers seemed more likely than assassination attempts, but she was beginning to realise that most of the truth about Cris Defoe was hidden from her. She wondered why. Either he was a very private man, or he had a sinister secret or he was deliberately keeping his distance from her.

'One more frequently than the other,' he murmured, as his lips moved down from her temple.' You have such a beautiful curve to your cheek.' His tongue swept over it. 'And you taste like salt on peaches.'

Somehow she found enough space to wriggle her hands between their bodies and catch hold of the knot that secured the sash of his robe. She wanted to see him naked again, not, as he had been last night, obscured by the half-darkness, tumbled in the coarse blankets. In response he pulled her in tighter, moved so that her hands slipped, found the thrust of his erection under the lush fabric.

She began to caress him through it, not attempting to push the sides of the robe apart. The silk slid over his hard, heated flesh and he made a sound between a growl and a groan as his teeth closed gently on the vulnerable angle between her neck and shoulder. The gesture was powerfully possessive and the image of a stallion she had once seen mounting a mare, his teeth bared as they closed on the arch of her neck, holding her for his domination, filled her mind with shocking clarity.

But she was no mare to be dominated. One-handed she pulled at the sash and the robe opened. She raked her nails lightly down the flat belly, into the dense tangle of coarse hair, down to touch him with a demand as fierce as his.

The response was instant. His right hand took her nightgown by the neck, twisted, tore it so that it gaped open, and he lifted her, stepped forward so she was trapped between his body and the door. Instinctively Tamsyn curled her legs around his hips, her arms around his neck as he held her there, open to him. She knew she was wet, was ready for him. She had been from the moment her tongue had touched the skin of his throat. With a growl as demanding as his she shifted and lunged, taking him into her in one glorious movement.

Cris made a sound of astonished pleasure and was still, his brow resting against hers, his forearms bracing him against the door on either side of her head. 'Vixen.' His voice was rough, naked, powerful and yet vulnerable. She had shaken him. Which was only fair. He had shaken her to her foundations and beyond.

The position was exquisitely, erotically, uncomfortable. The door was unyielding behind her shoulder blades, she had to lock her ankles together, harden her thigh muscles to keep from sliding on the silk that still draped across his hips, and she could scarcely move. It was bliss, but it couldn't last. Cris was so aroused that he would take them both over the edge in a few powerful thrusts.

He began to move and she realised that she was wrong. He had the strength to move slowly, agonisingly slowly. Tamsyn could feel his muscles lock rigid as she hung on to his shoulders, she could hear the effort of control in his breathing, but he did not break. He was relentless and she could do nothing but let him fill her, pleasure her, drive her insane.

'Cris…please.' She had no pride left, all she could do was beg and gasp and strive to break free from the ropes of desire that he was tying tighter and tighter around her.

'Not…yet.'

'I can't.'

'You will.' She felt his effort to breathe, to find more words. 'Look…up.'

'Why?' Somehow she lifted her head.

'I don't…want…you screaming.' His lips sealed over hers as he gave one more thrust and the ropes tightened and broke her into a thousand pieces and she screamed into the heat of his mouth and then she was flying, moving through the air, and the aurora burst behind her eyelids.

'Tamsyn.'

She had been flying, so now she was lying on clouds. When she looked down, what would she see? The whole

ocean spread out beneath her? She dragged open heavy
lids and found her nose was buried in the thick fluffy
coverlet, her body sprawled diagonally across the bed.
It was an effort to turn her head towards Cris's voice,
but she managed it. He was lying parallel with her, on
his back, his hands behind his head.

'That,' he said seriously as she blinked at him, 'was
infinitely preferable to having my throat cut.'

It made her choke with laughter, gave her enough
energy to roll over and curl up against him. 'I would
hope so.'

'Are you all right?' He sat up, giving her an admirable view of his muscles at work, and ran his hand down
her back. 'Have I bruised you?'

'Don't know,' she mumbled, kissing the only part of
him that she could without sitting up, which happened
to be his right hip bone. 'Don't care.'

'I do not think anyone has ever kissed me there before.' He sounded lazily content as he flopped back.
'Do you think you can find anywhere else like that?'

'I've got to do all the work of exploration, have I?'

'I did all the work just now,' he said reasonably, as
though he was negotiating a deal. The almost-dimple
was back at the corner of his mouth.

'Very well. Lie on your stomach.'

He rolled over obediently. Tamsyn thought for a moment, then got up on her knees, straddled his legs and
bent to kiss the tendon that ran up from his heel.

'That's one,' he conceded.

She switched position, leant down and nipped one
firm buttock, then soothed the sting with a kiss.

'No, those have had kisses lavished on them.'

'Don't be smug. Just because you have a very superior rump—'

He moved so fast that she was pinned beneath him before she had a chance to retaliate. 'Is it? Superior?'

'I think so.' Yes, he was definitely smug. 'Almost as superior as Mr Stone's.'

'Hussy.' He slid into her and she bowed up to meet him, loving the way her breasts were crushed against his chest, loving the darkness in his eyes, just before he closed them to hide the depths of his pleasure from her, loving the way their bodies moved together without shyness or hesitation.

Loving him.

The shock of finding herself in love distracted Tamsyn all through the next day. It was hard to focus on keeping the aunts calm, let alone on listening to the advice Cris was giving her, when all she wanted to do was to sit looking at him, trying to come to terms with what her unruly heart had done.

'I would suggest wearing something respectable and practical. You don't want to give the impression that you are attempting to act the fluttering female to sway the jury and they know you, I imagine, so pretending to be some helpless little thing won't work either.' He leaned back against the front of the summer house, rocking the bench a little on its spindly metal legs.

He is beautiful, but I haven't fallen in love with those blue eyes or that superior rump...

'Tamsyn?'

Or that decided voice or those well-formed lips... 'I thought my newest riding habit. I will have to ride over in any case and it is a severe cut and deep-blue colour.'

'Excellent. I imagine it will make you exceedingly angry, but—'

Although those all help. It is his courage and his kindness and...

'—it is essential that you keep calm. You are willing, of course, to help the authorities, but you are baffled—'

...as to why I love you when you keep secrets from me and I am not of your world, whatever it is, and you will be gone soon and I will never see you again.

'Are you listening to a word I'm saying, Tamsyn?'

'I am baffled,' she repeated obediently. *Although you make love like an angel. Or perhaps a devil and that helps, too.* 'I will try my best to keep my temper, be helpful but confused. And, if he persists in this nonsense, indignant. I'm a lady and respectable, whatever my late husband might have done. After all, a wife is a mere chattel of her husband's, is she not? I cannot be held responsible for what Jory did.'

'If you were ever any man's *mere chattel*, I will eat my hat.'

Oh, and I adore that rare, rare smile of his.

'I will have the advantage that, being men, they will assume I am incapable of organised thought or sophisticated planning,' she said and looked out across the garden to the sea. It was impossible to think when she was looking at Cris, all she could do was count the things about him that mysteriously merged together and made a miracle.

'I am trying to think of it as a duel, me against Franklin. I must keep a cool head and fight strongly but prudently.'

'Sensible,' Cris admitted. 'And when we do find out what he is about it will be my pleasure to make that duel a reality.'

'You cannot!' She spun round so fast that the bench rocked and almost tipped her off on to the grass.

'Why ever not?' Cris was suddenly the austerely aloof, distant man who sent a shiver of awe down her spine. 'He has behaved in the most appalling way to-wards a lady, therefore it is the duty of any gentleman to call him to account.'

'If he murdered poor Mr Ritchie, then he will hang. Would you cheat justice and spare him the ordeal of the courtroom and what follows?' she asked fiercely, knowing as she spoke that what she felt so passionate about was Cris's safety, not the abstract idea of justice.

'I doubt he pulled the trigger himself. Why should he when there are so many villains to hire in the rooker-ies of London who would cut their own grandmothers' throats if you made it worth their while?'

'You mean he could get away with this?'

'I think it very likely. After all, what proof do we have?'

'There may be some after the inquest,' Tamsyn told herself that rushing to meet trouble was not going to help, she had enough to cope with as it was, not least was the prospect of a broken heart in the very near future.

Chapter Fifteen

'This court will rise for Sir James Trelawney.'

Awkward in their best clothes and solemn with responsibility, the jury shuffled to their feet from their double row of benches. The audience, jam-packed into the main part of the Ram's Head Inn's little assembly room, stood, too, nudging and whispering and staring at the front row, where all those to be called as witnesses were seated.

Sir James took his seat behind the table set on the rather shaky dais that the local joiner and coffin-maker had knocked up hastily, fussed with his cushion, his pen and his papers, donned a pair of spectacles and cleared his throat.

'Silence in court!' The parish constable was enjoying himself. 'Be seated!' He turned to Sir James, who nodded. 'Call the first witness! Thomas Gedge!'

'I be 'ere, Fred Dare, you old fule. Sitting right in front of you. No call for yelling.' An elderly man in a smock and sea boots got to his feet.

'You stand there.' Red about the ears, the constable pointed to the witness stand, another of the carpenter's constructions. 'And here's the Bible.' He handed it over, read the oath, still at full volume, and sat down.

'…so help me God,' the old man concluded.

'You are Thomas Gedge, fisherman?'

'Aye, sir.'

'And you frequent Cat's Nose Bay?'

'Don't know about frequent it. I keeps me fishing boat there and me shed with me nets and all.'

Sir James glowered. 'And were you there on the night of Wednesday last and for what purpose?'

'Aye, I was there, having a bit of a smoke in me shed. The wife's mother had come to visit and a man can't get any peace in his own home with two women clacking. It was a good, warm night, so down I go to the cove. I was there from when the church clock struck eight to past one.'

'Aye, and with a brandy bottle, too, I'll be bound!' someone called from the back.

'Silence in court! And you could see the beach?'

'The door to the shed was open, but I can't see the beach on account of the shed's with the others, up aways. I could see the track down to the beach.'

'And did you see anyone go down it that night?'

'Aye, I did that.' A whisper of interest ran round the room. 'It was that new Riding Officer, Ritchie. Recognised his hat and the cocky way he has…had…of walking. And the moonlight caught his face as he went past. I thought to myself, you'll find no one down there to bother, you interfering devil, you.'

'Did you see anyone else?'

'I did. About ten minutes after, it was. Figure in a cloak, all muffled up and walking quietly, like they didn't want to be seen.'

'And is that person in this court?'

'How would I know, your worship? He was all muffled up, like I said.'

'Was it a man?'

'Could be. Might have been a tallish woman, I suppose.' He shrugged. 'I had a bit of a doze. Then I woke
up and was just thinking the mother-in-law would have
gone to bed and it'd be safe to go home when I heard
a shot. I thought about it a bit, then I closed the door
of the shed and waited until I heard footsteps going up
the track. Then I waits some more and then I went to
have a look and there was Ritchie on the beach in the
moonlight with a bullet in his back and blood all over
the stones.'

'Why did you wait before going out to look, man?'
Sir James asked irritably.

'Because I didn't want a bullet in me head, of course.
Then I went and got Fred Dare out of bed, much good
he was.'

'That will be all. You may go back to your seat. Fred-
erick Dare, take the stand.'

Gabriel Stone leant forward as the constable took the
oath and murmured across Tamsyn to Cris, 'And that is
it? One cloaked figure of indeterminate sex?'

'There will be more,' Cris said.

The constable recounted being woken, getting
dressed, fetching some of the local men in support and
finding the body on the beach.

'And were there any traces of the murderer to be
seen?'

'Aye, there was, your worship. There was an object
lying under the body. It's that there object in the black
bag before you, your worship. We carried the body up
to the church, and woke up the vicar, then I went to tell
you and you told me to search the neighbourhood for
any strangers or news of anyone behaving suspiciously,
and that I did. That night I didn't find anyone, but the

next day I came across this traveller in the inn and he said he'd been out for a walk and had seen something odd. So I brought him to see you, Sir James.'

'Thank you, Dare. You may stand down and call the next witness.'

The local doctor came to the stand and explained in lengthy and gruesome detail that the deceased had been killed by one bullet to the heart and showed no other signs of injury.

Tamsyn found she was watching the proceedings, slow and rustic and ponderous, as though they were a rather bad play. She ought to feel something, fear, or curiosity at least, but all she felt was numb.

Beside her Cris whispered, 'Now we come to the interesting witness.'

A thin man with a very ordinary, instantly forgettable face, took the oath and stood clutching his hat and staring stolidly at the coroner. He had brown hair pulled back in an old-fashioned queue, brown eyes, a brown suit of decent, but plain clothes.

'State your name and occupation and business in this parish.'

'Paul Goode, solicitor's clerk of Gray's Inn Road, London.' Tamsyn felt a sudden prickle of interest. The accent was southern, the man a total stranger. 'I was sent by my employer, Mr Ebenezer Howard, on a business enquiry, which took me further down the coast from here. I was making my way back and stayed overnight at this inn, your worship. I'd been hoping to get to Barnstaple, but the roads defeated my old horse, so I rested us both up.'

'Tell us what you might that will throw light on this business, Mr Goode.'

'I went for a walk after my supper, sir. I wasn't

sleepy. It was a nice moonlit night and the seaside is a novelty for a city man like myself. I wasn't sure where to go, but I saw a man walking down the track that I discovered later led to the beach and I followed, assuming if he was going down it, it must head somewhere. I got a stone in my shoe, so I sat down on the bank and took it off and someone else passed me. I followed along, rather cautiously, sir, because I thought maybe I would be interrupting a tryst and that would be a bit embarrassing.'

'A tryst?' Sir James looked at him over his spectacles and Tamsyn thought he was tense now, like a weasel about to leap on its prey. 'An odd word to choose, Mr Goode, for a possible meeting between two men. You may stand down, but do not leave the room.'

'Why doesn't he hear all the man's evidence?' Tamsyn whispered to Cris.

'No idea. He's stage-managing the whole performance.'

'Call Mrs Tamsyn Perowne to the stand.'

Cris rose with her, his hand under her arm until she turned with a smile and shook her head. 'I'll be fine.'

Once she was no longer waiting it was easier. She took the stand, repeated the oath, folded her hands on the rail in front of her and turned the calmest face she could manage on Sir James.

'You are Mrs Tamsyn Perowne, widow of Jory Perowne, leader of the Silver Hand gang of smugglers.'

'I am Jory Perowne's widow,' she agreed. 'But I have never heard his relationship with that gang confirmed in a court of law.'

'You knew the victim of this murderous attack?'

'I had met Lieutenant Ritchie on one occasion. He came to Barbary Combe House and introduced himself. A brief conversation on the front lawn was the extent of our encounter. I have not seen him before or after that.'

'And did he issue a warning to you?'

'He told us that a gang of smugglers was operating. I took that to be a caution in case they proved violent.'

'Did you, indeed? A curious construction to put on it, considering your late husband's business.' When she merely stood impassive and waited for the next question he snapped, 'And who is this *us* you speak of?'

'Myself, my relative Miss Holt, with whom I live, her companion, Miss Pritchard, our staff and two gentlemen who are our guests. You met them the day before yesterday. Mr Defoe and Mr Stone are sitting in the front row now.'

'Did your husband wear a charm around his neck?'

'Yes,' she agreed. 'A silver hand on a silver chain.'

'And is it unique?'

She had expected a question about the whereabouts of Jory's charm, but she answered immediately, knowing that hesitation would only create a bad impression. 'I owned one also. A replica with an engraved message that was a gift from my husband.'

'And where is it now?'

'I have no idea. It appears to have been stolen from the locked chest it was kept in.'

There was a whispering of excitement and speculation in the court. 'Stolen, you say? It must be a valuable piece, why has no reward been offered for it?'

'Because its loss has only just been discovered.' As soon as she spoke she felt a twinge of fear.

Sir James smiled. 'Indeed? Constable, show the witness the contents of the black bag, then pass it to the jury.'

Tamsyn did not need to see the river of silver links that spilled into Dare's calloused hand to know what this was, but she waited until he handed it to her and made a point of examining it carefully. 'This is the hand and chain given to me by my late husband. It is engraved J and T with a heart.' She let it run back into the constable's outstretched hand and wondered if she should remove her handkerchief and permit herself a brave sniff and a dab at her eyes, but the thought of play-acting sickened her. Let them believe her or not, she would give them the truth and nothing else.

The coroner waited until the hand had been passed along the rows of jurors and returned to him. 'This chain and the attached charm were found clasped in the dead hand of Lieutenant Ritchie as he lay on the beach at Cat's Nose Bay. As you have heard, gentlemen of the jury, the witness has identified them as her property.'

Put there to incriminate me. The words were almost out of her mouth before she caught them. The jury did not need her to underline the conclusion they were being led to.

'You know the cove in question, Mrs Perowne?'

'Certainly. I visit it occasionally. I believe the last time this year was in March when a fishing boat belonging to me was washed up there.' It felt like standing on a frozen pond, hearing the ice cracking, feeling it shift under her feet, wanting to run. But she had to stand there, stay calm, not defensive.

'Mr Goode, return to the front of the court. Remember you are still on oath.'

The whispering increased as the thin man made his way forward and stood, perfectly composed in his respectable drabness, looking at the coroner.

'You told the court that you saw a cloaked figure following Lieutenant Ritchie down to the beach. Can you describe that man?'

'I can, sir. But it was no man, it was a woman. She was wearing a cloak, but the hood was down and I could see her plain in the moonlight. Quite tall she was.'

The whispering broke out into exclamations. Tamsyn's hands hurt and she looked down to see them locked on the rough bar at the front of the stand. A split ran all along the seam of the right index finger of her glove.

'Silence in court! And can you see that woman in this courtroom?'

Goode hesitated, bit his lip. 'It bleaches the colour out, does the moonlight.'

A nice touch, she thought, wondering at her own detachment.

'Try, Mr Goode,' the coroner said with an encouraging smile.

The man turned to the stand and made a show of studying her. She made herself stare back, expressionless, while her stomach seemed to drop into a pit and her heart rate kicked up to a gallop.

'Er…if the lady could turn sideways to me?'

'Mrs Perowne, please do as the witness asks.'

She made her feet move although her legs were trembling, turned to face Sir James, lifted her chin and met the coroner's gaze steadily.

'That's her! That's the lady I saw. I couldn't mistake that profile, the moonlight lit her up, clear as day.'

Tamsyn turned back slowly to face him. 'Liar,' she said without emphasis, wondering if she was about to faint. The coroner's words to the witness were a blur of sound as she focused on breathing, on keeping the blackness at the edge of her vision from moving in.

'Mrs Perowne, you heard the witness. What have you to say?'

'He is either lying or he is mistaken. I was not at the cove, I was at home at Barbary Combe House.' As she spoke the reality hit her. She had been at home, but not in the house. She had been in the lookout with Cris, making love, lying in his arms, tiptoeing back into the house at three in the morning.

Something must have shown in her face, for Sir James leaned forward. 'Are you certain of that, Mrs Perowne?' When she nodded he smiled, thinly. 'And can you prove it?'

'No,' she said bleakly.

'Yes,' said Cris Defoe, coming to his feet.

Sir James narrowed his eyes at him. 'You wish to present evidence, sir?'

'I wish to take the stand and swear to an alibi for Mrs Perowne.'

'Very well. Mrs Perowne, return to your seat. Mr… Defoe, is it not? Take the stand.'

'No,' she whispered as Cris passed her. *'It will ruin me.'*

Cris took the oath. She stared, uncomprehending, as Gabriel Stone sat beside her muttering, 'Bloody fool, he must know where this will end up.'

'Give the court your name, if you please, sir.'

'Anthony Maxim Charles St Crispin de Feaux of Avenmore Park and St James's Square.'

'The—'

'Yes,' Cris said abruptly and with emphasis. 'I believe that is sufficient to identify me.'

'I understand. Well, m…sir, what have you to add to the proceedings?'

'I do not know who Mr Goode saw, but Mrs Perowne was with me that night.'

'We are aware that you are a guest in the house and that you would expect your hostess to be there in her own chamber after the party had broken up and gone to bed. However, the shooting occurred at past one in the morning.'

'When I say that Mrs Perowne was me that night, I mean that I was with her,' Cris said, his face an austere mask. 'We were together. All night. Do you require me to draw you a diagram, Sir James?'

The courtroom exploded into a hubbub. Tamsyn knew she had gone white, she felt as though there was no blood left in her head at all. What was he thinking? He had ruined her.

After much banging of the coroner's gavel and shouting by the constable, order was restored.

'Do I understand you to mean that Mrs Perowne is your mistress, my…sir?'

'Certainly not,' Cris snapped. 'The lady is my affianced bride.'

Beside her Gabriel Stone was swearing under his breath, a litany of obscenities that, mercifully, she could hardly make out through her fog of relief, dismay and confusion.

'Ah. In that case, naturally, it becomes apparent that Mr Goode must be mistaken. Mr Goode?'

The constable looked round wildly as people began to crane their necks. 'He's gone, sir.'

'Then you must see that he was lying, that he had been put up to this by the real criminal—or that he himself was the murderer?' Cris demanded.

Sir James hesitated, then snapped, 'Constable, find that man Goode and arrest him! Gentlemen of the jury, you must disregard everything you heard from that witness. Thank you, sir, you may stand down.'

'But I will not.' Tamsyn found she could think, speak, and that she was on her feet. 'Sir James, Mr Defoe has most gallantly spoken out to save me from this accusation, but the inference you have drawn from his words is incorrect, as he intended it to be. Yes, I spent that night in his company, late into the night, in fact. But we were up on the cliffs walking because I was distressed over a family matter and could not sleep, and Mr Defoe was protecting me with his escort when I insisted on going out so late.'

'But he has said you are betrothed to him.'

'What else could a gentleman say when he has, for the best of reasons, ruined a lady's reputation? He was not lying—after all, having led you to believe the worst he obviously felt himself honour-bound to make me his wife, even though he has said nothing to me.'

'I see. This is all most unfortunate. The witness may stand down and the court accepts that there is no stain on Mrs Perowne's virtue and therefore no need for… er… Mr Defoe's gallant action.' For a moment Sir James appeared flustered, then he cleared his throat. 'Gentlemen of the jury, you have heard the evidence, you must now decide your verdict.'

Tamsyn sat numb as Cris came back to the seat beside her. He had put himself in a position where, in order to safeguard her reputation, he had offered to marry her. Did that mean, could it mean, that he loved her? She hardly dared think beyond the burgeoning warmth that was defeating the numbness now.

Nothing was said as the jurymen trooped out to debate their verdict. It took them all of ten minutes.

'Your worship, we do find that Lieutenant Ritchie was foully and deliberately murdered by a gunshot fired by a person or persons unknown. And we are all agreed it ain't likely to be a woman, neither, and specially not Mrs Perowne, who's a lady we all know of and respect. And we agrees with you and Mr Defoe that that man Goode was lying. And that's the opinion of us all.' The foreman sat down with a thump and was patted on the back by his fellow jurors.

Cris stood, took Tamsyn by the arm and walked her out, Gabriel on their heels. He led them to the stables, stood in silence while their horses were brought, then boosted her up into the saddle, mounted himself and headed out of the stable yard at a trot that turned into a canter the moment they were clear of the street.

When they reached the open space at the crossroads, he reined in and waited for Tamsyn and Gabriel to catch up.

'Cris, why on earth did you do that?'

Please tell me you realised you love me...

'I have saved you a trial,' Cris said, getting Jackdaw under control as the stallion plunged and backed as Gabriel thundered up. 'They would have put you in prison and I could not allow them to do that to you. And it exposed Goode as a liar and probably as the man who pulled the trigger.'

'Of all the damn-fool things to have done!' Gabriel exploded into speech the moment he was within earshot. 'Couldn't you have done something that didn't almost involve you marrying a totally unsuitable woman?'

'Mind your tongue, Stone.' Jackdaw plunged again as Cris wheeled him to face Gabriel. 'You will not speak disrespectfully of Mrs Perowne in my hearing.'

'Disrespectful? She is a charming lady, an intelligent, beautiful lady, a wonderful hostess and great company.' Gabriel, his face grim, sketched a bow from the saddle to Tamsyn. 'She is also a smuggler's window and, forgive me, ma'am, of simple gentry stock. She is not a suitable wife for a man in your position and you know it.'

'Will you both please stop discussing me as though I am not here?' Foxy had caught Jackdaw's restlessness and was sidling away from the other horses, tossing his head. 'What *is* Cris's position?' An awful thought struck her. 'No, you aren't going to tell me he is a duke and that you were not joking the other day.'

'No, he is not a duke,' Gabriel said furiously. 'Allow me to introduce the Marquess of Avenmore.'

Chapter Sixteen

'A marquess?' It was a joke, of course. They would both laugh in a moment.

They did not.

And then it all began to make sense. Cris's fine clothes, his superior manservant, his air of utter confidence, his foreign travels. His whole attitude of assurance.

'My name is de Feaux.' He gave it a slight French intonation. 'Not Defoe. I was not trying to lie to you, but my voice was hoarse.'

She waved away the explanation with an irritable flick of her hand. 'You could have told the coroner anything—that we had both been up looking after a sick horse, that Mr Stone played cards with us all night— anything than let everyone think we were lovers.'

'But that would not be true,' Cris said with maddening reasonableness. 'I do not lie under oath. If I could have seen a way to prevaricate, I would have done. If what I said was going to ruin you, then I would have had to keep silent for now. But once I said I intended to marry you there was no danger of that, Tamsyn.'

'And thanks to my own willingness to tell half-truths you are not leg-shackled to a wife your close friend regards as a disaster! Why did you do it?'

'Because it was an explanation that convinced both the coroner and the jury and, as for your reputation, almost anything will be forgiven to the betrothed of a marquess.'

'And anything at all will be forgiven of a marquess, I suppose?'

'It is the way of the world.'

'Maddening, but true,' Gabriel observed.

'Thank you, Mr Stone, I do not need you to point that out to me,' she snapped.

'I am the Earl of Edenbridge, actually,' he said with a rueful grimace. 'I suppose I had better tell you while we are laying our cards on the table.'

'And the ruse served its purpose. Goode ran, exposing his own guilt.' Cris shrugged. 'No one has to marry anyone.'

'I suppose I got in with my explanation just as you were about to explain your cunning deception to the coroner.'

'Yes, of course.' Cris had both his voice and his horse under perfect control now.

She was so angry that she was unsure whether it was with him, or with herself for being so shamefully weak in wanting him to love her, to tell her it had been no ruse at all, but a ploy to make a humble country girl the wife of a marquess. Tamsyn gathered up the reins, dug her heel into Foxy's side and gave the gelding his head, thundering along the road that led back towards Stibworthy. Anything but think, anything but risk him reading the feelings in her face.

'We must keep her in sight.' Cris spurred Jackdaw in pursuit.

'But I would advise you not to actually catch her.'

Gabriel jammed his hat on his head and drew level with Cris. 'That is not a happy woman.'

'She is an unhappy woman who is not sitting in a cell awaiting the next assizes,' Cris said grimly.

'She might not be in a cell, but you as near as damn it landed yourself in a parson's mousetrap. And don't tell me you were about to tell the coroner it was all a ploy—you didn't think of that until she was on her feet digging you out of the hole you'd made for yourself.'

What in Hades was I thinking? I do not need Gabe to tell me that I was risking creating a storm in London, in the diplomatic corps, at Court.

But he had simply been incapable of watching Tamsyn stand there, brave and honest and truthful, while the snare tightened around her. 'So I should have let her be accused by the coroner's jury, allowed her to be carted off like a felon to prison and let her languish there with prostitutes and Lord knows what scum while I worked out how to disprove that so-called solicitor's clerk?'

'Yes.'

'I can always rely on you for the ruthless answer, can't I?'

'You can. Tamsyn would have survived a few weeks in gaol. She's not some sheltered society miss.' They reined in as a flock of sheep swept across their path, spooked by a circling buzzard. Gabriel pushed his mount in front of Jackdaw. 'Cris, listen to me, I am worried about you. You are half-tempted to tell her you won't withdraw your offer, aren't you? You've slept with her and I know you when you've a fit of gallantry on you.

'But think what you owe to your name, your reputation. You might not want to help out the Foreign Office again and you certainly don't need the money, but you enjoy the work. You'd lose that—which ambassador's wife is going to want to receive a smuggler's widow? The Queen most certainly wouldn't have her at Court. Let Tamsyn go now, let her calm down. Ride back slowly, take her at her word that she doesn't want you.'

'I know all that. Don't think I haven't had what is expected of me dinned into me since I was old enough to understand.'

But she didn't say she did not want me. What if she loves me? What have I done?

The frustration and anger came down like a red mist in front of his vision. Cris urged Jackdaw forward alongside his friend's mount, bunched his right fist and hit Gabe square on the jaw. He held his panicked horse in check for long enough to see Gabriel sit up on the heather, rubbing his chin and swearing, then kicked into a gallop after Tamsyn.

He had no time for thinking as he raced after her. She knew this country like the back of her hand, and so did Foxy, but he did not and the track was treacherous. He caught sight of her only as Jackdaw plunged skidding and sweating down Stibworthy's cobbled street past the inn, and by then she was already vanishing down the track to Barbary Cove.

He reined in, reassured that she was going home and that nothing much could happen between there and the house. Jackdaw was tired, but game, and proved a handful to keep to a trot. On impulse, when they reached the fork that led to the clifftop where they had picnicked, he dismounted, tied the reins up and slapped Jackdaw's rump. When the big black trotted on down to the stable Cris walked up to the summit, then made for the almost hidden path to the lookout hut.

Inside, he shut the lower half of the door, sat down

on the bench and stared out at the square of blue sea, blue sky, until his anger with Gabriel subsided and his brain started working clearly again. He had done the only possible thing, he told himself. The only honourable thing. He had slept with Tamsyn and that had put him even more under an obligation to defend her. But he had no obligation to marry her now. Unless she expected it. But she had rejected him in court when she thought he was plain Mr Defoe and had been horrified to discover he was a marquess.

The crunch of feet on stone was the only warning he had before the hut door opened and someone ducked inside. For a moment there was simply a figure in silhouette against the brightness, then he recognised her at the same moment that she saw him. 'Tamsyn.'

'You.' She recoiled in shock and he leapt for her, his stomach clenching in fear at the thought of the closeness of the cliff edge, the narrowness of the path. He caught her by both wrists as she teetered on the brink, yanked her back into the hut and fell with her in a tangle of limbs on the hard wooden bench.

She was quivering in his arms and he realised he was shaking with the sheer horror of that moment when he thought she was going over the edge. Then his mouth was on hers and her hands were clenched in his hair and they were kissing with a ferocity that swept everything away but the urgency to mate, there, then, on the hard wooden bench.

Tamsyn's hands were on his falls and he twisted to give her access even as he dragged up her skirts and found the hot, wet core of her. She pressed into his hand as she freed him from the tangle of shirt tails, the constriction of breeches that had become too tight on his aroused flesh.

'Cris.' It was a demand, a plea, an order, and he came down over her, into her with a single thrust. She came apart on the instant and her cry, the hot, tight grasp of her, almost sent him over the edge before he could withdraw.

There was a moment's perfect bliss as they lay in a hot, tangled, sticky heap, the aftershocks of his release sending spikes of pleasure through him. Then Tamsyn shoved at his shoulders, hit out, writhed beneath him.

'Stop fighting me, damn it.' He sprawled on top of her as she bucked against his weight and in sheer self-defence he caught her wrists above her head.

'Let me go.'

'The moment you promise not to scratch my eyes out or go rushing out on to that cliff edge again. You took ten years off my life, woman.'

She subsided, panting, and Cris sat up, keeping his distance as much as possible in the cramped space as he stuffed his shirt back into his breeches and fastened his falls.

Tamsyn wrenched down her skirts as she struggled up. 'You lied to me.'

'A moment ago you were crying out in ecstasy in my arms.'

She buried her face in her hands, then pushed back her hair impatiently. 'I don't know what that was.'

'Fright, relief, sheer irrational lust. And I did not lie to you. I withheld information.'

'Why?'

Cris had asked himself the same question often enough over the past few days. Now, as the mists of sexual release began to clear, he forced himself to focus. 'Because I found I enjoyed being Mr No One in Particular. I can hardly recall what it was like not being the Marquess of Avenmore. This is the first time, as an adult, that I have ever experienced that freedom. I found I liked Barbary Combe House and its inhabitants. I found I valued the peace and the informality and the lack of fuss. If I had said who I was, what I was, you would all have treated me differently. I did you no harm by not telling you my title.'

'I would never have slept with you if I had known.'

'Why not? A naked marquess is no different from any other man in a bed.'

'Don't be disingenuous.' Tamsyn sounded more weary than angry now. She was flushed and he could see a red mark where the collar of his riding coat must have chafed her neck. 'You know perfectly well why not. You might like to take a holiday from who you are now and again, but the rest of us cannot. You had the arrogance to think that it did not matter, deceiving me. You enjoyed playing the knight in shining armour and setting out to protect me, and now your pride has almost landed you with a scandal that you have escaped by the skin of your teeth.' She drew up her legs and wrapped her arms around them, rested her head on her knees so he could only see part of her face.

'Tamsyn, you should take no notice of Gabriel. He is my friend and he is simply trying to protect me. Dukes have married actresses before now and the heavens have not fallen.'

'But presumably they both wished to be married to each other.'

The sarcasm in her voice was like a slap on the face. Cris realised that he had believed, deep down, that Tamsyn *would* want to marry him, and her rejection, whilst it had to be a relief, was an assault on his pride. He was eligible beyond her wildest dreams, they were good in bed together, they seemed to get on well—yes, she was angry and upset about him implying that they were lovers in open court, but once she had got past that…

'You wouldn't want to be married to me?' He should take her rejection thankfully, and leave it, leave her. He was free to marry the right wife for the Marquess of Avenmore. And yet some demon had control of his tongue. 'Leaving aside my title for a moment—' He ignored her muttered response to that, ignored his own common sense telling him not to pursue this argument. 'What else makes you react like this?'

'I cannot marry you.' There was something desolate in her tone before her chin came up and her voice hardened. 'One of the benefits of being an ordinary peasant, dust beneath your lordship's boots, is that one can marry whom one loves, someone who loves you back. And ours would have been no love match, would it, my lord?'

'I am not sure what being in love means.' That was certainly true. He had almost died because he had got his head into such a mess over Katerina. 'I like you, I desire you, I would have tried to make you happy.'

Leave it, drop the matter, you have done all that honour demands.

The memory came of his father's voice as they had walked down the long gallery at Avenmore Park together. He had pointed out each ancestral portrait and enumerated the reasons why each wife had been chosen, her bloodlines, her connections, her dowry.

'Each marriage strengthens our house, our line. There is nothing more important than the choice of your marchioness, the mother of your children.'

'You cannot.' Tamsyn gave a deep, shuddering sigh. 'And I know it, even if you cannot accept that you would not be every woman's dream husband.'

*Well, that answers that. She is not in love with me,
she doesn't want to marry me. I am, quite definitely,
free.* Perversely it did not make him feel any happier,
but presumably that was his wounded pride.

'What do you want to do now?' Cris asked. He knew
what he wanted, which was to take her into his arms and
let her weep, something he suspected she was fighting
against with every ounce of her willpower. He wanted
to tell her to look after herself, cosset herself against
the stress of the day, but she would only fling that back
in his face as patronising.

'I will go back down to Barbary, tell the aunts that
everything is all right, tell them…tell them what happened in court so they do not hear rumours and gossip
and be taken unawares.'

'Will you tell them who I am?'

'No. Not until you have gone and perhaps not even
then. They would not understand why you could not tell
us.' She stood up, hunched under the low roof. 'And you
are going, aren't you, Cris? Soon.'

He followed her out along the narrow ledge, up on
to the cliff, acutely conscious of the drop to his right,
of the sea crashing on the rocks beneath as she stood
looking out to sea, the wind whipping her uncovered
hair back into a ragged banner behind her, her skirts
tight around the long horsewoman's legs.

'You want me to leave?'

'Yes. I want you gone.' She said it without apparent anger, with a weariness that hurt more than harsh
words would have done.

'And I want you safe.'

'I will pay the two chairmen to stay here as bodyguards, I will puzzle out what it is that Franklin wants
so badly he will kill for it. I will employ more of the

villagers to guard the farm and the flocks. I will do all those things I would have done before you ever came into my life, my lord.'

My lord. She uses the title like an insult. Yes, he would go and he would pursue Chelford with every resource he could muster and, if he could not find out what the man wanted with Barbary Combe House and its occupants, if he could find no proof that would stand up in law, then Franklin Holt was going to find himself in the hold of a ship bound for Australia.

He watched Tamsyn walk away from him, back straight, head up. This was the woman who had seen her husband leap to his death like a hunted stag, who had faced down a courtroom, who had dragged him from the sea. And she was walking out of his life, and he must be glad because that was what she wanted.

She could not face the aunts, not yet. Tamsyn closed the door of the summer house and struggled to find some composure. What was she becoming? What was this nightmare doing to her? One moment all she wanted was to be part of Cris in the most carnal way possible, the next she was seized with disgust at herself for throwing herself at a man who wanted her only for the moment.

This mystery had brought her Cris, and love, but she could not be glad, not even for the memories of those two perfect nights in his arms. He would be gone soon, back to London and the world that he belonged to and to the search for a wife who was a well-bred, well-dowered, well-connected virgin who would bear his children. *All the things I am not and cannot be.*

Eventually, when she had her hair and her clothing and her face under as much control as she could manage, she ran across the lawn and slipped in through the front door. There was no sound of anyone talking, the aunts must be in their room. She reached the foot of the stairs when a heavy tread made her turn. 'You.'

'Yes, me, the nasty Lord Edenbridge.' He leaned against the table on which she had left her flower arrangement, his gypsy-dark, dangerously masculine looks a startling contrast to the wispy grasses and the lush femininity of roses. 'Where is Cris?'

She shrugged. 'Up on the cliff.'

'Where you made love and had a thundering row, I suppose. Tamsyn—'

'Mrs Perowne to you, my lord.'

How does he know what we have been doing? I suppose I still look as though I've been tumbled like some country trollop. Which is what he thinks I am anyway.

'Mrs Perowne. I mean you no ill, but Cris is my friend and I'll not see him brought down by an entanglement.'

She held up a hand to stop him. 'I have *un*tangled him from my lures, such as they are. He will go back to London very soon, rest assured, my lord. You will have him safely back in his rightful environment, far from scandal and unsuitable women.'

Something changed in his expression, some slight shift towards sympathy. 'Are you in love with him, Tamsyn?' He did not wait for an answer. 'It is better this way, believe me. Cris is a prisoner of his responsibilities to Avenmore and he would not thank you for freeing him from those chains.' He turned abruptly and walked away, his elbow catching a spray of roses, sending the soft crimson petals shaking and tumbling on to the polished oak.

Tamsyn picked up the trailing skirts of her riding

habit and climbed slowly up the stairs to her aunts' door, tapped and went in.

Izzy, always demonstrative, jumped up from her embroidery and ran across to hug her. 'Oh, my dear, that nice Mr Stone looked in to tell us it was all right and that you were on your way home, safe and sound. He said you'd found it rather upsetting, so not to expect you back immediately.' She went back to her chair beside the sofa where Rosie was lying and the pair of them gazed at her expectantly.

Tamsyn found a chair, took a deep breath and began to recount the story of the day, accompanied by gasps and exclamations from Izzy, solemn nods and shakes of the head from Rosie.

When she finished with the jury's verdict they looked at each other in one of the silent exchanges that Tamsyn had never been able to interpret. Behind them on the wall above the bed, the two small oil paintings that were Aunt Rosie's favourites glowed with the vibrancy of rich red fabrics against the lustrous naked flesh of gods and goddesses feasting and loving, and she thought of the fallen rose petals on the table below, of the texture of Cris's skin against hers.

'So,' she said briskly, 'with that out of the way Mr Defoe will be going back to London very soon.' She even managed a smile.

Chapter Seventeen

'But he asked you to marry him.' Aunt Izzy shook her head in puzzlement. 'That is wonderful. Yet you refused him?'

'It was a ruse and I would prefer not to be seen as the woman who entrapped a man who had to marry her to save her reputation,' Tamsyn said firmly.

'Yes, dear. But surely he wouldn't have thought of it if he hadn't already been considering asking you. Don't you want to marry him?'

'No, certainly not.'

Aunt Rosie's eyebrows rose in disbelief, but Tamsyn stared her out until she shook her head and turned to look out the window. 'There he is now, walking across the front lawn.' She pushed the window a little wider. 'Mr Defoe! Do come up. We are both so anxious to speak to you.'

'You won't say anything…?' Tamsyn began, panicking at the thought of the two of them assuring Cris that she really did want to marry him and that they thought it would be an excellent idea.

'Naturally we will thank him,' Aunt Rosie said, then called, 'Come in,' in answer to a tap on the door. 'Mr

Defoe, thank you so much for taking care of Tamsyn today,' she said, beaming as he entered.

To Tamsyn's eye he looked less than his usual elegant, unruffled self, but neither of the aunts appeared to see anything amiss, let alone the mild dishevelment of a man who had been making love in a hut half an hour before.

'Things became a trifle fraught,' he said with a smile for Rosie and without a glance at Tamsyn sitting at the foot of the sofa. 'But we brushed through all right in the end. Mrs Perowne is held in esteem by many people around here, even if the authorities are still determined to visit her late husband's sins on her head.'

'You consider not being required by your stratagem to marry Tamsyn is *brushing through*?' Rosie enquired, with no attempt to hide the tartness in her voice.

Cris turned a level blue gaze on her and his expression assumed a polite aloofness that sent a shiver down Tamsyn's spine and made Aunt Izzy's eyes widen in surprise. 'Mrs Perowne's wishes in the matter are paramount. It will, no doubt, help reduce any further speculation if I remove myself back to London tomorrow. I have presumed on your hospitality more than enough.' Izzy opened her mouth, and he added, 'I will, of course, continue to investigate Lord Chelford's involvement in the problems you have been experiencing. I may well be better placed to do so in London in any case.'

'We will miss you,' Izzy declared with a reproving glance at Rosie for her acid tone.

'And I, you.' Cris's smile returned, the chill vanished. 'You have made me very welcome here—as well as saved my life. I will miss your company and this charming house.' Tamsyn saw him look up at the paintings on the wall over the bed. 'Its endless small treasures are a constant pleasure.'

The three of them began to talk about art and the handsome set of Hogarth engravings on the walls of the landing and Tamsyn indulged herself by watching Cris's face. He was enjoying talking to the aunts, she realised, recognising the deepening of the laughter lines at the corner of his eyes, the softening of the severe line of his mouth with its betrayingly sensual lower lip.

She pulled her attention back as he shifted his position to gesture to the pictures over the bed. 'Those two oils, for example. Magnificent, like gems.'

'I know,' Izzy said with satisfaction. 'They are perhaps a trifle *warm* for display in the public rooms, but the colours and the energy in them have always pleased me.' She shook her head. 'One cannot wonder at the classical gods having so much energy for, er…'

'Life?' Cris supplied, the crease at the corner of his mouth deepening.

'Exactly. They used to hang in Papa's study, but he knew I liked them, so in his will he said I must have them to give me colour through our windswept winters here on the coast. I have no idea who the artist was, but dear Papa always said they had been in the family for a long time.'

'May I?' Cris stood and reached for the left-hand painting, lifting it down when Izzy nodded. He carried it to the window, looked at it closely, then propped it up on the sill and went back for the other. 'You know, these are not just good, they are exceptional. and I have seen this artist's work before, I think.' He looked at Izzy whose smile faded at his seriousness. 'I think they may be by Rubens.'

'*Rubens?* But that would mean they are worth thousands,' Rosie gasped. Then her expression hardened. 'That is what Franklin wants, those paintings.'

'They will be listed in the inventory of Holt Hall, won't they?' Tamsyn moved to sit by Izzy, taking her hand in hers.

'I am sure they will be,' Aunt Rosie said. 'And that is in Franklin's hands now.'

'They belong to him?' Cris asked.

'They do, as virtually everything in this house does, but he cannot touch them, let alone sell them, during my aunt's lifetime,' Tamsyn said thoughtfully. 'You must be right, Aunt Rosie. We always knew he had debts. What if they have become pressing? What if he has read the inventory, noted that we have something very valuable here and decided to get his hands on it? Moving us out of here into a small house on the estate would mean Izzy would have to reduce the furnishings and pictures. Or two little paintings might get lost in the move…if you did not know what they were.'

'And then we refused to move so he tried to scare us away and when that failed he attacked you. If something dreadful had happened to you, then I do not know if we would have been able to carry on alone here. We might well have agreed to move to the dower house. It all makes perfect sense now.' Aunt Izzy clasped her hands to her chest. 'But to murder a man to incriminate you, Tamsyn! I cannot conceive of such wickedness.'

'He must be desperate,' Tamsyn said. 'I hate to think of him getting away with it, but unless anyone can lay hands on that so-called solicitor's clerk who gave evidence at the inquest there is nothing but our suspicions to go on.'

'Let me take the paintings to London and get them appraised by experts,' Cris offered. 'Then at least you will know where you stand. If I am wrong, you can let Franklin know they are not valuable, make a story out of your excitement and then disappointment.'

'But what if they *are* genuine?' Izzy asked. 'What will we do then?'

'Cross that bridge when you come to it,' Cris advised and Izzy smiled, soothed, as she always seemed to be, by Cris. 'At least you will know why the attacks have been happening. You will have the facts and that puts you in a position of strength.'

Tamsyn slipped out of the room. She needed to think and she needed to calm the churning anger that her cousin could act that way, kill a man, threaten her, because of his own weakness and cupidity.

Cris would charm the aunts and smooth their ruffled feathers and when he was gone they would talk often of 'dear Mr Defoe', she thought as she went to her room, fighting the desire to simply get into bed, pull the covers over her head and pretend the whole exhausting, bitter day had not happened. She would not tell them they had taken a marquess and an earl under their humble roof, she decided. They would worry that they had not entertained them in style and that would spoil their innocent pleasure in the little adventure of Cris's arrival.

He would write with news of the pictures and of Franklin's activities. That would hurt, she accepted as she changed out of her riding habit and into something suitable for the evening. She didn't want to see his handwriting, to imagine his voice as she read his words. She wanted to forget him and she knew she never would, however angry she was with his secrecy and his wretched, wretched title.

A marquess, for goodness' sake! One step below a duke and I have to go and fall in love with him.

He must not guess for a moment how she had felt when he had declared that they were betrothed, how the treacherous little flame of hope that this was a declaration from his heart and not his honour had burned clear through the fog of fear, only to be quenched when she remembered that her daydreams could never be, however he felt about her.

She finished dressing, put up her hair with more care than usual and donned her few pieces of jewellery along with a smile that she was almost confident looked genuine. Cris would see that she was perfectly happy to see him leave and the hostile Lord Edenbridge would see that, despite his opinion, she had the manners and the poise to match the Marquess of Avenmore.

'You will take care?' Cris stood by the gate, Jackdaw fidgeting beside him. Gabriel himself sat on his horse by the stable-yard entrance, all too obviously not watching them. His carriage was already on its slow way up the rough track with Cris's vehicle following it.

'Of course. I told you, I will hire the two chairmen to guard the house.'

'It is already taken care of.'

'I do not need or want your charity, my lord.' They were safely out of earshot of the aunts who were watching from the drawing-room window.

'Do not call me that.'

'Why not? Your dear friend Lord Edenbridge would tell me I should curtsy respectfully as well.' She did so, with grace and a straight back.

'Gabriel will learn to watch his tongue one of these days. But if we are to be formal, Mrs Perowne, it is not you who has the say in the matter of hiring. I consulted your aunt Isobel, who is, after all, the mistress here, and convinced her that this was a good way to protect you and that I would be deeply hurt if she did not allow me to make the gesture.'

'You always get your own way, do you not?' She said it politely, with a smile on her lips, both for her own pride and for the watchers in the house.

'Not always.' He was smiling, too, a charming expression that did not reach his eyes. 'And sometimes it is right that I do not.'

She would never see him again, that must be the explanation for her reckless question. 'There is someone, isn't there? Someone you are in love with and cannot have.'

'I thought so.' He spoke readily, but his eyes were bleak. 'I was wrong, but it clouded my judgement badly enough to almost get me drowned through sheer inattention.' He turned and mounted, collected the restless horse with a light hand on the reins. 'I would have done my best to make you happy, if marriage was what you wanted.'

'What I want, my lord, is my old life back. I wish you a safe journey and a happy return to your old life. Thank you for your help and for taking the pictures to be appraised.' She could still hardly think of them without feeling ill.

He inclined his head, turned Jackdaw and spurred off up the lane, not slowing as he drew alongside his friend, but cantering on. She waited, but Cris did not look back.

Thank you for your help. Thank you for two nights of bliss in your arms. I wish I had never seen you, because I do not know how my heart will heal.

It was more difficult than she could have imagined to walk back briskly into the house and join the aunts in the drawing room, but it was good discipline, Tamsyn told herself. Soon, if she kept on smiling and pretending everything was all right, she would begin to get used to this hollow ache.

'Such nice young men,' Izzy said, patting the sofa beside her. 'I will miss them.'

'We will hear from Mr Defoe soon enough, I expect,' Rosie said. 'He did not think it would take the expert long to assess the paintings.'

'Dear Mr Defoe will know what to do,' Izzy said, apparently comforted by the thought.

'*Dear* Mr Defoe is having the pictures valued for you, not investigating the crime,' Tamsyn pointed out.

'If Franklin had come to me in the first place, told me he needed the money and wanted to sell the pictures, then I would have given them back,' Izzy lamented. 'I still would if it were not for that poor man's death.'

'With no proof, there is not a lot we can do, although I hate to admit it,' Tamsyn mused. 'We must be on the alert here and hope some way to deal with Franklin occurs to us.'

As she spoke the bulky figure of Seamus the chairman passed the window. He was apparently strolling casually, but Tamsyn noticed the truncheon hanging at his side when his coat was blown back by the breeze. At least their bodyguards were in place, but unless she could come up with some plan then they were never going to be free of Franklin's shadow.

The London papers arrived, courtesy of the vicar, four days after publication. A week after Cris and Gabriel had left, Tamsyn sat and attempted to read an account of the antiquities of Devon—also thanks to the vicar, who was generous with his library—and told herself that she was managing very well without Cris de

Feaux. She'd hardly thought of him at all—not more than every hour or so—although it was unaccountably difficult to concentrate on manorial history for some reason. It was hard to sleep as well, but that must be because of her worries over the pictures and what Franklin might do next, and the faint crunch of footsteps as one or other of the Irishmen made their nightly patrols.

'Franklin's name is in the paper,' Izzy announced suddenly, making Tamsyn jump.

'It is?'

Her aunt folded the *Morning Post,* pushed her spectacles further down her nose and peered at the small print. 'Here, I glimpsed his name somewhere under "Fashionable Arrivals and Departures". In "Arrivals" it says, "The Duchess of Devonshire to Ashbourne's Hotel; the Marquess of Avenmore to St James's Square; the Earl of Edenbridge to Half Moon Street; Dowager Countess of…" Here it is. "The Viscount Chelford from Holt Hall."'

So Cris and Gabriel were in London. She wondered what Cris's house was like. It must be very grand, she supposed. Even if she had never been to London she knew that the St James's area was fashionable and that the legendary Almack's was just off St James's Square, which was convenient for Cris in his pursuit of an eligible wife. With Franklin out of town, at least there was no risk of the two meeting.

'Here comes the post,' Rosie observed before Izzy could launch into futile speculation on Franklin's movements and motives.

A few minutes later Jason brought in the letters. Tamsyn's correspondence was all exceedingly dull until she reached the letter from Mr Pentire, their man of business, who was delighted to report that since their banker had received a letter of guarantee from no less a person than the Marquess of Avenmore, he had been energetically quashing all rumours about the state of finances at Barbary Combe House.

It should have been a huge relief, of course. *Damn him*, Tamsyn fumed. *In he strolls, setting my life straight with the bank as well.* Dear Mr Defoe, *says Izzy*. Interfering, patronising marquess, *I say*.

It was unworthy and ungrateful and she should think of the aunts' security and happiness, not her own wounded heart and dented pride. She was still talking herself out of the sullens when Rosie gave a shriek.

'They *are* by Rubens! The oil paintings, Mr Defoe says they are by Rubens and worth—oh, my goodness, I must be misreading his handwriting. Isobel, dear, you see what it says.'

Izzy took one look, added her own shriek. 'I don't believe it! That much, for two little pictures? Whatever am I going to do? I am very fond of the paintings, but hardly to the extent that I would see anyone hurt to keep them.' She looked as though she might weep at the thought.

'Nothing,' said Rosie fiercely. 'If your nephew had been a decent young man and you had discovered this, then of course you would tell him. But he is responsible for that poor man's death, whether he intended it or not. Your father wanted you to have the pictures. That should be enough—it is not as though you could or would sell them and they will go back to the estate eventually.'

'If he takes them, he will only be stealing his own property,' Tamsyn said thoughtfully. She got up and went to sit beside Izzy, put an arm around her and gave her a hug. 'I am trying to think of what we could accuse him of if there is no evidence about the murder. He would be breaking the terms of your father's will and he would be breaking and entering, I suppose.'

'We must think on it when we have got over the shock,' Rosie said. 'Ring for some tea, Tamsyn dear, and let us open the rest of our post.'

Even tea did not entirely stop Izzy's agitated murmurings, but eventually she opened the remainder of her letters. 'This is from Cousin Harriet—do you recall her, Rosie? Sylvia's daughter, such a nice girl, and she made a good marriage, to Lord Pirton, and had three sons and a daughter, Julia. I haven't heard from her in an age, but she says she has been in a whirl with her daughter's come-out and marriage! Goodness...to Lord Dewington. And she—Harriet, that is—says she was quite cast down with anti-climax and Pirton is insisting on staying in London during the summer because of some government business and she's been meaning for an age to invite us all to stay, but couldn't because of Julia—' Izzy paused for breath '—and would we like to come now?'

'But—' Tamsyn began.

'But neither Rosie nor I enjoy cities,' Izzy continued. 'You could go, though, dear. You have never been to London, after all.'

'I couldn't leave, not now, with all this going on. And surely Lady Pirton knows about my marriage and Jory. She wouldn't want me visiting, surely?'

'Yes, she knows and she was very sympathetic and understanding at the time. And it is not as though the season is under way,' Rosie said. 'You could see the sights and keep her company for a week or so, do a little shopping. We will be quite safe here with our two sturdy bodyguards. And Mr Defoe says in his letter something about the dealer he took the pictures to.' She searched painfully through the scattered sheets in her lap until her arthritic fingers found the page she was looking for.

'Yes, here it is. He says that the dealer has put the pictures into his own strong room until we decide what to do about them. I really think it would be best to go and talk to this Mr Masterson and get all the details, don't you? He may have advice about looking after them.'

But... No, she couldn't just sit there mouthing the same word over and over. Tamsyn made herself look at the issue objectively. The aunts had their large and capable bodyguards and she was certain that if she asked him, Dr Tregarth would call in daily. She had strengthened the security on the farm and the livestock. It would be sensible to talk to the dealer about the paintings now that they knew what a responsibility they were. She might even find out more about Franklin and whatever mess he had got himself into. Which left the real reason she did not want to go to London—Cris was there.

Coward. 'Yes, I will go,' she found herself saying before she could think about it any more. 'I will go to London.'

Chapter Eighteen

'Excellent,' Aunt Rosie said. 'You deserve a holiday, my dear, and you will enjoy London.'

Will I? Tamsyn had her doubts, starting with the risk of encountering Cris, through qualms about her lack of familiarity with society beyond the local gentry and assemblies at the nearby towns, to the prospect of making the longest journey she had ever attempted.

She mentally stiffened her spine and told herself not to be feeble. She could do this. 'Will you write at once, Aunt Izzy, and say I would be delighted to come for a week? And I will send a note to the Golden Lion in Barnstaple and book a seat on the stage for the day after tomorrow.'

'I will say a month,' Aunt Izzy said from her seat at the writing desk. 'It is too far to make a week's stay worthwhile. The roads are better than the last time I went to London, but they are still poor as far as Tiverton, so you will be a good two days on the road, besides having to set out from here the day before to stay at the Golden Lion. You had best take Harris with you, you can't go staying at inns by yourself and we can manage with Molly. I can always get in more help from the village if necessary.' Purposeful now the decision had been made, she was writing rapidly as she talked.

Tamsyn went to her own desk and wrote a note for the doctor, then another to the inn to reserve a room and two inside seats on the stage, and finally a list of things to do that took up three sheets of notepaper. It was not until she fell into bed that night with a grateful sigh that she realised that she had not thought about Crispin de Feaux for at least eight hours. That seemed like a small, but significant, victory.

Tamsyn swam up through clouds of sleep into a pale blue light and, for a moment, had no idea where she was. She fought her way upright against a heap of pillows, looked around and remembered. She was in London. Had arrived yesterday afternoon and had been swept into the warmth of Lady Pirton's welcome.

'My dear Tamsyn! May I call you Tamsyn? Such a pretty name. Welcome to London!'

Her hostess, in a flurry of silken skirts, had come across the drawing room, hands outstretched as Tamsyn collected her scattered and travel-tossed wits and executed a respectable curtsy, trying not to stare like a yokel at the elegance of Lady Pirton and her drawing room. 'Lady Pirton, thank you for your invitation.'

'Harriet, dear. Why, we are almost cousins, are we not? Now then, are you exhausted? What would you like best? A nice bath and your bed? A little something to eat? A walk in the fresh air? You must tell me just what would suit you.'

'A bath, something to eat and my bed, Cousin Harriet,' Tamsyn had admitted honestly. 'I do apologise, but I have to confess that the room is jolting up and down and I forget when I last had more than a few hours' sleep together.' And when she had closed her eyes it had been to fall into a restless doze, full of anxious dreams about the aunts and disturbingly erotic fantasies of Cris.

As she had travelled, grown more weary of the jolting, crowded coach, the hectic, grubby inns, the constant need to look out for their possessions and to find their way in unfamiliar places, she had felt both her uncertainty about what to do deepening but her determination to do *something* about Franklin strengthening.

'You are a heroine for even attempting a stagecoach journey of that length,' Cousin Harriet said with a shudder. 'Now, up to your suite and I will send my woman to look after you. I have no doubt yours is in as much need of a rest as you are.'

And now it was full morning, judging by the light. A bell pull hung by the bed and she tugged it, wary of just who might appear and hoping it would not be Cousin Harriet's very superior lady's maid, Fielding, who had helped her into her bath, unpacked her battered valises and had refrained with crashing tact from showing any reaction to her workaday, unfashionable wardrobe.

But, thank goodness, it was Harris who came in, neat as a pin as usual and looking as rested as Tamsyn felt. 'How are you feeling, Harris?'

'Much better, Mizz Tamsyn. Sorry—madam, I should say.' Harris wrinkled her nose. 'Lord, but they're a starched-up lot below stairs, for all they've made me very comfortable. All precedence and Miss Fielding this and Miss Harris that. And a butler called Pearson with a poker up his—yes, well, you know what I mean.'

Tamsyn snorted with laughter and felt better. 'It is all very grand, is it not? What is the time?'

'Eight o'clock, madam. Her ladyship says, would you

care for breakfast in your chamber or will you join her in the breakfast parlour in half an hour?'

'I'll go down, I can't lie about in my room any longer.' Tamsyn slid out of bed. 'It will have to be the green morning dress, I think, Harris. It is the better of the two.'

Cousin Harriet was just entering the breakfast parlour as Pearson, the stately butler, showed Tamsyn to the door. She managed to say, 'Thank you, Pearson', without giggling over Harris's pungent description of him and took her seat.

'Now then, what would you like to do, my dear? I have all kinds of suggestions, but this is your visit.' Lady Pirton heaped her plate from the buffet with an enthusiasm that belied her slender figure and gestured to Tamsyn to help herself.

'I have a few errands, and some shopping for myself and my aunts, but you must tell me how I might be of use to you, Cousin Harriet.'

'By keeping me company and letting me come shopping with you. I miss my darling Julia and you must stop me moping and keep me young. Now, what are your errands?'

'There is a picture dealer I must visit on behalf of Aunt Isobel and a shopping list of alarming proportions for both her and Aunt Rosie—I suspect I will be visiting every bookshop in London.'

'And dress shops for yourself?' Lady Pirton buttered another slice of toast and reached for the strawberry conserve.

'Yes, I fear my wardrobe is hopelessly out of date and provincial,' Tamsyn confessed. 'Not that we have an extravagant social life in Devon, but I would like something pretty for the occasional assembly and certainly for local dinner parties. And perhaps a new riding habit and a walking dress or two.' She looked down at her sprigged green skirts. 'And a morning dress.'

'And shoes and shawls and all the trimmings. Excellent.' Lady Pirton beamed. 'And I have invitations to some select little parties you will enjoy, so I suggest we visit my *modiste* first so she can make a start and then we can go to your art dealer and the bookshops. You won't need to dress up for either of those.'

Which implies that I'm not yet fit to be seen in any of the fashionable lounges like Bond Street or Hyde Park, Tamsyn thought with an inward smile.

The visit to the *modiste*, who proved to be the famous Mrs Bell, much to Tamsyn's alarm, was thoroughly embarrassing. She was stripped down to her plain and functional underwear, which was *tutted* over, then she was measured, peered at, discussed and turned around like a doll in the hands of a group of little girls.

'I think I might... Do I really need...? But how much...?' All was ignored until she pulled herself together, put up both hands and said, 'Stop, please! I need to know how much each garment will be before I commit myself. And I most certainly do not require a ball gown.' It was not as though she could not afford a new wardrobe, but her practical soul revolted at the idea of wasting her money on things she did not need and would never use.

Finally she escaped with an order that satisfied both practicality and a purely feminine desire for a few frills and furbelows that were, perhaps, not entirely necessary.

'That is a reasonable start,' Cousin Harriet commented as they took their places in her smart town carriage with its hood down.

Tamsyn tried hard not to stare about her like a yokel. Bond Street, Albemarle Street, fashionable squares and elegant town houses. And the traffic…and the people and the noise. By the time they reached the pleasant side street close to Grosvenor Square she was both dizzy and exhilarated and had to calm herself down in case she let slip too much slip in front of Cousin Harriet when they entered the dealer's shop.

Fortunately the older woman appeared to think that Aunt Izzy was thinking of selling the paintings and therefore took herself off discreetly to one side to study a Fragonard while Tamsyn spoke to the dealer.

'Yes, Mrs Perowne, they are undoubtedly by Rubens. I took the precaution of seeking a second opinion from an expert who considers them excellent, although small. If your aunt wishes to place them on the marketplace, I would be happy to act as her agent.' His eyes gleamed, presumably, Tamsyn thought, with the prospect of the commission.

'The disposal is not entirely in my aunt's hands,' she said carefully. 'Will you be able to keep them securely for a few more weeks? Would there be a charge for that?'

'As I am acting on behalf of the Marquess of Avenmore in this matter, and he is an excellent customer of mine, it would be entirely *gratis*, ma'am, I assure you.'

It niggled at her pride to be beholden, yet again, to Cris, but common sense told her this was the safest place. All she had to do now was to try to think of a way of dealing with Franklin, which was proving as hard here in London as it had in Devon. With a mental shrug, Tamsyn allowed herself to be swept off by Cousin Harriet for more shopping. The important thing, she assured herself, with half an ear on Harriet's discourse on the best place to buy ribbons, shawls and lace, was to keep calm, and then a solution would present itself.

Three days later the only things that presented themselves were a pile of dress boxes from Mrs Bell, Lady Pirton's *coiffeuse* to give her a fashionable crop and an alarming pile of invitations.

'Now that your hair has a modish touch and you are outfitted in style, what is to stop you from going to parties? Lady Ancaster's informal supper dance tomorrow will be just the thing. It will not be a crush, the food and music will be excellent and Hermione's little gatherings are always delightfully unstuffy.'

'*Hermione's little gathering*' appeared to consist of about two hundred beautifully dressed people all talking at the top of their voices. Tamsyn told herself that she, too, was beautifully dressed, in sea-foam-green net over matching silk with cream lace at neck, sleeves and hem. She had borrowed pearls at her neck and in her earlobes and a simple ribbon threaded through her smart new crop. She found her smile and her poise and lunged into the throng.

Half an hour later her hair ribbon slipped. 'Just through the arch on the left,' Harriet advised. 'Then down the passageway and you'll find the ladies' retiring room. I won't have moved far when you come back.'

Tamsyn found the arch and then discovered three possible passages. She took the left one at random, rounded a corner and walked into the back of someone large, solid and male.

'I do beg your pardon, sir.' He turned. 'Oh. Lord Edenbridge.'

Behind Gabriel a tall blonde girl with lovely blue eyes put her hand to her mouth, turned and hurried away.

'Come back!'

The young woman stopped, looked back with something close to despair in her eyes.

'Don't be a fool. You don't have to marry him and you don't have to…damn it, I've burned the thing.'

'A promise is a promise,' the blonde said, chin up. Tamsyn recognised someone holding back tears by sheer pride and willpower. 'But if you do not want me—' She shrugged, turned and walked away.

What on earth was that all about? Tamsyn eyed Gabriel's furious expression and began to back warily away.

'What in Hades are you doing here?' he demanded as the brown gaze focused into recognition. 'Does Cris know?'

'Certainly not. I do not need Lord Avenmore's permission to visit a relative.'

'Come with me.' He took her arm and swept her back into the main reception room and up to a handsome couple who were in the middle of what looked like a heated, but amiable, discussion.

'Alex, Tess, stop bickering.'

'But Alex says I must not cut my hair.' The woman Gabriel had addressed as Tess turned deep-blue eyes on him. 'And I want to be in the mode.' She smiled at Tamsyn. 'I want a crop like yours, with the curls at the front and long at the back. Who did it for you?'

Tamsyn made a dab at her slipping hair ribbon as the man called Alex smiled at her apologetically. 'Darling, we haven't been introduced. You cannot interrogate people about their hairdressers without an introduction.'

'Don't be stuffy—'

'Alex, Teresa, allow me to present Mrs Perowne,' Gabriel cut in, earning a rap over the knuckles with Teresa's fan. 'Mrs Perowne, the Viscount Weybourn, Lady Weybourn. This,' he said, turning to his friends and ignoring Tamsyn attempting to curtsy, 'is the person I told you about. Cris's problem.'

'Gabriel,' Lady Weybourn gasped.

'I am no one's problem,' Tamsyn said hotly at the same time.

'In here, I think.' The viscount, smiling amiably, took Tamsyn's arm with his right hand and a firm grip on Gabriel's elbow with his left and walked with apparent casualness towards one of the small retiring rooms. Lady Weybourn came, too, muttering under her breath about *overbearing men.*

The room was, thankfully, empty. Lord Weybourn, showing rather more decision than Tamsyn had assumed from his amiable appearance, promptly locked the door. 'Now, what's going on?'

His wife took Tamsyn's hand and urged her to sit next to her on the sofa. 'Yes, what *is* going on? That was rude, even by your standards, Gabriel.'

'Mrs Perowne is the widow of a smuggler who cheated the gallows only by a lethal leap from a cliff. She is embroiled in a feud with Lord Chelford and she has seduced Cris into a declaration of marriage in front of a courtroom full of yokels.'

'They were not yokels and I have not seduced anyone,' Tamsyn said, furious.

Lord Weybourn studied her face, which she could feel was pink with anger. 'No? I must say, I had not thought anyone was capable of seducing de Feaux against his will. I was about to congratulate you, ma'am.'

'Cris is to marry you?' Lady Weybourn caught Tamsyn totally off guard by planting a kiss on her cheek. 'Kate and I told you he was in love,' she added triumphantly to the two men.

Who on earth is Kate? 'No, he is not! At least, not with me. It was a ploy, because otherwise I was going to be accused of murder and he was establishing an alibi for me.'

'Murder?' Lord Weybourn sat down. 'You told us that Cris had formed an unsuitable attachment—and I must say, coming from you, Gabe, that is rather rich— but you said nothing about the lady in question being a murderous seductress.' His smile to Tamsyn was teasing and she realised he thought her neither of those things.

'Cris might show the world a façade of ice, he might be a marquess and none of us have ever seen him put a foot wrong, but that does not mean he isn't vulnerable and that when he is, that we don't guard his back, just as he guards ours.' For once Lord Edenbridge's air of care-for-nothing cynicism had slipped and Tamsyn found herself liking him for his fierce loyalty, if nothing else.

She stood up. 'If you are Cris's friends, then ask him to tell you all about his time in Devon, but believe me, I want nothing to do with him, ever again. Will you kindly unlock that door, my lord?' Stepping out into the crowded reception was like plunging into roaring surf. Tamsyn took a deep breath, fixed a smile on her face and went in search of the retiring room once again.

Chapter Nineteen

Cris regarded the stolid figure of the Bow Street Runner seated across the desk from him as he finished his description of the lying witness.

'Thin, forgettable face and brown hair? Shabby, respectable and with an Essex accent? Aye, I know that one. What's he calling himself, my lord?'

'Paul Goode, solicitor's clerk.'

'That's what he was before he went to the bad.' Jem Clarke, the Runner, nodded, his satisfied smile holding a wealth of promises for Mr Goode. 'I'll be glad to lay my hands on Paul Gooding, which is what his real name is. What's he done this time?'

'Murder and perjury, for a start,' Cris said.

'Hanging crimes.' The Runner was beaming now. 'How strong is the evidence?'

'The perjury, good enough. For the murder, I think we'll need to trick a confession out of him and do that by confronting him with the man who paid him. And he, I fear, is a viscount.'

'Tricky. The corners of the Runner's mouth turned down, then he brightened. 'But you're a marquess.'

'I am. Let me tell you the background to this.'

* * *

He was almost finished with the explanation when Dyson, his butler, scratched on the door and opened it just enough to slide inside. 'I know you did not want to be disturbed, my lord, but Lord Edenbridge—'

'Insists.' Gabriel followed the indignant butler into the room. 'Sorry to interrupt. You entertaining, de Feaux?' His intelligent gaze skimmed over the Runner in his blue coat and red waistcoat. 'Or investigating?'

Tempting though it was to try to eject Gabe, he would be as persistent as a dog with a stolen bone. Cris waved him to a seat and introduced him to the Runner. 'My thought was to get hold of Chelford, let him think we have evidence of what are actually only suspicions and confront him with Goode, after telling him the man's turned King's Evidence. With any luck they'll both say too much.'

'I'm with you on that. How do we get hold of them both?'

'I'm relying on Clarke here to find Goode, or Gooding or whatever he's calling himself this week. When he has, then I'll invite Chelford to a nice intimate dinner.'

'I can't condone kidnapping, my lord.' The Runner did not look too worried at the thought.

'Heaven forfend,' Cris said piously, making Gabriel snort. 'The doors in this house have locks that are prone to stick, but that's a minor inconvenience. I'm sure they would prove easy to open if you, for example, were to try one.'

'I'll get right on to Gooding's tail now, my lord.' The Runner got to his feet. 'I know who'll know where to find him, if you follow my meaning.'

'Let me know if you need to grease any tongues,' Cris said as the man took his leave.

'Right, now we're alone, you can help me think through how to handle Chelford.'

'Later.' Gabriel strolled over to the decanters and splashed out two brandies. 'Your Mrs Perowne is in town.'

'She is not my—*what* did you say?'

'Bumped into her at Hermione Ancaster's little affair last night. Dressed to the nines with a fashionable hairdo that Tess admires. Spitting tacks in my direction.'

'Why should she be doing that?' he asked as he grappled with the news. Tamsyn in London. Tamsyn within reach of Chelford. He stared at the glass in his hand and found it was empty.

'I warned her off you again.' Gabriel sat down at a safe distance, which was sensible.

Cris put down the glass. 'Why? You are acting like an hysterical society mother whose little lamb is straying into the jaws of some rake like…you. I, in case you haven't noticed, am male, almost thirty and no one's little lamb.'

'But you are an honourable man and she is a not-unattractive lady in distress who has turned up virtually on your doorstep for no good reason that I can see. If you are not exceedingly careful you are going to find yourself leg-shackled to her. And, if my memory is not failing me, you were only saying a few months ago that you'll be looking for a bride this coming season.' Gabriel, on the receiving end of Cris's most icy stare, smiled innocently. 'And I'm your friend, so I must look out for your interests.'

'What is she doing here?'

Gabriel shrugged. 'Said something about visiting a relative, but not who. Or where. Just as long as she is not chasing a husband.'

Landing his infuriating friend another facer was tempting, but not constructive. Cris got to his feet. 'I'm going out. Do help yourself.' He gestured ironically towards the decanters.

An hour later, after a visit to Masterson in the Albemarle Street shop, Cris used the knocker on the door of an elegant town house in Grosvenor Street.

'Lord Avenmore to see Mrs Perowne,' he said as the butler opened the door.

'I am not sure Mrs Perowne is at home, my lord.' Cris stepped forward, the man gave way before him and he found himself in the hallway.

'No? Perhaps you would check. If she is not, then I will wait.'

The man looked as though he would protest. Cris dropped his card on to the silver salver on the side table, raised one eyebrow and waited.

'Perhaps if your lordship would care to take a seat in here, I will make enquiries.'

Cris settled himself in the small salon and summoned up some patience. He had hardly crossed one booted leg over the other when the door burst open.

'What are you doing here?'

He stood up, taking his time about it, admiring the vision of fashionable womanhood who had swirled to a halt in front of him. 'I could ask the same of you.'

'I am visiting a relative of Aunt Isobel's, doing some shopping and consulting the picture dealer. Why have you called?'

'Gabriel told me you were in London. I was concerned about you.'

'Concerned that I might be pursuing you?'

'No. Concerned for your safety. You are looking very fine.'

She did not sit, but swept over to take a stand in front of the fireplace, giving him an admirable view of pale primrose skirts and upswept hair that exposed the temptingly soft skin at the nape of her neck. 'Thank you. I can look respectable if I wish, you see.'

'I was going to say, I preferred you as I remember you.'

'Why?'

He was only a stride away, too close to give himself the opportunity for second thoughts. She was in his arms before he was aware of moving, straining back against his hold, but not struggling, her eyes wide, dark, as she searched his face. 'I remember you naked in the sea, in my arms. I remember you windblown and laughing on the cliffs, I remember your long legs, strong and lovely as the old riding habit blew back against them.'

'Oh.' It was a gasp and she wrenched out of his hold and retreated across the room to take refuge behind a low armchair. 'Do you have to remind me?'

'I don't need reminding and I don't believe you do either.'

'You arrogant man!'

'Why is it arrogant to praise your passion and your beauty?' He stayed where he was, not wanting to provoke her into fleeing the room or ringing for a chaperone.

'Stop it, you are flustering me.'

'Good.' She turned her head away, but not before he saw the colour flooding her cheeks. The movement gave him an excellent view of the vulnerable soft nape of her neck, the elegance of her figure in the well-made gown. *Damn, but I want her...*

'Your friends have made it very clear to me that I should not be associating with you.'

'No doubt Gabriel has, but I'm not so sure about Tess and Alex. I am not going to be barred from Court simply for knowing you, Tamsyn.'

'No?' She sounded wistful, but her back was still ramrod straight, her head still averted.

'I missed you. Did you miss me?' As he spoke he moved closer, skirted the chair.

'Of course I did.' Still she would not look at him. 'But it will pass.'

He should go. She was right. It would pass, this feeling, whatever it was. And he could not, must not, court another woman with his mind distracted by Tamsyn Perowne. 'I wish it would not, Tamsyn.' And he touched her arm, curled his fingers over the smooth, warm flesh and saw her eyes widen as she started and turned at the touch.

Then she flung her arms around his neck and brought his head down so she could reach his lips and they were lost. He could have sworn he smelled the sea salt on her skin, in her hair, that he could hear the surf pounding on the beach and the gulls crying overhead. The taste of her, the feel of her in his arms, was familiar, yet different, right and yet unsettling. As he swept his tongue into her mouth, finding her again, claiming her, the salt scent yielded to rose water. As his hands spanned the familiar curve of her waist and hip, his fingers encountered fine lawn and the structure of stays.

Tamsyn broke the kiss, laid her head against his chest, held him. 'You overwhelm me.' But she did not let him go. 'I did not want this.'

'I did,' he admitted, his mouth buried in her hair.

'I will not be your mistress.' It was a fierce declaration and he wished he could see her face.

'No. I would not ask it.' Lovers, yes, but he could not bear to see her brought to a position of a dependent, living on his whim, obligated to please him, to pleasure him. Tamsyn was wild and free and her own woman.

'And I am not negotiating, that was not a demand for something more.' She broke away, seemingly angry with herself, not with him. 'I should never have come.'

'Why *did* you come? And do not tell me, shopping.'

'I wanted to deal with Franklin, to make him stop, to find a solution to this.'

She sat down and he pulled up a stool so he could sit close, catch her expression. 'It is dangerous for you. I am dealing with it.'

'Cris, it is not your problem to deal with.'

'No?' He reached out and cupped her cheek. 'It has become so.' When she shook her head he added, 'Let me tell you what I have been doing.'

'Lord Edenbridge—' Tamsyn said when he had finished telling her about the Runner and his discussion with Gabriel.

'Ignore Gabriel. He is going to find my right fist in his teeth if he does not stop this nonsense. It is insulting to you and it is driving me to distraction. You need have nothing to do with him and he'll pull himself together soon enough and be of some use.'

'There is a woman, I think. I don't know her name, but she is…upsetting him. I saw them at Lady Ancaster's reception. I do not know what exactly is going on, but I do not think he knows how to deal with her.'

'Excellent. That will be the first time a woman has tied Gabriel in a knot. It might stop him attempting to nursemaid me.' What was it that Gabriel had said when he arrived at Barbary Combe House?

A sudden impulse of decency in regard to a woman. A lady. I thought it better to remove myself before I discovered that I was on the verge of becoming reformed.

'I can help,' Tamsyn said.

'No.' It made his blood run cold to think what might happen if she sailed in to attack Chelford, all indignation, banners flying. 'It is bad enough that you've been flitting about London unguarded as it is. You could have bumped into him at any time.' He wanted to keep her in the house, wrapped in cotton wool, protected.

Tamsyn snapped, 'He is not going to make me a prisoner, or afraid, any more than he is going to make me a pawn in his selfish, greedy plans.' Her eyes were narrowed, her mouth set and her chin was up.

A warrior queen, Cris thought with a sudden jolt under his sternum. To treat her like a victim was to deny who she was, a fighter. 'We need to get our hands on Gooding first, otherwise all we have is pure speculation. Even when we do, it will be his word against Chelford's unless we can trick him into some kind of confession before witnesses, preferably our Runner.'

'If he discovers I am in London then that will unnerve him, surely?' Tamsyn turned to him, caught his hands in hers in her eagerness. Cris quietly closed his fingers and enjoyed the flutter of her pulse, the warmth of her palm against his. 'He'll wonder what on earth I am doing here and it might provoke him into rash action.'

'If he tries rash action in your direction, I'll break his neck.' He discovered he meant it. 'But it might be a good tactic. What we need is for both of you to be at the same party, one we can control and where I can keep you safe. I'll see what I can persuade Tess and Alex to put on, I doubt Chelford knows we are friends.'

'Thank you.' She looked down at their clasped hands and made no move to free herself. 'And thank you for agreeing to involve me. I know your instincts are all to shut up the women and children and man the barricades.'

'I only want to shut *you* up safely.' He lifted his hands until he could kiss her knuckles. 'But it would be like caging a wild hawk, and besides, you wouldn't let me do it.'

Tamsyn made a tiny, inarticulate sound and sought his mouth, fiercely urgent, pushing away the knot of their hands so she could find his lips. The heat surged through him as he caught her by the shoulders and pulled her on to his knee.

Mine. The word beat in his brain, drowning out common sense and caution.

'Tamsyn!'

She recoiled from his grip back into her chair, sending the stool he was sitting on rocking. Cris got to his feet with a twist and regained his balance to find a trim matron in her forties regarding the pair of them with something between horror and amusement.

'Lord Avenmore.'

'Lady Pirton.' How in Hades a grown man was supposed to maintain his dignity when he was caught in an amorous tangle by the chaperone of the lady concerned he had no idea. 'I can explain.'

'There is absolutely no need. Mrs Perowne may naturally count on my protection if she feels in need of it, but as she appears to be an entirely willing participant in your, er, conversation I will retire to the Green Salon and ring for tea. Perhaps you can both join me shortly?'

Cris found himself without words as the door clicked shut behind Lady Pirton. Then, as Tamsyn collapsed into a fit of helpless giggles, he caught sight of his own rigid expression in the over-mantel mirror and gave way to laughter, too.

He folded up on the floor by Tamsyn's chair and groped for a handkerchief. 'Will she send you home, do you think?' he managed when they had both sobered up enough to speak.

'I'm sure not and if she should ask me to leave, why, I will hire myself a lady companion and take us both off to a respectable hotel.' Tamsyn got up, mopped her eyes and held out a hand to him. 'Stop sprawling on the floor. It is conduct unbefitting a marquess, as I am certain the very respectable Earl of Edenbridge would remind you.'

That was a glimpse of a different man altogether, Tamsyn thought as she sat sipping tea with perfect decorum, and a suspiciously pink nose, ten minutes later. She would never have believed the cool and collected man she thought she knew could have given way to amusement in quite such an uninhibited manner. It was, she decided ruefully as she watched him accept a cucumber sandwich with perfect composure, exceedingly attractive.

'I was not aware that you were acquainted with Mrs Perowne, Lord Avenmore.' Cousin Harriet poured tea with a steady hand, but Tamsyn could almost see the calculation going on behind her bland expression.

'We met in Devon. Mrs Perowne came to my aid when I almost drowned. I was delighted, but surprised, to discover she was visiting London.'

'Oh, then you were not expecting to meet?' Harriet

was apparently having trouble controlling her curiosity as her gaze flickered back and forth between the pair of them.

'No,' Tamsyn said, softening the flat negative with a smile. 'It quite took us by surprise.'

'So I see.' Cousin Harriet blushed and put down the tea pot with a clatter. 'Will you be leaving London for the summer, Lord Avenmore? Your country estates, perhaps? Or the seaside?'

'Later, no doubt. I have some business to complete first.'

Tamsyn felt his gaze resting on her and slid him a sideways glance. His mouth was just twitching into a hint of a smile. Then he ran the tip of his tongue over his lips in pursuit of an errant crumb and a wave of desire hit her like a rogue wave. She was mad to have kissed him just now, to have incited that outburst of passion. It seemed he felt as ardently as she did— about making love, at least. Parting again was going to be hellish.

To her relief Cousin Harriet appeared to expect her to see Cris to the door and stayed behind in the salon after shaking hands. But with the butler waiting with Cris's hat in his hands there was no opportunity for conversation, let alone any more stolen kisses.

Cris stopped her with a hand on her arm, just out of earshot. 'I will let you know how things progress, but do not go out alone, or with only a maid. Take a hefty footman, at the very least.'

She didn't point out that Cousin Harriet appeared to employ footmen for smart good looks and not for bulk. 'I will take care. I just wish I knew the best thing to do about those pictures.'

'We'll think of something.' Cris caught her hand in

his, raised it to his lips, the courtly, almost old-fashioned gesture at odds with the heat of his mouth as he lingered a moment longer than decency allowed. 'Do not worry.'

Chapter Twenty

Tamsyn got through the next few days by a mixture of intensive shopping, sightseeing and sheer willpower. She added a flirty little veil to her bonnet, intriguing Cousin Harriet, who teased her about trying to set a new vogue, but soothing to her nerves when she was outside. Surely Franklin would not recognise her dressed to the nines, veiled and hundreds of miles from where he thought her to be?

Lady Weybourn came to call, fortunately while Cousin Harriet was out, because she proved to be charmingly frank. 'Let's use first names, shall we? You mustn't mind Gabriel, he's in a muddle with some woman, which is doing nothing for his mood, and he is worried about Cris.'

'But why? I am not trying to entrap him, and besides, Lord Avenmore is a grown man of experience. He can look after himself.'

'He has changed since he went to Devon. No...' Tess shook her head, contradicting herself. 'No, he had changed before that, when we were up in Northumberland visiting Kate and Grant—Lord and Lady Allundale. Kate thought he was in love. He seemed on the surface his usual self, all cool detachment and lofty self-confidence, but there was something in his eyes, some…bleakness. I wondered if she had died, now I suspect he had to give her up, leave her.'

'I think so, too,' Tamsyn said. The other woman looked a question. 'We became close.' Tess smiled and Tamsyn shrugged. 'Oh, very well, we became lovers. But he does not love me, I knew that from the beginning and I never expected it, or marriage. I knew it was an affair of the moment and he would leave, we both did. And I do not need Gabriel Stone to tell me I am not the wife a marquess should be looking for. He needs someone with a pedigree of note, a young woman who will give him an heir.'

'You are not some rural bumpkin,' Tess said. 'You may live in the depths of the country and you may have married a smuggler, but you are perfectly well connected. Don't pretend otherwise,' she added sternly when Tamsyn began to protest. 'Country gentry, I presume? There's nothing wrong with that. I'm illegitimate and I'm married to a viscount who'll be an earl one day.' She settled back more comfortably into the corner of the sofa and Tamsyn saw the way she rested one hand protectively over her stomach for a moment.

'Does he know he's going to be a papa next year?' Tamsyn asked.

'Oh! How did you know?' She followed the direction of Tamsyn's gaze to where her hands had settled again and laughed. 'No, he doesn't. I wanted to be certain, and now I am and I will tell him tonight.'

Tamsyn was happy for her, she truly was, and she thought her smile showed nothing but delight for the other woman, but Tess was both observant and sensitive. 'Tamsyn? Have you—have you a child from your marriage?'

'No.' Now her smile was too bright, she could feel it. 'No, I was not so fortunate. Jory and I were not married long. Just nine months before he died.'

'I heard what happened, Gabriel told me. You were there?'

Tamsyn nodded.

'It must have been appalling.'

'It was…quick. Better than prison and a trial and a noose. But it was a terrible shock.'

She kept her tone as neutral as she could, but Tess was intuitive. 'It was more than a shock, wasn't it? Were you pregnant?'

'Yes.' She looked down at her hands, willed them to stillness.

There was a little silence, then Tess turned the subject and began to talk about the reception Cris had asked them to hold in order to entrap Franklin. 'He said to make it for a week today. He seems very confident he can amass the evidence he needs for then.'

'I have the suspicion that if he hasn't he will bluff and I'm sure he will be excellent at that. But if his Bow Street Runner can lay hands on the so-called Mr Goode, then I think it will be all right.'

They chatted about decorations and the menu for supper and whether a string quartet or Pandean pipes would be best and by the time Tess took her leave, off to give her husband her glad news, Tamsyn found that the need to retreat to her room and weep that she had been fighting for an hour had left her.

You see, she told herself. *You can manage this. You can leave him without your heart breaking.*

* * *

Five days passed. Tamsyn fretted about the pictures, wrote long, chatty letters home, spent too much on clothes and helped Tess with the planning for the reception.

Despite it being July there were still enough people in London to garner a respectable number of acceptances, including, to everyone's relief, Lord Chelford's.

'I made sure he heard there would be plenty of card tables and some heavy play.' Alex sat on the arm of his wife's chair, his hand possessive on her shoulder. He was having to fight not to fuss over her as though she was spun glass, Tess had confided.

They were at the Weybourns' town house, expecting Cris and Gabriel for a council of war, as Alex termed it. 'And about time,' he added as the two were announced. 'There's only four days to go.'

'Jem Clarke, the Runner, has got Goode safely locked up at Bow Street,' Cris said, dropping into the chair next to Tamsyn's and sending her a rapid assessing glance followed by a hint of a smile. 'He is singing like a canary because the magistrate has hinted that if he only meant to wound Ritchie, and if he gives us the full story, then he will be transported, not hanged. It means that we'll not be able to get Chelford for conspiracy to murder, because I doubt any jury is going to believe that Goode would be hired to kill and not carry it out, not with his record.'

'If this is the only way he is going to be brought to justice—' Tamsyn broke off, shivered. 'I hate the thought of anyone hanging. One thing worries me, though.'

'Only one?' Cris reached across and took her hand, ignoring the interested stares of the other three.

'Aunt Izzy is going to be devastated by the scandal. Franklin is her nephew, after all, and if he comes to trial I do not know how she will cope with it.'

'So we had best make certain he finds a pressing necessity to leave the country and not come back,' Gabriel said dryly.

'It is hardly justice,' Alex commented. 'What of Ritchie's family?'

'I have made enquiries,' Cris said. 'Fortunately he was not married, had no parents living and I can't locate any dependents. He seems to have been something of a loner, which is one small mercy.'

'Who is Chelford's heir?' Tess asked.

'His younger brother, Michael. A nice young man as I seem to remember,' Tamsyn said. 'I haven't seen him for years, but Aunt Izzy said he is a lawyer somewhere in Somerset and is married with a family.'

'Couldn't Chelford discover he has weak lungs and must go and live in Italy, or the South of France or Greece or somewhere hot?' Tess said. 'I am only thinking aloud, but if he hands over the estate to his brother in return for a pension—'

'A modest one,' Alex said.

'Yes, although the world at large need not know that. Then the brother could take over and have the benefit of the estate and Chelford would be exiled for the rest of his days.'

'We could see to that, certainly,' Cris said with a thin smile that made Tamsyn shiver. 'There would be no scandal for the family.'

'What about his debts? They must be serious if he is prepared to do what he has and if he needs to sell a pair of Rubens's paintings to cover it.'

'Yes, those must be paid.' Cris pinched the bridge

of his nose in thought. 'I'll cover them, then talk to the brother about making it a long-term loan on the estate. He's a lawyer, he can sort something out.'

'Now we just need to make sure Goode doesn't name Chelford in court,' Gabriel said. 'And hope his brother will see this the same way as we do. He has a young family and the opportunity to save the estate and family name for them. That should do it.'

'We are conspiring to help a criminal to escape justice,' Tamsyn said worriedly. 'Just because the family is going to hate the scandal… Is this really the right thing to do?'

'We are conspiring to subvert the law,' Cris said. He was still holding her hand. 'But I think *this* is justice. We cannot be certain Chelford would be convicted in court—it would be the word of a habitual criminal against a peer of the realm.'

'But we have got to convince him that it will go to trial, that he *will* be convicted,' Gabriel said. 'Then we can *reluctantly* offer him a way out and he should snatch at it.'

'It's a plan,' Cris agreed. 'And this is what we will do on the night—'

'But not Tess,' Alex said.

'Alex, I am not ill,' his wife protested. 'It is a perfectly normal state of affairs.'

'You've news for us?' Gabriel asked with a grin.

Tess blushed, but nodded. Gabriel got up and shook Alex's hand, but Cris, to Tamsyn's surprise, went to Tess and bent and kissed her cheek. 'Can I hope to be a godfather?'

'Of course!' Tess laughed.

Gabriel took Cris's seat and leant towards Tamsyn. 'Cris is as soft as butter over children. You wouldn't think it, would you? He's going to make an excellent father.'

'Yes,' Tamsyn said, a growing hollowness below her diaphragm. 'I am sure he will.' Why was she upset? She had known all along he was not for her. Why should this revelation hurt so much? Perhaps she had been harbouring ridiculous dreams after all, she thought drearily. And all the time she had told herself she was being realistic and keeping control of her emotions.

Cris reclaimed his seat and she pulled herself together. 'I know what to do about the paintings, if we can't get Franklin out of the country. When we meet at the reception he will want to know why I am in London. I will tell him and while he is reeling from that, you men can spring your trap.'

'Tell us,' Cris said. 'Then we can weave our noose.'

Tess had planned a glittering reception with an orchestra in the gallery of their town house, masses of flowers and greenery in every corner, card tables set out in one room and little sitting areas scattered throughout to allow for intimate conversations.

The staff were hurrying back and forth, setting out the buffet tables, when Tamsyn arrived early to find Cris waiting for her.

'You look like a mermaid,' he said as he drew her into an alcove screened by a vast display of ferns and orchids. He studied her gown of sea-green silk with a mass of white net foaming over it and an edging of tiny pearls and little shells made of mother of pearl. His eyes darkened, his lids lowered with what she was all too aware was arousal and she found herself short of breath in the confined space.

'That was rather the idea,' she confessed. 'I simply

could not resist it when I saw the fabric and the trimming.'

Cris reached out and trailed one ungloved fingertip along the edge of the scooped neckline, over the curve of her breasts. He made no attempt to delve beneath it, or to pull her closer, but the gesture was both possessive and provocative.

'You will spoil my concentration,' she murmured. 'I need all my wits about me tonight.' It was difficult not to sway towards him, to beg with her body for his hands, his mouth.

'Come, then, see what we have arranged.' He led her to a little grouping of chairs. 'That is the door to the card room just there. We are certain Chelford will make directly for it when he arrives—it is his normal pattern of behaviour. You will be seated here, talking to Gabriel, who will inevitably gather a small group around him. He appears to have a magnetic attraction for a certain kind of young lady and for rakish young men who wish they were just like him.'

'He is very attractive,' Tamsyn said, with deliberate intent to provoke.

'I know,' Cris said grimly. 'There should be a law against it, at least according to most anxious mothers.'

'You are very attractive, too,' she conceded, still in a teasing tone, meaning every word.

'I am exceedingly respectable, boringly eligible, debt-free and apparently sober, most of the time. I could have the looks of a horse as far as the ambitious mothers are concerned.'

He probably has to beat the fluttering debutantes off with sticks, Tamsyn thought, suddenly plunged into gloom.

'Anyway, you are seated here, facing the way he will

come. Even if he doesn't recognise you and react, you will see him. Call him over with no sign that you've the slightest suspicion of him, drop your bombshell about the pictures and one of two things will happen. Either he'll make a scene, in which case Gabriel and I will get hold of him and steer him out of the room, which will make an unfortunate, but hopefully small, disturbance. It will be better if he is thrown into confusion by your revelation and so distracted that we can quietly cut him out as he goes into the card room and get him away without a fuss.'

'And the Bow Street Runner and Goode are here?'

'Yes, with Sir Peter Hughes, a magistrate, behind a screen with another Runner on guard.'

She nodded, as much to quiet the butterflies in her stomach as to reassure Cris that she had it all clear.

'Nervous?' They were in full sight of the bustling servants now and the sounds from the entrance were signalling the first arrivals. He did not touch her, but the concern in his expression was enough to bring her chin up.

'Certainly not. Just excited and keyed up.' Cris's left eyebrow rose and she had to laugh. 'Oh, all right! I admit it. I am quivering like a jelly inside.'

'No one would ever guess.' He stepped in close as the servants began to leave the room, or take up position around the walls. 'You've got courage, Mrs Perowne. Your Jory would be proud of you.' Cris's kiss was swift, hard, scandalous, a moment of affirmation and desire, then he was striding away across the room towards the card room. He paused in the doorway, turned and looked back. 'I won't let anything happen to you, I swear.'

Then he was gone. Tamsyn sat down, tried another

chair, told herself to relax and instead fidgeted with her gloves. They were new, made of pearl-grey kid as soft as satin, and they fastened above the elbow with ribbons. Cousin Harriet had assured her that the slightly loose fit was perfectly fashionable, but, unused to evening gloves, she found the sensation that they might slide off at any moment unsettling.

Worrying the ribbons until they were even looser occupied her for a frustrating five minutes, then Gabriel wandered over, two young bucks on his heels. 'Mrs Perowne.'

'Lord Edenbridge. On your way to play cards?' The young men, who had not been introduced, looked enthusiastic at the thought.

'Later, perhaps. There does not appear to be anyone to make up a serious game, as yet.' The young men wilted. 'May I?' He indicated the seat beside him and, at Tamsyn's smiling gesture, folded his length into it. He should have looked out of place in a formal setting, Tamsyn thought. His evening dress had been beautifully cut, but was worn with a carelessness that included slightly wilted collar points, a loosely tied neckcloth, an off-centre stick pin in its folds and a crimson silk handkerchief escaping from the pocket in his coat-tails.

Against the two young men, starched and groomed to a point of utter perfection, he looked feral, dangerous and, she acknowledged, worryingly attractive. No wonder anxious mamas kept their daughters away and wise fathers forbade their sons to follow him into gaming hells or even less reputable places.

She smiled at the two lads and Gabriel obligingly said, 'Mrs Perowne, may I make known to you Lord Brendon and Mr Elliott. Gentlemen, Mrs Perowne, a visitor from Devon.'

She shook hands, encouraged them to sit and no sooner had they embarked on a careful conversation about the beauties of Devon and the possibilities for stag hunting than three young ladies fluttered past, giggling, just as Cris had predicted.

'Oh, Lord Brendon, good evening.' The boldest, a plump and pretty blonde, came to a halt, smiled at the young man and managed, at the same time, to bat her eyelashes at Gabriel.

Hiding her own smile, Tamsyn obligingly invited Lord Brendon's friends to join them and, camouflage complete, settled down to make conversation and watch the entrance door without appearing to do so.

Guests began to arrive, the room filled up and Tamsyn stayed in place, resisting all invitations to take a turn around the room, admire the paintings in the gallery or accompany any of the young ladies on an expedition to find the retiring room.

How long was it since she had seen Franklin? Only months, she realised, calculating while she tried to keep at least part of her mind on social chitchat. 'Yes, indeed, Miss Wilberforce, a very striking colour for a gown.' It had been when he came to invite the Barbary household to take up residence in his dower house so he could 'watch over them'. 'Thank you, Lord Brendon, I think I will sit a little longer. No, some ratafia a little later, perhaps.' So she couldn't have failed to recognise him. But where was he?

The crowd shifted and he was walking directly towards her. Tamsyn suppressed a gasp. He looked changed and not for the better. His blond hair was still carefully groomed, yet somehow seemed lank. He had put on weight and at only medium height could ill afford it. There were dark circles under his eyes and his gaze shifted restlessly around the room as though he expected an attack at any moment. It passed over her without recognition so she fluttered her fan in a clear gesture of greeting.

He stopped, looked and took a step backwards. Then he seemed to recover himself and came forward to make a jerky half-bow. '*Tamsyn*. Mrs Perowne! What a surprise to see you here.'

Beside her she felt Gabriel gathering himself, although he still sat elegantly at his ease. 'So formal, Cousin Franklin. Or must I call you Lord Chelford?' she chided him. 'It was Cousin Tamsyn last time we met. But doubtless you will tell me I am showing my country manners.' This was the man behind the 'accidents' on the farm, the man who had tried to implicate her in murder. She had no doubts now she was face-to-face with him, his eyes failing to meet hers, his mouth hardly capable of maintaining a social smile.

'Not at all, not at all. But I must confess my surprise at seeing you here.' The smile was more successful now.

'Shopping, you know.' She smiled vaguely. 'Oh, and tasks for my aunts. I must go down to Dulwich soon.'

'Dulwich?'

'The picture gallery, surely you know of it? Aunt Isobel has a pair of paintings at Barbary Combe House that she thinks deserve to be shown to a wider public, and I believe the gallery could accept them on a long loan. So much safer as well, don't you think?' She appealed to the men in the group. 'Do you agree, gentlemen? Works of art deserve an audience, and, besides, I am not certain a remote country house is the best place for treasures.'

There was a chorus of agreement and some flattering remarks about the generosity and vision of Tamsyn's aunt.

Franklin was sweating. He pushed his hair back from his forehead, seemed to realise what he was doing and patted it flat again. 'But dear Aunt Isobel is not—'

'She is the custodian for her lifetime,' Tamsyn said, turning to the others in the group with a proud, affectionate smile. 'She takes her responsibilities very seriously. Oh, you are leaving us, Lord Chelford?'

'I am meeting someone in the card room, excuse me.' He gave a jerky bow and strode off.

'Excuse me, Mrs Perowne, ladies.' Gabriel got to his feet. 'I am reminded that I, too, have a rendezvous.' He followed Franklin into the card room and Tamsyn wished her imagination was not conjuring up images of silent black panthers padding in pursuit of their prey.

There was no point in worrying. She had done her part, she told herself. Franklin was unsettled and off balance. It was all in Cris's hands now. Cris's hands and Justice's scales.

'Do you know, Lord Brendon, I think I will accept that drink you offered me. But a glass of champagne, if you would.' Ratafia was nowhere near sustaining enough.

Chapter Twenty-One

Cris watched the exchange between Tamsyn and Chelford, then crossed the card room to intercept the man just as Gabriel reached his side. As he passed he took a glass from the tray a footman was holding, stumbled and spilled the contents down Chelford's waistcoat.

'My dear fellow! So clumsy of me, here, let me help.' He dabbed heavily at the stain, took the furious viscount by the arm and marched him towards a door leading to the corridor. 'Retiring room through here, we'll have that sponged off in no time.'

Cris was conscious of Gabriel on the other side, exclaiming about his carelessness, taking Chelford's arm, despite the man's attempts to bat him away. Then they were out and into the corridor without anyone noticing anything amiss beyond a tipsy encounter and an accident.

Gabriel took Chelford's wrist, wrenched his arm up his back at a painful angle and, as Cris held the door, pushed him into the room where Jem Clarke sat stolidly at a table, Goode next to him. A screen stood across one corner. There was silence, broken only by the click of the key in the lock and Chelford's heavy breathing.

'What is this?' he demanded.

The Runner introduced himself. 'And I believe you know this man, Goode, or Gooding, my lord.'

'Never seen him before. This is an outrage. I'll have the lot of you for kidnapping.'

'Do you recognise him?' Clarke asked Gooding.

'Aye, I do that. Paid me fifty guineas to injure that Revenue man down in Devon, then swear in court I saw some female do it.'

'That's a lie,' Chelford spat.

'And that's on top of the money he gave me to fire a rick and some other things like that.'

'That'll be the Revenue man you killed. Conspiracy to murder, that is, my lord.'

'This is outrageous. I never—'

'Him dying was an accident,' Gooding said hastily.

'You can't take any notice of the things a criminal like that says. With his record, he's...' His voice trailed off as he realised what he had just betrayed.

'So you admit you know him?' The Runner made a note in his Occurrences book. 'So what was it? A set-up that went wrong, or murder?'

'Neither, I have nothing to do with this.'

'Met me at the Waterman's Tavern, down near Tower Steps,' Gooding said. 'I gave you the dates and times. The landlord will remember him.'

'Nonsense,' Chelford blustered. 'How could he, in a crowded place like that and weeks ago?'

'You really aren't very good at this lying business, are you, Chelford?' Cris moved away from the wall and came to stand beside the man. 'Or is it just because your nerves are shot to pieces with wondering what Dapper Geordie's enforcers are going to do with you when they track you down? Oh, yes, we found out about your debts. The last man I know of who welshed on Dapper Geordie had both thumbs cut off. Devilishly difficult to hold a hand of cards when you've no thumbs.'

Chelford moaned and sagged at the knees. Gabriel caught him and pushed him unceremoniously into a chair. 'Gooding has turned King's Evidence. We've got witnesses, we've got hard evidence and circumstantial evidence. We know about the Rubens oils. You might as well make a clean breast of it.'

At the mention of the paintings Chelford's head came up and his sagging features hardened into fury. 'It's Tamsyn behind this, isn't it? She's influenced Aunt Isobel to stay down there, squatting on all those things that ought to be mine to do what I want to with. I offered them a home, the unnatural coven that they are. Those two old women—disgusting, living together like that— and she's as bad. I offered her marriage, honoured her with my attention and what does she do? Turned me down and married that criminal Jory Perowne!'

'So you tried to get your hands on what's yours by rights,' the Runner said, sympathetically. 'I mean, seems unfair they turned their noses up at a perfectly good home you'd offered them. No wonder you tried to shake them up a bit, show them some real life.'

'That's it exactly.' Chelford leaned forward, apparently thankful to find someone who understood. 'Tamsyn trying to run an estate, a farm, as if she was a man. Turning me down. Like I said, it's unnatural.'

'Still, getting her blamed for smuggling, that attack on the Revenue man—that's going a bit far.'

The Runner was playing him like a master, Cris thought, gesturing to Gabriel to keep back, out of Chelford's line of sight.

'Of course she's mixed up in the smuggling. Where

do you think Perowne's ill-gotten gains have gone? There's some hidey-hole she knows about. If the Revenue man had got any closer, she'd have dealt with him, mind my words.'

'That's what you said to me when you paid me to have a go at him,' Gooding said suddenly. '"Make it look like that fool woman's done it," you said.'

'Almost worked, too,' Chelford said. 'Still don't understand how she got out of it.'

'By being innocent, no doubt.' The dry voice came from behind the screen. Chelford jumped to his feet as it was moved back to reveal an elderly gentleman in an old-fashioned bagwig. 'I've no doubt of your implication in this matter, Lord Chelford. I am Sir Peter Hughes of the Bow Street magistrates' court. The question remains of the exact charges to be brought, which cannot be settled here.'

Got him, Cris thought on a wave of relief. *We've got him scared of the court on one hand and Dapper Geordie on the other. He'll agree to whatever escape route we offer him.*

The elderly magistrate moved forward. The Runner stood up, sending the table rocking, made a grab for it, knocked the screen with his elbow and suddenly Chelford moved, pushing the old man into the screen, shoving the table back into the Runner, who fell against Gooding. Cris reached for him and found his arms full of furious, flailing magistrate. The unlocked door behind the screen banged back and Chelford was gone.

'Servants' stair,' Cris snapped as he and Gabe forced their way through the bodies and furniture and out into the passageway. 'You follow it down, I'll take the main staircase, then we'll catch him in the middle when he comes out into the hall.'

As he ran, bursting out into the corner of the reception room, heads turned. 'Cris?' It was Tamsyn, pushing her way to the front of the crowd, who were craning and jostling to see what was happening.

'Stay there.' He turned his back on her and ran out on to the wide landing at the head of the sweeping curve of the main staircase, deserted now except for a few footmen.

He took the stairs two at a time, landed skidding on the marble floor of the hall and came face-to-face with Gabriel, who erupted from the green baize-covered door to the servants' area. 'Where the hell is he?'

'Don't know.' Gabriel swivelled, searching the hall. 'The staff say no one went through there, there wasn't time for him to have got through the front door—'

He broke off as someone screamed on the landing above. Then there was silence. They turned as one to the foot of the stairs.

'Stay where you are.' Chelford had Tamsyn by the arm, one-handed, the other holding a long knife. The blade glittered in the candlelight, lethally sharp against the pale skin of her neck.

'Carving knife from the refreshment buffet.' Gabriel moved to one side to let Cris come up beside him, three steps from the hall. It felt like a hundred miles from Tamsyn.

'You can't escape. Put the knife down before someone is hurt,' Cris said, pitching his voice to reach the shocked crowd who filled the doorway into the reception room. He could only pray none of them made a rash move.

'I don't give a damn who is hurt,' Chelford snarled. He looked almost hysterical with fear and anger.

'He bolted before we could tell him there's a way out,

that he could leave the country,' Gabriel said to Cris, his voice low. 'He thinks he's going to hang.'

'He will if he hurts Tamsyn,' Cris snapped back. 'If there's anything left of him to hang.' He raised his voice again. 'Chelford, let her go. Something can be arranged. You can leave the country.'

'Liar!' It was almost a scream.

'He's beyond reason,' Gabriel said, taking a step back. 'I'll get round the back, see if I can find a pistol, take him out from up there.'

'Don't move!' Chelford yelled and Gabriel froze as he moved towards the head of the stairs, dragging Tamsyn with him by the arm, the knife waving at the cringing onlookers.

Cris strained to see Tamsyn, who was twisting and turning, trying to free herself. It must be agony; Chelford had large hands that looked strong, for all his dissipation. Then he saw what she was doing. Her long evening glove was loose, twisting on her arm as she distracted Chelford by screeching in his ear. In a moment, unless he realised what she was about, she could slide her arm out of his grip, leaving him holding the glove.

Gabriel realised, too. 'There's nowhere for her to go when she frees herself. That part of the landing is effectively a balcony and he's between her and the door. He'll cut her throat or stab her. If she jumps...'

Cris eyed the distance between balustrade and floor. The height was too great, the floor, without so much as a carpet, was mercilessly hard marble. If she jumped without anything to break her fall, she would die.

He stepped backwards to the floor, making Chelford shout and brandish the knife.

'Tamsyn!' Her head turned. 'Remember Jory. Do what he did,' he shouted.

For a moment her eyes widened in shock, then she gave a frantic twist and pulled her arm from the glove, wrenched away from Chelford and swung herself over the rail. *She's strong*, he told himself as he ran to stand beneath her.

Tamsyn balanced on the far side of the balustrade, her toes on the narrow ledge, then she crouched, seized two of the wrought-iron uprights and swung down to hang over him.

He couldn't touch her even if he stretched. A shoe fell off, hit him a glancing blow as Chelford leaned over the rail and swung at her with the knife.

'Let go! I'll catch you.'

The jolt to her shoulder joints as she swung free with all her weight hanging from her hands made her cry out. Tamsyn risked a glance down and almost passed out, the floor beneath her a shifting pattern of black and white moving dizzily as she swung. *Too far, I'll break my neck, my back.* The memory of Jory's broken body in the seconds before the wave took it came back with sickening force.

Franklin leaned over, white with fear and anger, swiped at her with the long blade, slicing her knuckles. Tamsyn clenched her fingers in agony as the blood welled and he shifted to try again.

'Let go! I'll catch you.' Below her, out of sight. *Cris.* He had told her to jump and she had trusted him. He must have got something for her to land on, a sofa, some cushions. As the knife whistled down she forced her fingers to open and fell.

She crashed into something, something solid that collapsed down with her. Hands held her, she was pulled hard against cloth and she was still falling and then, seconds after she had let go, she was down, jolting and gasping on to a solid, yet yielding object. Something lashed around her ribs, holding her tight, then fell away.

The fall knocked the breath out of her for a moment, sheer shock kept her eyes closed, then the rising volume of shouts and screams forced her to open them. She was lying face down, her nose pressed into white fabric. She lifted her head and discovered it was a neckcloth and above it was Cris's face, eyes closed. He was quite still. He had caught her with nothing to break his own fall.

'Cris!' Gabriel was on his knees beside them. 'Are you all right, Tamsyn? Is anything broken?' He was not looking at her, his fingers busy loosening Cris's neck-cloth, then sliding underneath to search for the pulse in his neck.

'No.' She rolled off Cris's body, landing in a sprawling heap on the floor, the hard, unyielding floor that he had crashed down on to without his hands free to save himself. Down on to his head, his spine, with her whole dead weight on him. She ignored the pain to her overstretched arms, the blood from the knife cut on her hand, as she scrambled to her knees. All she was conscious of was terror. 'Is he dead?'

'No.' Gabriel sat back and shouted, 'Get a doctor!' Then he bent to look closely at the side of Cris's head. 'No blood from this ear. Your side?'

'No.' She knew that was a bad sign if blood came from the ears, but there was so much else to worry about.

Someone came rushing up with a rug, pillows. 'Don't raise him or touch his head. Keep him flat.' Dr Tregarth had told her that when she had helped him with three boys who had fallen from a barn roof. She spread the rug over him and looked across at Gabriel, whose expression was grim. 'His head, his spine… Gabriel, do you know what to do?'

'I know not to move him and I know not to let some damned leech of a doctor bleed him.' His fingers were still against Cris's jugular.

Tamsyn hardly dare touch the unconscious body. Carefully she threaded her bloodstained fingers through his still left hand and tried to send every ounce of her strength, of her love, to him. Someone brought more rugs, spoke to her. Alex.

'Our doctor's coming. He used to be an army surgeon, he'll know what to do.' He, too, reached out and laid his fingers on the column of Cris's neck. 'The pulse is strong. Chelford's dead. He tried to struggle with the Runner and the knife—' Alex broke off as Cris's lips moved.

'Curses,' he whispered. 'I wanted to break his neck myself.'

'Cris.' Her voice wavered and she bit down on her lip until she could master it. 'Don't move.'

'I don't intend to.' Incredibly there was the thread of a laugh in his voice. 'Who is fondling my neck with those cold hands?' His eyes were still closed.

'Gabriel and Alex.' She managed a smile for them both and they lifted their hands away. 'Can you move your fingers?' There was a pause, as though he was recalling where they were, then the hand in hers contracted, squeezing her fingers.

'Tamsyn, are you hurt?' He opened his eyes, dark with pain or shock.

'No, I am perfectly all right, thanks to you. And your feet?'

That time the pause was longer, but after an eternity that was probably only five seconds, the rugs over his legs shifted. 'Wish I hadn't done that,' Cris remarked as his eyes rolled up and he lost consciousness.

'The doctor, my lord.' Both the men got to their feet, helped Tamsyn to hers. Gabriel swept her up in his arms, carried her across to the bench against the wall and set her down on it, keeping one hand on her arm as she tried to get up again.

'Let the dog see the rabbit,' he said mildly.

Someone had moved screens around Cris's sprawled body. Beyond them she could hear the guests making their way down the stairs, Tess's voice as she reassured them, thanked them for their understanding, wished them a good night. The doctor, lean and white-haired, knelt beside Cris, his hands running lightly over his body while Alex told him what had happened, how Cris had moved his hands and feet. She found she was praying under her breath, 'Let him live, let him live, don't let him be crippled.'

'Ah, you're with us,' the doctor remarked and she realised Cris was conscious again. 'We'll have you off this floor soon, just tell me if this hurts…and can you move that? Good, and now, I'll just try bending this.'

Cris's muttered comments sounded profane, but Tamsyn was just happy he was conscious and able to swear. Tess came in, wrapped a shawl around her shoulders. 'Come along, we'll get you undressed and check you over.'

'I can't leave him.'

'Yes, you can. Look, Dr Langridge is organising the footmen to put him on a tabletop and carry him to a bed-chamber. He wouldn't do that if there was any danger. And you can't follow him in, they'll be stripping him.'

'I've—'

'Yes, I know you have, but we don't want the doctor

being shocked, do we? Come on.' Tess coaxed her to her feet, away from Cris, slowly up the stairs. 'There's a nice bedchamber just here.'

Tamsyn managed to get through the door and then, for only the second time in her life, she fainted.

Chapter Twenty-Two

'Cris?' Tamsyn demanded as Tess slipped back into the bedchamber. Her ferocious lady's maid, White, carried on easing her into a borrowed nightgown, positioning herself firmly so that Tamsyn could not get out of bed.

'Battered, but there is nothing seriously wrong, I promise,' Tess said before she even had the door closed. As Tamsyn sagged back against the pillows she added, 'Twisted ankle and knee on the right, several broken ribs, a lump the size of a plum on the back of his head and apparently bruises in just about every place possible.'

'I feel dreadful,' Tamsyn confessed. 'What the marble floor didn't do, I must have, landing on him like a sack of potatoes.' She tried to smile and hide the fact that she wanted to burst into tears of sheer relief after twenty minutes of imagining Cris with a broken spine or a fractured skull.

'You aren't *that* heavy,' Tess said, laughing.

'I'm not some dainty little debutante either.' White moved away and she promptly threw back the covers. 'I want to see him.'

'You stay right there, ma'am.' White tucked in the covers like a straitjacket. 'The doctor said you were to rest and the marquess is not to be disturbed until at least tomorrow.'

'Franklin.' The memory of why all this had happened came back with an unpleasant lurch in her stomach. 'They said he was dead or did I imagine it?'

'He is. Perhaps it is for the best,' Tess said, although she sounded dubious.

'The scandal…and your lovely party ruined.'

'We're putting it around that he suffered a brainstorm and was experiencing delusions.' Tess perched on the edge of the bed, ignoring White's's disapproving expression at such bad deportment. 'It is early yet, but so far, from what I can hear, people are accepting that. Apparently he has been acting oddly recently—Alex said he was in the grip of a really frightening money lender and most of the gentlemen are quite prepared to believe that was enough to drive anyone insane.'

'I must write to my aunts before they hear this in the newspapers.'

'Just a note then. In fact, I will do it for you now and send it to catch the next post. I'll reassure them everyone else is safe and make sure they know about the brainstorm story.' She slid off the bed and took Tamsyn's hand. 'You rest and I'll just go and tell Cris he can stop worrying about you. Try to sleep,' she added as White blew out all the candles, leaving only the little oil lamp by the bed. 'All is well.'

All is well. Tamsyn lay, eyes wide open. When she closed them she could see Franklin's face, contorted by fear and rage, see the marble floor far below her dangling feet, see Cris's face, white and still.

The trial for the murder of poor Lieutenant Ritchie

would go ahead with, she suspected, no mention of Franklin's involvement. The aunts were safe and so was the estate and everyone on it. The worthy lawyer cousin and his family would move into Holt Hall, which could only be a good thing for that estate, and soon Franklin would be a fading memory, an unsatisfactory nobleman who had gone to the bad and suffered for it.

And she would go home, back to Barbary Combe House, back to her life at the edge of the sea, to remember two men. One who had married her as he might have adopted a stray kitten and whom she had loved as a friend, the other who had shown her gallantry and the glories of physical love and whom she loved with what she feared was everything she had in her heart and her soul.

Tamsyn drifted off to sleep at last and woke, stiff and sore and confused in a strange bed with the light seeping through the curtains on the wrong side of the room. Then she recalled where she was and the events of the night before came back to her like a hammer blow. Next door to her chamber she could hear doors opening and closing carefully, a murmur of voices, footsteps on the landing and then silence. Perhaps that was where Cris was.

She needed him, she needed to see him just one more time, touch him, reassure herself that he truly was not seriously injured, store a few more precious memories away. She got out of bed, clumsy and sore from the fall, and pulled on the wrapper Prescott had left for her. There were no slippers, but then, she was not supposed to be wandering around. The clock on the mantelshelf struck five with thin, silvery notes as she eased open the door and found the corridor outside deserted.

The door to the next room opened with well-oiled silence, but even so, the man on the bed turned his head towards her as she slipped inside. 'Tamsyn.'

'Don't move.' His hand when she took it was warm and his grip reassuringly strong. Tamsyn sat down on the chair beside the bed without letting go.

'I didn't know whether they were telling me the truth when they said you were unhurt,' Cris said. He was lying completely flat with no pillows and there was a hump in the bed where some sort of framework had been put over his injured leg. 'Tell me the truth. Were you injured?'

'No, of course not.' She managed to smile and adopt a rallying tone rather than throw herself on his battered body and just hug him as she wanted to. 'How could I be injured when I had a large man between me and the floor? I could wish you were rather better padded with fat and not solid muscle, though. It was like hitting a horsehair sofa.'

Cris snorted with amusement and winced. 'Do not, I beg you, make me laugh. Tamsyn, tell me truthfully, how do you feel about yesterday?'

She thought for a moment, then answered him honestly. 'I am sorry for Franklin, that his own weakness and folly led him to such an end. Part of me is relieved, because he cannot threaten Aunt Izzy any longer, but I cannot be glad, not at the loss of a life, however wasted. Tess says the scandal can be contained, explained, but I hate bringing violence and death into her home, especially now.'

'Now?' Cris raised an interrogative eyebrow.

'Now she is expecting a baby.'

He grinned. 'Alex is almost tying himself in knots trying not to fuss over her, the lucky devil.'

'You want children.' Of course he did, she knew that. He needed an heir, but beyond that, she could tell he wanted to be a father, with all that entailed.

'Naturally.' Cris shrugged, a thoughtless, nonchalant gesture that made him gasp. 'Have you any idea how much everything itches the moment you can't reach to scratch it?'

She forced a smile for him. 'When will the doctor let you get up?'

'He's calling again this afternoon to make certain my skull's all right, then I can sit up, he says. The man's seen too many head injuries during the war, it makes him over-cautious.'

'I would rather he was. I thought…I thought for a moment that you…were dead, or had broken your back.'

'Would you care very much?' The austere, cool expression was back on his face and he was looking up at the underside of the bed canopy, not at her.

'Of course I care! You saved my life, Cris. That was an incredibly brave thing to do, to risk. And I couldn't have jumped for anyone else, there is no one else I would have trusted. How did you think of telling me to do what Jory did? It confused Franklin, stopped him guessing for a few vital seconds.'

'I thought that would penetrate the noise, and the confusion, and reach you in a way that just shouting *Jump!* would not. If I thought at all. But I do not want your gratitude, Tamsyn.'

'Why not?' she asked softly. He seemed somehow angry and all she got for a reply was a shake of the head. 'You are in pain and I am making you irritable. I'll go, I just wanted to see for myself that you are alive and are going to get better.' She released his hand and got to her feet.

'I am not irritable,' Cris snapped.

'No?'

'No. I am working out how to propose to you from this ludicrous position.' He sounded completely exasperated.

'*Propose?* But, Cris, why?' Of all the unromantic offers of marriage she could imagine, being snapped at by a man flat on his back and in a foul temper must be top of the list. 'We have discussed this.'

'I love you.'

'Just because—' Her brain caught up with her ears. 'No, you do not.' How much more did this have to hurt?

'I think I may know better than you how I feel.' His eyes, blue and dark and unfathomable, watched her as he lay, unmoving.

'You are being gallant again. The scandal does not matter, I am leaving today.'

'*Today?*' Cris came up off the bed, cursing with pain, and twisted to take her by the shoulders with both hands.

'Lie down, *please*.' She tried to push him back, but he yanked her against him, kissed her until she stopped struggling and began to kiss him back. It was the last time, she justified to herself with what was left of her powers of reasoning. When they finally broke apart she reached for the pillows and piled them behind him in the hope he would at least lie back.

She moved the chair safely out of range. 'That is not love—that is desire. We know we feel it. What about the woman you were in love with before? Is this just the rebound from her?'

'How did you know about Katerina?' Cris was controlling his breathing with a visible effort.

'I did not, you have just told me her name. I guessed there was someone. Your friends thought so, too.'

'I believed I was in love with her. She was married and it was impossible. We exchanged one kiss—that was all. I think the very impossibility of it made me believe it was love. That first time I kissed you, in the sea, there was something that made me doubt my feelings for her and the more I thought about it, the more I realised it was not love I had felt.'

She should not ask him any more, because even if this was the truth, he was not for her. She was not for him. *But I am only human.* 'What makes you think what you feel for me is love?' she asked, her voice steady, her body shaking with the effort of will that took.

'The ache when I came to London and you were not here. The sense that something was missing, as if I had lost a limb, or a sense. And then last night, when I saw you fighting to be free from Franklin, when I saw you blazing with courage and determination and a refusal to give in and I thought I was going to lose you. Then I knew.'

'I am not the wife for you, for a marquess. You know that.'

He loves me. I love him and I cannot, must not, marry him.

'All my life I have thought I knew not whom I must marry, but what kind of woman. It was a certainty, like knowing that the land was entailed, or that I had a seat in the House of Lords. But I lay here last night, unable to sleep, and made myself listen to reason, to reality, to what I felt. I realised I could marry a yeoman's daughter tomorrow and a few eyebrows might be raised. And they would be lowered again if she proved to be elegant and cultured and knew how to behave in society.

And before you mention last night's uproar, the scandal is Chelford's. Only a small inner circle know how you are involved.'

'Jory—'

'Was a youthful love. A romance that happened a long way away from any of those raised eyebrows. Tamsyn, I do not have to marry for money, I do not have to marry for political alliances. I have only myself to please if I fall in love with a lady who can only enhance the family name, be a life's partner to me, a wonderful mother to my children.'

Her control did break then, as though he had hit ice, sending cracks and fissures spreading out, taking pain with them. Of course he did not know what had happened on that clifftop that day, not all of it.

'But I do not love you,' she lied as she stood up, sending the chair to the floor behind her. He was white to the lips as he stared at her, his hands already clenching on the bedclothes as though he would throw them off, try to follow her as she backed across the room to the door.

'I'll always remember you, but I cannot…'

Cannot lie to you any more.

'Goodbye, Cris.'

My love.

She was halfway across the room and he was half out of bed, the frame over his injured leg knocked away, one foot on the floor. Behind her the door banged open and Alex strode in.

'What the devil is going on in here? There was an almighty crash, I thought you'd fallen out of bed.'

'Tamsyn is trying to leave. Stop her.'

'I must go home, Lord Weybourn. Please could you ask someone to secure me a post chaise to leave at ten?

I must call at the dealer's shop and retrieve the paintings and I can hardly take them on the stage.'

'I'll send you in one of my carriages,' Alex said over his shoulder as he advanced on Cris. 'Get back into bed, man, for heaven's sake, or Tess will have my guts for harp strings.'

Tamsyn closed the door on them and ran. Tess and Gabriel would help her get away before she did something unforgivable and agreed to marry the man she loved.

It was good to be home. There was a peace to be found in the endlessly changing weather, the finality of land meeting ocean, the timeless rhythms of the farms and the fisheries.

A week after she'd returned home Tamsyn made herself walk to the clifftop where Jory had gone to his death. It was the first time since that afternoon and she knew now it was finally time to lay that ghost to rest. She sat down on a rock that pushed out of the rabbit-nibbled turf, its base fringed with purple thrift, and gazed out to sea. One day people would walk on these cliffs and look out at this view and they would know nothing of her, or her love or of tragedies long ago. That was strangely comforting.

The grass muffled footsteps and the man was almost on her before she heard him and turned. The tall figure was silhouetted against the bright sky and for a second her pulse stuttered and a wild hope ran through her, only to be crushed a moment later when Dr Tregarth stopped at her side.

'Tamsyn. They told me you were home again.' He sat down on the rock, took off his hat and let the wind ruffle through his hair. 'It is good to see you again.'

'And you. Is everything well in the village? The aunts knew of no problems to recount to me.' He was such a comfortable presence at her side that she was almost tempted to lean against his shoulder.

'Little Willie Stephens broke his arm falling out of Mr Pendleton's apple tree, the Penwiths' pigs got out and rooted up old Mrs Fallon's vegetable patch, and Lucy Williams was brought to bed of a fine pair of boy twins, which would be a cause for rejoicing if only she could work out who the father is.'

'The field of candidates being somewhat large, I expect.'

'Somewhat,' he agreed drily. 'Are you back to stay?'

'I am.' If anywhere could heal her, this place could. Or, rather, she could learn to live with the loss of Cris de Feaux here better than anywhere else.

'So…' He heaved a sigh as though exasperated with his own hesitation. 'Defoe. I thought you might marry him.'

'Mr Defoe is, in fact, Crispin de Feaux, Marquess of Avenmore.'

'Is he indeed! And so he did not ask you?'

'Yes. He did and I refused him.'

'Why on earth would you do that?'

Probably Michael Tregarth was the only man she could talk to about this. She was so healthy that she had never had to consult him, but if she needed a doctor, then he was the one she would go to.

'I cannot have children. I was pregnant when Jory died. I was there and the shock brought on a miscarriage and the doctor told me that I could never…' She swallowed the lump in her throat and pressed on, determinedly matter of fact and sensible. 'So there is no way that I could, in all conscience, marry a nobleman who needs heirs. Besides all the other things, like the disparity in our ranks and his friends disapproving.' Although it occurred to her that Tess and Alex did not seem to be against her and Gabriel had definitely softened.

'Who told you that you could not carry another child?' Tregarth demanded.

'Dr Philpott, who was here before you came. You never met him, of course, he had a stroke and there was several months before you arrived. I was quite ill after Jory died, with the shock and the miscarriage. I was in a fever for almost a week. When I was recovering he said I would be…'

'Sterile. Hmm. How did Defoe—sorry, the marquess—take that?'

'I didn't tell him.'

'Why not?'

'He is a very stubborn man and he is used to getting what he wants. He would have brushed it aside and then, later, regretted it bitterly.'

'So what reason did you give him for refusing?'

'I told him I do not love him.' A kittiwake soared up from the cliff face, stiff-winged, white and free, its gentle dark eye warily watching the human intruders in its world.

'You lied. Hmm.'

'I wish you would stop going *hmm*! What do you mean?'

'That perhaps you should have told him. It might have made it easier for him to accept your rejection if he knew there was a reason behind it, not simply that you could not return his affection.' He shifted and she knew he was studying her profile. Tamsyn kept her gaze fixed out to sea. 'Which, of course, you do.'

'Yes.'

'I thought you did. Think on it.' Tregarth got to his feet and clapped his hat back on his wind-tangled hair. 'I'll bid you good day. I'm off to see how young Stephens is getting on, the little devil.'

Tamsyn watched him go, striding easily over the clifftop towards the precipitous path down to the bay. A good man, and a good doctor, so his advice was worth pondering on, however difficult it might be to take.

Chapter Twenty-Three

...and so, you see, even were things different, it would not be right for me to accept your proposal.

I hope your injuries are improving rapidly and that you are out of pain. Please give my warmest regards to Lord and Lady Weybourn and to Mr Stone—I cannot think of him as Lord Edenbridge, I fear.

Yours for ever

Tamsyn scrubbed at the words with her nib.

Your friend,
Tamsyn Perowne

There, it was done, and as near the truth as she could get without admitting to Cris that she loved him. Tamsyn sealed and addressed the letter and put it on the hall table to be taken up with the rest of the post.

She stood for a moment, her fingertips resting on the letter, then with a shake of her head, turned back to the drawing room. A line had been drawn, as it had when Jory had died and she had lost the baby. She would start again and she would get through this, just as she had before.

The tide was just on the turn, the sun was beating down and a more beautiful mid-August day for a swim would be hard to imagine, Tamsyn thought as she carried her rug and her armful of towels down the lane to the beach. The aunts had gone off on a picnic with Izzy riding and Rosie in the sedan chair, that was now carried by two of the village lads who had proved apt pupils for the brawny Irishmen who had returned to Bath two weeks before, much to the regret of several of the village girls.

There was no one at the house. Mrs Tape had gone to Barnstaple, shopping with Molly and Michael, and Jason was with Izzy and Rosie. Which meant she could yield to temptation and swim naked.

It would strike cold, even this far into the summer. Tamsyn ran, the breeze cool on her sun-warmed skin. There was no one but the gulls to hear her shriek as the water hit her stomach and no one to watch as she struck out for the Flatiron Rock that was above water now and would be until the tide was halfway in.

When Jory was twelve he had cut rough steps in the side of the rock after a summer of hard labour with a hammer and chisel and as children they used to clamber out and sun themselves on the smooth, wave-polished top. But it was years since Tamsyn had done so and certainly not since Jory died. She clambered up at the cost of a scraped knee on the barnacles that covered the sides and sat down, legs stretched out, and wriggled her toes in a big clump of bladderwrack seaweed clinging to the far edge.

Her toe caught painfully on a rough surface. 'Ouch!' She jerked back her foot. Behind her something splashed, but when she turned there was only a swirl of water close to the beach, lost immediately as a wave came in, its crest creaming as it built up to break. Then a head broke the surface, an arm came out, powered forward in a long, cutting stroke, and she came up on her knees, heedless of the scrape of barnacles and sand, as the swimmer reached the Flatiron. He trod water, looking up at her, and she could not help the shock of pleasure, of excitement.

'Cris.' He should not be here, it would all be unimaginably painful, but now, in this moment, all she could feel was joy.

'How do I get up?' He was smiling at her, her own happiness reflected in his face.

'There are footholds, just there.' She watched him climb easily, with none of her fumbling and scraped knees. Muscles taut, skin streaming water, hair slicked back to expose the austere planes of his face, he was like some sea god rising from the deep.

'Tamsyn.' She stumbled into his arms, heedless of sense or of anything but the moment. His body, under the chill of the water, was hot and so was his mouth on hers. *Oh, the taste of him. Cris.* Under her palms his back was smooth, broad, infinitely masculine, and she clung to him, taking and giving in a kiss that was trying to make up for over a month's separation.

When the necessity to breathe finally broke the kiss, they stayed locked together, not speaking, reading each other through their eyes. Finally Tamsyn could pretend no longer. 'Why are you here?'

'Because I love you.' Cris sat down, pulled her with him, knee to knee, his hand still on her arm.

'I told you that this is not possible.'

'You told me that you did not love me. And at first, I believed you.' He held her gaze, not hiding the pain in his eyes, not shielding his feelings as he always had before. 'Then you wrote to me.'

'But I explained why I cannot marry you. And it makes no difference to my feelings.' Now she was the one veiling her gaze, trying to keep him from seeing the futile hope.

'I know.' He lifted his other hand and cupped the fingers around her averted face, turning her back to face him. 'I asked myself why you would have written and told me something so painful to you, when, if you did not love me, it could make no difference. And the only answer I could find was that you *did* love me and that this tragedy in your past was why you were refusing to marry me.'

'But it is not in my past. It will be my future, too. It cannot be yours.'

'Tamsyn. Do not lie to me, because here, now, I will know, believe me. Do you love me?'

'Yes,' she burst out. 'Yes, I love you. And what difference does knowing it make, except to worsen the pain for both of us of what we cannot have?'

The tender expression in his eyes became something else, something hot and intense and possessive. 'I knew it, I could sense it. I knew you were lying to me before. Tamsyn, my love.'

She pushed back against his naked chest, even though it was like pushing against the Flatiron itself. 'It makes no difference.'

'You cannot have a child whether or not you marry me. I do not want one unless it is yours. It will be a grief for both of us, one we will share,' he said fiercely. 'I do not want children with any other woman because I *want* no other woman. Only you, Tamsyn. Only you.'

'But your heir—'

'He is a perfectly pleasant, intelligent young cousin who would have inherited if the woman I married bore only daughters, or if I had a son who died, or if I married someone else and we had no children anyway. I love you, you love me. We can be happy for the rest of our lives. We can build a good marriage and you will make a wonderful marchioness.' When she stared at him, wordless, he pulled her to him, breast to breast, mouth to mouth.

'I love you,' he said against her lips. 'I was washed up on this beach because I thought I had lost love and all the time I was on the verge of finding it. Don't deny us this happiness, my darling.'

Something broke inside her as if a dam had been breached, a stone wall that had been holding back her love for him. 'No,' she said. 'No, I won't. I love you too much.'

A bare rock, covered in limpets and seaweed and water, in the middle of a rising sea, was not the most comfortable place to make love, Tamsyn thought hazily. Cris lifted her on to his thighs, entered her with a gasp that held relief and joy and intensity, and then she forgot to think, or to feel the sun on her back or the friction against her knees or the slap of wet seaweed tossed up by the wind. All that was real was the power of Cris's body and the need to use hers to show him how much she loved him.

They broke together, clinging as they had done when they had first found each other in the sea, locked together now by love and the promise of a future.

Finally Cris moved and they untangled their limbs,

laughing a little at themselves, touching again and again, as though unable to believe this was real. He flopped back, full length on the rock. 'Lord, but I do love you. What the blazes?' He sat up again, rubbing his head and twisted to glare at the lump of bladderwrack that Tamsyn had been exploring with her foot earlier.

'Is it a crab?' She shifted to sit beside him, legs dangling, as he poked at the mass.

'No, it's hard.' He pushed the weed aside. 'Look— it's a ring bolt and a chain.'

'Pull it up.' A certainty that she knew what this was began to creep over her.

Cris hauled, his muscles bunching as he took the weight of whatever was at the end of the chain. He stood, braced his feet apart and hauled and suddenly a small, square, metal box broke the surface. He dumped it on the rock and stared at it. 'If I didn't know better, I'd think we'd found a pirate's treasure.'

'No. A smuggler's. This rock was Jory's place, ours when we were young.' Tamsyn ran her hands over the rusting iron bands that bound the box. 'There is no padlock, only a staple through the hasp.'

'You open it, you are his heir,' Cris said. In the end it took both of them to force it open, lift the lid, creaking, to reveal a canvas bag no bigger than a lady's reticule. 'Hardly pieces of eight and golden doubloons.'

'If it was full of money I suppose we'd have to give it to the Revenue,' Tamsyn said, trying to cover her disappointment with a show of reasonableness.

Cris put the bag in her hands and helped her open it. Inside was a gold chain and a handful of crystals. 'Cris, these aren't—?'

'Diamonds? Yes, I think they are. I think your first husband has left you jewels where no one else but you would ever find them.' They sparkled in his palm like the foam on the sand in the moment the sunlight caught it. 'You can have these made into a necklace you'll always remember him by.'

'You wouldn't mind?' she asked as he tipped them back into the bag, knotted it securely and hung it around his neck.

'That he made you happy? That he kept you safe? Of course I don't mind.' He stood up and reached down to help her to her feet. 'Come, we had best get ashore and decent before your aunts discover us disporting.'

'That's a good word, *disporting*.' But he had already dived into the sea and was treading water, waiting for her. She dived in, too, and swam slowly back to the point where their feet could touch bottom. 'We disported here before,' she said and slipped her arms around his neck and curled her legs around his waist. 'Shall we try it again?'

Later that evening, as they sat, hand in hand on the sofa, trying to make conversation with a deliriously happy Isobel and Rosie and not simply sit staring into each other's eyes, Molly came in.

'Letter for Mizz Tamsyn, just been delivered by the doctor's man.'

'Will you excuse me, I had better read it now. I can't imagine what it might be.'

The others talked while she took the letter to the table where the oil lamp stood and cracked open the seal.

Dear Mrs Perowne,
I have been meaning to read my predecessor's di-
aries, which I found stored in a trunk in the attic
of the house when I took over the practice, but

have never found the time. After our discussion on the clifftop I looked at the one relating to the date of your husband's death and the following weeks.

I find that the late Dr Philpott was a believer in the old theories of health and medicine, now thankfully becoming a thing of the past. He wrote that your bodily humours were unbalanced by shock and grief and that your womb had no doubt 'wandered' as a result.

You may be familiar with the idiotic but widely held theory that a 'wandering' womb is the cause of feminine hysteria. No doubt at the time you were understandably distraught at the tragic loss of your husband and might be thought, by an old-fashioned doctor, to be hysterical.

He wrote that it was very regrettable, but he expected you to be rendered infertile as a result. I can assure you that nothing in his notes leads me to the same conclusion.

I would recommend you to attend a specialist in these matters, possibly a London doctor—I can suggest some names. Or you may simply wish to let nature take its course.

I am, dear Mrs Perowne, your obedient servant, Michael Tregarth, MD

'Is anything wrong?' Izzy asked.

'No. Nothing is wrong at all. Dr Tregarth was simply recommending a certain course of action to deal with a problem I had discussed with him.'

Cris stood up and held out his hand to her. 'Shall we take a stroll in the moonlight before bedtime?'

She let him lead her out on to the lawn and, out of sight of the windows, curled into his embrace.

'Should I be concerned?' Cris asked her, holding her a little away so he could look down into her face as she smiled up at him.

'No, not at all.' She told him what the letter had said. 'I don't want to be prodded about by London doctors. I shall follow his advice and let nature take its course.'

Five minutes later, emerging breathless from his embrace, she murmured, 'My bedchamber is still the same one as before, my love.'

'Excellent,' Cris growled. 'Because after that kiss, my darling Tamsyn, I, too, fully intend to let nature take its course.'

* * * * *

*If you enjoyed this story,
don't miss these other great reads in
Louise Allen's* LORDS OF DISGRACE *quartet,*
HIS HOUSEKEEPER'S CHRISTMAS WISH
HIS CHRISTMAS COUNTESS.

And watch out for
THE UNEXPECTED MARRIAGE
OF GABRIEL STONE
coming soon!

COMING NEXT MONTH FROM

⬨HARLEQUIN®

ℌISTORICAL

Available June 21, 2016

THE INNOCENT AND THE OUTLAW (Western)
Outlaws of the Wild West • by Harper St. George

Innocent Emmaline Drake knows Hunter Jameson is trouble the second he walks into her saloon. He's on the path of revenge, but she can't escape his captivating gaze!

THE UNEXPECTED MARRIAGE OF GABRIEL STONE
(Regency) *Lords of Disgrace* • by Louise Allen

Gabriel Stone, Earl of Edenbridge, resolves to help respectable Lady Caroline Holt. But then his mission takes him somewhere he *never* thought he'd end up—down the aisle!

UNBUTTONING THE INNOCENT MISS (Regency)
Wallflowers to Wives • by Bronwyn Scott

How can Jonathon Lashley concentrate on his French lessons with Miss Claire Welton when all he wants is to claim her delectable mouth with a heart-stopping kiss?

COMMANDED BY THE FRENCH DUKE (Medieval)
by Meriel Fuller

Alinor of Claverstock risks her life to rescue Bianca d'Attalens. But when Alinor encounters Guilhem, Duc d'Attalens, it's not just her life that's in danger...

Available via Reader Service and online:

THE OUTCAST'S REDEMPTION (Regency)
The Infamous Arrandales • by Sarah Mallory

Wolfgang Arrandale has lived as a fugitive for ten years, until the revelation that he's a father changes everything. Can parson's daughter Grace Duncombe help him prove his innocence?

CLAIMING THE CHAPERON'S HEART (Regency)
by Anne Herries

For Lord Frant, haunted by his experiences in India, love is definitely the last thing on his mind! Until, that is, he meets his ward's beautiful new chaperon, Lady Jane March...

YOU CAN FIND MORE INFORMATION ON UPCOMING HARLEQUIN® TITLES, FREE EXCERPTS AND MORE AT WWW.HARLEQUIN.COM.

HHCNM0616

REQUEST YOUR FREE BOOKS!

HARLEQUIN

HISTORICAL

Where love is timeless

2 FREE NOVELS PLUS 2 FREE GIFTS!

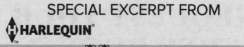
He was leaving? No. Unacceptable. She was not losing
him after one lesson. Jonathon Lashley could learn to
speak French and she could teach him. But she had to act
fast. He was already halfway to the door. Something fiery
and stubborn flared inside Claire. He was not leaving this
room.

She fixed herself in the doorway, hands on hips to take up
the entire space, blocking the exit. He would not elude her.
"I never figured you for a quitter, Mr. Lashley, or perhaps
you have simply never met with a challenge you could not
immediately overcome?"

"Do you know me so well as to make such a
pronouncement?" Lashley folded his arms across his chest,
his eyes boring into her. This was a colder, harsher Jonathon
Lashley than the one she knew. The laughing golden boy of
the *ton* had been transformed into something dangerously
exciting. Her pulse raced, but she stood her ground.

What ground it was! She'd never been this close to him before—so close she had to look up to see his face, so close her breasts might actually brush the lapels of his coat without any contrivance on her part, so close she could smell his morning soap, all cedar and sandalwood and entirely masculine, entirely him. She'd waited her whole life to stand this close to Jonathon Lashley and, of course, it was her luck that when it happened it was because of a quarrel—a quarrel she'd provoked.

She'd never thought she'd fight with him, the supposed "man of her dreams." She'd been thinking *never* a lot since this all started. Yesterday, she'd never thought they would have desperation in common. Today, she'd never dreamed his French would be this bad, or that she'd have trouble teaching him or that she'd quarrel with him.

"You are a very bold woman, Miss Welton." His tone was one of cold caution. "Yesterday you mopped up my trousers and today you are preventing me from leaving a room. One can only wonder what you might do to my person next. Perhaps tomorrow I will find myself tied to a chair and at your mercies."

Don't miss
UNBUTTONING THE INNOCENT MISS
by Bronwyn Scott, available July 2016 wherever
Harlequin® Historical books and ebooks are sold.

www.Harlequin.com

Turn your love of reading into rewards you'll love with
Harlequin My Rewards

**Join for FREE today at
www.HarlequinMyRewards.com**

Earn **FREE BOOKS** of your choice.

Experience **EXCLUSIVE OFFERS** and contests.

Enjoy **BOOK RECOMMENDATIONS**
selected just for you.

PLUS! Sign up now
and get **500** points
right away!

Earn
FREE
REWARDS
HarlequinMyRewards.com
Join
Today!

MYR16R